RAVE REVIEW

"T. M. Wright is a rare and blazing talent."
—Stephen King

"T. M. Wright has a unique imagination."
—Dean Koontz

"Like Stephen King at his best, Wright can hold us shivering on the edge between laughter and fear."
—*Newsday*

"T. M. Wright is a master of the subtle fright that catches you by surprise and never quite lets you go."
—Whitley Strieber

"Wright convincingly proves that he understands, as few do, how to give a scare without spilling blood all over the page."
—*Publishers Weekly*

"T. M. Wright is more than a master of quiet horror—he is a one-man definition of the term."
—Ramsey Campbell

"T. M. Wright's nose for horror is as acute as Stephen King's."
—*Fear*

"I have been an unabashed fan of T. M. Wright's since reading his first novel."
—Charles L. Grant

MORE PRAISE FOR T. M. WRIGHT!

"Without doubt, Wright is one of the most interesting horror writers out there."

—*At World's End*

"A producer of work of the highest caliber. While many other authors may be sweating over their next supernatural extravaganza, Wright seems to deliver these delicious pockets almost effortlessly. His narrative is so sharp it makes a lot of writers seem clumsy by comparison."

—*Horrorworld.com*

"T. M. Wright is a brilliant writer. His impeccable prose is hypnotic and the rhythm of his words entrancing."

—*2 A.M. Magazine*

"Keep an eye on T. M. Wright."

—*The Philadelphia Inquirer*

"Wright's slow escalation of terror is masterly."

—*The Sun Times* (U.K.)

PREDATOR AND PREY

The bus was empty, except for the woman and the bus driver, and he was taking the bus back to the bus barn because his shift was done. He hadn't yet noticed her, but he did now, and he called, "You gotta get off the bus, lady." He pulled over and opened the rear doors.

She said nothing. She didn't look at him. The blast of cold air made her muscles tense. And it started in her, as well, an instinct, a capacity, and a power which she had used often since coming to this city, though not in a way that could draw much attention to her.

The driver said again, "You gotta get off the bus, lady." He looked at her in the rearview mirror, saw that she wasn't looking back at him, stood and started walking back to her. He stopped walking. She had looked up at him, had leveled her gaze on him.

He started backing away from her, tried to keep his eyes on her, but couldn't because she wasn't there. Then she *was* there. Then she wasn't. She was a part of the bus seat, a part of the advertising placard overhead—Bacardi rum—a part of the dark floor, a part of the rear window and the blowing snow, the headlights, the neon, the streetlamps, the wind, the black sky. But she was teeth, as well, and breasts, hips, sky-blue eyes and dark pubic hair. She was a naked phantom, and she was a living woman, dressed garishly for an evening in cheap hotels. She was a part of the dark floor, the neon, the blowing snow and the black sky.

The bus driver fell backwards in the desperation to get away from her. He muttered little pleading obscenities at her, saw her coalesce with the air itself, saw her reappear—teeth and hands and breasts and pubic hair.

Then she was upon him.

LAUGHING MAN

T. M. WRIGHT

LEISURE BOOKS NEW YORK CITY

A LEISURE BOOK®

February 2003

Published by

Dorchester Publishing Co., Inc.
276 Fifth Avenue
New York, NY 10001

ISBN 0-8439-5084-6

The name "Leisure Books" and the stylized "L" with design are trademarks of Dorchester Publishing Co., Inc.

Printed in the United States of America.

Visit us on the web at www.dorchesterpub.com.

LAUGHING MAN

Book One
The House on Four
Mile Creek

Chapter One

Jack Erthmun remembered being left alone in a cave when he was a child. He maintained that he was less than a year old when this happened, although everyone else in his large family told him that it was pure fantasy. Some of them even laughed, which Erthmun thought bordered on cruelty, because childhood memories were sacred, after all. Childhood itself was sacred. Adulthood wasn't. Adulthood was profane, violent, and perverse. Erthmun sometimes wondered why nature allowed human beings to grow beyond the purity of childhood.

He remembered that, as a child, he had owned pets. This was fantasy, too, according to the other members of his family. They reminded him that Erthmun's father had harbored no particular fondness for animals, and was—according to family legend—not above shooting stray cats and dogs that happened onto the family property.

T. M. Wright

The cave that Erthmun remembered was small and dark, and it smelled of newly mown grass. This memory was particularly strong for him, as memories of smells are for everyone. It haunted his nights and clouded his days, though not all of his nights, nor all of his days.

"Do you remember if you were alone in the cave?" his sister Lila once asked.

"Alone in the cave," Erthmun said; it was not a question. He was repeating what she had said.

"Yes," Lila said, and grinned.

"Yes," Erthmun said.

"You were?" Lila said, still smiling. "Alone in the cave, I mean."

"I was alone," Erthmun said. "Yes."

"You know, of course," she told him, "that this memory is something you've concocted to take the place of another memory. One that's probably even worse."

Erthmun nodded. "Even worse," he said.

"Jack, it's a widely accepted concept," Lila told him. She smiled again, though Erthmun could not imagine why she was doing so much smiling. She finished, "Manufactured memories to take the place of other memories. It's a widely accepted concept."

"A widely accepted concept," Erthmun said, and when she smiled yet again, he wanted suddenly to bash her head against a wall. The impulse came and went as quickly as a twitch; he found it very confusing—though it was far from the first time that such an impulse had come to him, in many situations—and he was ashamed of himself for it.

Erthmun did not often see the other members of his family, though two of his sisters lived within an easy commute of Manhattan, and his mother lived in a comfortable

4

Cape Cod in White Plains, also an easy commute. He got along with his sisters, and his mother, when he saw them on Christmas and Thanksgiving because, according to social convention, holidays are times when people should get along.

The man that Erthmun had known as his father died when Erthmun was five years old. This had been the impetus for his mother to pack up their belongings and move him and sisters out of their house on Four Mile Creek, in the Adirondacks (the house near which Erthmun was born). It was a move she had been wanting desperately to make for a long time, but one which Erthmun's authoritarian father had denied her because the house on Four Mile Creek was, as he put it, "safely removed from the muck and mire and moral decay of the cities."

Erthmun did not remember much about his father. He remembered only that there were many times that he saw himself in his mind's eye stealing into his parents' bedroom late at night, or stealing up behind his father while the man sprayed weed killer on his small, mannered garden, and reaching into the man's back and tearing his spine out. Then Erthmun saw himself running through the fields with the spine held high over his head, as if it were a great and dangerous snake and he had defeated it in battle.

Erthmun did not feel connected to his surviving sisters, or to his mother. They clearly sensed this; his sister, Sylvia, once told him, "Molasses is thick, Jack, but blood is thicker, and if you ask me, families should be as thick as thieves."

"Thick as thieves," Erthmun said, though he had not understood it. The whole concept of families was odd to him. He could sense how his sister felt when she talked about families. He sensed much. But he did not feel the same warmth that she obviously felt when she talked about families, and he told her so.

"You're a strange duck," she said.

"I'm not a duck at all," he said, and though she cracked a smile, she knew that Erthmun was not trying to be funny.

Erthmun's impulses to violence were quick, and he rarely acted upon them. His own reflection—in a mirror, in a pond, in the polished metal surface of a car—often made his muscles tense, and made his hands ball up into fists. He had once hit a bathroom mirror with his fist, in response to his reflection. It made him feel foolish because, when he dwelt upon it, he could think of no good reason for having hit the mirror. His reflection had . . . excited him, or angered him, he guessed. It was as if it had been a stranger, and an enemy, not merely the reflection of his own square and essentially pleasant face, brown eyes, and thick, reddish hair.

People who smiled surreptitiously when he repeated their words also made him angry. He had been told by many that he had the annoying habit of repeating the words and sentences of those to whom he was speaking, but he could never remember doing it. Consequently, when people smiled at him because of it, he had no idea why they were smiling—he thought they were amused by him, or that they harbored a secret they weren't sharing with him. So he got angry, and saw himself doing some quick and bloody act of violence to them. But this was an impulse he had never acted upon because he was almost religiously concerned with being a civilized man, and with reacting in a civilized way to all that went on around him.

"It's called echolalia," Sylvia told him. "Jack, you have echolalia."

"Echolalia," he said.

She smiled. "See there, that's what I mean. You repeated what I said."

"No, I didn't."

"But you did, Jack."

"No, I didn't," he said, which was another facet of the problem; sometimes he repeated his *own* words.

Now, at the age of thirty-seven, his echolalia seemed to be fading, he thought. Or maybe people had gotten used to it, because there were fewer surreptitious smiles.

He also felt an impulse to violence when he ate. His sister Lila noticed one Thanksgiving—and not for the first time—that he seemed very tense as he ate his turkey, cranberries, and mashed potatoes, and she told him later that he looked like he was protecting his food.

"Protecting my food?" he said.

"Sure," she said. "So no one will steal it."

"Who's going to steal it?" he said.

She said, "How often do you eat out?"

"Eat out?"

"With friends."

He thought a moment. "What friends?"

"I know you have friends, Jack. Everyone has friends."

"They do?"

"Of course. What about the people you work with?"

He thought a moment, and said, "They're just people at work, Lila."

"But don't you . . . go out to lunch with your buddies? Don't all men do that? Don't you go to a bar and have lunch?"

"No."

"That's very sad," she said.

"Sad?" Erthmun said. "I don't know. Is it?"

She assured him that it was sad.

He said no, it wasn't.

Chapter Two

Erthmun lived alone in a three-room, fourth-floor apartment in Manhattan's West Village. His building was sturdy, old, and dreary, and the other people who shared the building with him were of various ages and occupations. One was an assistant editor at *Elle* Magazine, another was a postal worker, another a retired professor of biochemistry. Several were self-proclaimed artists and writers looking for their big break in the city that had given more than a few big breaks to others like them. All of these people nodded at one another in the hallways and on the elevators, but none of them had developed friendships with anyone else in the building.

Erthmun had no pets. He had long ago found that he possessed a strange ambivalence toward animals, and that they apparently possessed the same sort of ambivalence toward him. He looked with awe at the stray cats that roamed his neighborhood, and he thought of them as survivors. He respected them for this, and felt an uneasy kinship with them, but they eyed him warily, as if unsure if he was friend or foe.

Erthmun had been named after a maternal uncle who was a favorite of his and of his siblings. Uncle Jack had been a bear of a man who did a lot of hearty laughing and had brought presents whenever he'd visited. He had been partial to Erthmun, but he'd hidden it well.

As an adult, Erthmun was haunted by the memory of Uncle Jack's death. The man's last words, heard only by Erthmun himself, were, "Oh, shit!" Uncle Jack said this as if at a fleeting annoyance—a missed turn while driving, a name forgotten, a passing rain shower on a sunny day. Erthmun thought that it was a strange attitude in the face of death—annoyance—and found himself ashamed of Uncle Jack for it. He would have preferred that the man died kicking and screaming in anger because his life was coming to an end. What else was there, after all, but life?

Uncle Jack was also a man who told stories that made his young nieces and his nephew huddle together in delicious fright. These stories also caused Erthmun to stand at his bedroom window for hours and hours in search of the marvelous, misty, and dangerous creatures that, according to Uncle Jack, inhabited the hills and fields around the house on Four Mile Creek.

"It's like this," Uncle Jack said. "You can't see them if you're actually looking at them. You won't see them that way. That would be too easy, wouldn't it?" He laughed. "You can only see them if you're *not* looking at them."

Eight-year-old Lila said, "But Uncle Jack, how can you see them if you're not looking at them?"

"Yeah, how can you see them?" asked six-year-old Jocelyn.

Uncle Jack laughed again and explained, "Well, try this one night. Go out and look up at the starry sky and then find a patch of sky where there doesn't appear to be any stars. Look hard into this patch of black sky, and if you look long enough, after a while, very, very faint stars will appear, but not exactly where you're looking. They'll appear only where you're *not* looking."

Lila smiled. "I did that once, Uncle Jack."

"Of course you did," he said. "And that's how you see these creatures I'm talking about, too. Because they're so fast, because they run so fast—faster than anything you've ever seen, faster than the wind—and because they can look like the things around them. They can look like the grass, or the trees, or the sky and the clouds. You can't see them unless you look just ahead of them or just behind them."

"Behind them," Erthmun repeated.

"Behind them," Uncle Jack repeated. "Or above them, even."

Lila said, wide-eyed, "What do they look like, Uncle Jack?"

"They look like you"—he touched her nose gently—"and you"—Sylvia's nose. Then he looked hard at Erthmun and continued, "And they look like you especially, Jack." He touched Erthmun's nose. He lingered with his finger on Erthmun's nose. Then he gave him a small, secretive smile, as if the two of them shared a secret, although Erthmun had no idea what that secret might be. Uncle Jack laughed again and added, "And some of them even look like me!"

Lila, still wide-eyed, asked, "Where do they come from, Uncle Jack?"

"Well, Lila," Uncle Jack said, "where does *anything* come from?"

"Where does anything come from?" Erthmun said.

"I don't know," Lila said, clearly perplexed.

"From heaven," Sylvia offered.

"From heaven," Erthmun said.

Uncle Jack said, "Where do the plants come from, and the cows, and the fish in the sea?"

The three children looked in wonderment and confusion at him.

And Uncle Jack declared, "Why from *here*, of course. From the earth itself."

"The earth itself," Erthmun repeated.

"From *every*where!" Lila said, as if in awe.

Erthmun was a homicide detective in Manhattan's 20th Precinct. He was almost preternaturally good at his work, but his methods had aroused suspicion among the powers that be because, as far as everyone else was concerned, Erthmun's ideas of "probable cause" for search and arrest often amounted to no more than hunches.

PARTIAL TRANSCRIPT OF CRIMINAL TRIAL HELD AT RICHMOND COUNTY SUPERIOR COURT, STATEN ISLAND, 1993:

C.E. (Counsel for the Defense): "Could you describe what you saw there, Detective Erthmun, at the end of the driveway, that morning, when you arrived at 18 Morningside Lane?"

Jack Erthmun: "18 Morningside Lane? Yes, sir. I saw the body of a very obese Caucasian male dressed in a white shirt, black pants, and black shoes. He was lying on his stomach, and there appeared to be a bullet wound at the base of his neck—"

C.E.: "Did you do a direct examination of this

11

wound, Detective, to determine if it was an exit wound or an entrance wound?"

J.E.: "Not as such. No, sir."

C.E.: "Why not?"

J.E.: "Because only the medical examiner is allowed to touch the body."

C.E.: "Which would not have precluded you from doing a visual examination, isn't that right?"

J.E.: "I didn't think it was necessary."

C.E.: "You didn't think it was necessary?"

J.E.: "Yes, sir."

C.E.: "You didn't think it was necessary to try and determine whether this wound, which was apparently the victim's cause of death, occurred as the result of a bullet fired from in front of the victim, or from behind the victim?"

J.E.: "No, I didn't."

C.E.: "Could you tell the court why, Detective?"

J.E.: "Because I knew that the victim had been killed by a bullet that entered his body from the front."

C.E.: "You *knew* [emphasis] that the bullet had entered from the front *before* [emphasis] you actually did a close visual examination of the body?"

J.E.: "Yes."

C.E.: "How did you know this, Detective?"

J.E.: "I knew because of the victim's [witness hesitates] demeanor."

C.E.: "His demeanor? Could you explain that?"

J.E.: (hesitates) "Yes. I would say that it was in the nature of . . . instinct or intuition."

C.E.: "I'm still unclear as to what you mean. Could you try to be a little more forthcoming, Detective?"

J.E.: "I'm not sure. I mean [witness hesitates], I mean

that the victim, within the crime scene, was [witness hesitates] expressive."

J.K.: "In what way, Detective?"

J.E.: "I think in a holistic way. The victim at the crime scene was expressive in a holistic way."

J.K.: "Detective, are you trying to be confrontational?"

J.E.: "No."

C.E.: "Isn't it true, Detective, that your methods of investigation have been described as unusual?"

Erthmun thought that dead bodies were exquisite. They were so articulate, so passionless, and so passionate. They spoke volumes, not only about the victim, but about the perpetrator, too—all in shades of red and pink and white and brown.

Chapter Three

Early Winter

The snow was deep in Manhattan, and the air was cold, still, and dense. It smelled of exhaust fumes, deli sandwiches, urine. Erthmun's joints hurt on days as cold as this. He had thought often of moving south, and as often as he had thought of it, he had wondered why he simply didn't do it.

He was in a dreary little park at East 7th Street and Avenue C, and he was looking at a body lying in the snow. The body was that of a white male, about thirty-five years old, clean-shaven, black-haired. It was dressed for winter, in a bright blue parka, heavy pants, orange mittens, and a red cap with a tassel. It lay faceup, arms wide, left leg bent. The body wore black buckle boots, and had a rictus grin that had snow in it. The eyes were open, and they were muddy gray and green. There were no obvious signs of violence, and no clear indication as to the cause of the man's death. He looked like he had simply fallen asleep in the snow.

The little park was bordered by a tall, wrought-iron fence. Various posters had been put up on this fence, and they advertised strip shows, night clubs, Off-Broadway plays. They were attached to the fence by strips of wire or tape. The borough of Manhattan was supposed to see to the maintenance of the park, which included keeping posters off the fence, but this was unimportant work in a city that had much larger problems, so it was work that did not get done.

Erthmun, who was kneeling over the body of the man in the snow, nodded at one of the posters, and said to a uniformed cop standing nearby, "Could you get that for me, please."

The cop looked in the direction Erthmun had nodded, and said, "Get what?"

"Get what?" Erthmun said. "That yellow poster. Bring it to me."

The cop said, "Sure," and did as he was asked.

Erthmun studied the poster a moment. It advertised a revue playing in SoHo called *The Brown Bag Blues*. The letters were in black script. A graphic of a naked woman caressing the letter S in the word *Blues* was in purple. Erthmun gave the poster back to the uniformed cop, said, "Get me that one," and pointed at a smaller poster.

Erthmun's partner was a tall, long-haired woman who dressed well, in tweeds and trendy hats. Her name was Patricia David and she had been standing at the other end of the body in the snow during Erthmun's exchange with the uniformed cop. She smiled—although Erthmun couldn't see it because he was looking at the uniformed

15

cop—and said, "What are you up to, Jack?"

Erthmun said, without looking at her, "I don't know." It was the truth.

The uniformed cop came back and handed Erthmun a white poster. Erthmun looked at it. Patricia David came around the body to look at it, too. She read the poster aloud. "Mortality Makes Mulch of Us All." She grinned. "Pithy."

Erthmun glanced silently at her, then looked at the poster again. The brown words on a white background were neatly handwritten and they were the only words on the poster. A small, hand-drawn graphic of a devil's head lay at the bottom center. Erthmun stared at this devil's head. He touched it, felt nothing. The words and graphic had been done with red marking pen. He held the poster to his nose, sniffed, smelled the unmistakable and stinging aroma of marker ink.

Patricia David said, "Do you think that's important, Jack?"

He looked at her—he had his mouth open a little, like a dog savoring an odor. He closed his mouth and said, "You mean smelling this poster?"

She shook her head. "No, the poster itself. Do you think it's important?"

Erthmun shrugged. "I don't think so."

The uniformed cop said, "They're all over the city."

"Yes, I know," Erthmun said, and handed the poster to Patricia David. "Put this in the car, would you?"

She scowled, took the poster from him, said, "When we're done here, *then* I'll put it in the car."

Erthmun nodded distractedly—he hadn't heard the annoyance in her voice—and turned back to the body. He thought that the snow had melted from the man's rictus grin. This was odd. Surely the body hadn't gotten warmer. He glanced questioningly at Patricia David, then at the body again. He saw that he had been mistaken. The snow hadn't melted.

He bent over and put his ear to the man's mouth, as if the man were going to whisper to him.

"Christ," said the uniformed cop, "what in the hell is he doing?"

Patricia David said nothing.

Erthmun straightened and held his hand out for the white poster. Patricia gave it to him; he stared hard at it for a long moment, then gave it back. "Could you put that in the car," he said again.

She sighed. "When we *go* back to the car, Jack, *then* I'll—"

"Yes," he cut in. "I'm sorry." He looked down at the body and said nothing for a full minute. Patricia David and the uniformed cop glanced questioningly at one another. At last Erthmun said, "I'm very hungry."

"You're *hungry*?" Patricia said.

Erthmun pointed at the dead man's stomach. "*He's* very hungry."

"Shit," whispered the uniformed cop.

"Shit," Jack whispered.

Patricia asked, "What do you mean he's hungry?"

Erthmun shook his head. "I don't know." It was the truth. He bent over the man's body again, put his hand on the man's belly, pushed hard. The snow around the man's mouth fluttered; a dime-sized clot of snow fell from the man's lips.

"Jesus Christ," said the uniformed cop.

"Jack, is there a reason for all this?" Patricia asked. "We *are* still waiting for the M.E., you know."

Erthmun didn't answer. He pushed on the man's belly again, harder, with similar results. A small groan escaped

17

the man's throat—his vocal chords responding to the passage of air.

Erthmun straightened, shook his head, as if in confusion, glanced at Patricia David, then looked at the dead man's face again. "Did anyone call the Medical Examiner?"

Patricia David said, "Jack, you're the detective in charge; I'd assumed you'd already done that."

Erthmun looked blankly at her a moment, then said, "Oh, yes." He glanced at the uniformed cop. "Call him, would you?"

The uniformed cop said, "Right away," and went to his patrol car.

Erthmun bent over the body again, sniffed at the dead man's mouth, and, again, his own mouth opened a little.

Patricia David said, "Something, Jack?"

He whispered, his lips close to the man's nose, "It was a stupid thing you did, my friend."

Chapter Four

Erthmun did not believe that the dead actually spoke to him. He did not believe that the corpse in the bright blue parka and orange mittens had told him in so many words about the balloons filled with cocaine that he'd swallowed. Erthmun did not, in fact, believe in an afterlife—in heaven, hell, or in the talking dead. He believed that the corpse in the bright blue parka was eloquent in the way that the earth itself was eloquent. Because that, after all, was what the corpse was becoming—the earth. The earth had created the man, the man had died—because one of the cocaine-filled balloons in his stomach had broken open—and now the corpse, which had once been a man, was becoming one with the earth again. This was a fact as obvious to Erthmun as the fact of gravity, but he had never tried to share it with anyone. He wasn't sure why. He thought it may have been because most of the

T. M. Wright

people he knew—the people he worked with; his social life was nonexistent—seemed to have their own strongly held beliefs, and those beliefs were not much in tune with his own. And he could see no need to convince others that his beliefs were more valid than theirs, even though he knew, of course, that they were.

In winter, Erthmun kept his apartment very hot. He had received complaints about this from the tenant above him, a young and overweight man named Henry.

"Why do you keep your apartment so fucking hot?" Henry asked once.

"I need to," Erthmun answered. He was not a man who engaged in long explanations of his eccentric behavior because, simply enough, he did not view it as eccentric.

"Well maybe you want to pay my fucking air-conditioning bill, then!" Henry said.

"Why would I want to do that?" Erthmun said.

Henry sputtered something incoherent and went away. He did not speak to Erthmun again because he thought Erthmun was crazy. "He's got a maniacal glint in his eye," Henry told his friends.

Erthmun slept naked under several blankets and quilts, even when his apartment was hot. He slept naked because he did not believe there was any other way to sleep. In sleep, he maintained, he was drawn closer to the earth, and because he had sprung naked from the earth, that was the way the earth wanted him to sleep. He slept deeply, and long, and was very difficult to awaken. He claimed also that he never dreamed. People told him that he indeed did dream, but that he simply did not remember his dreams. His sister Lila explained, "We dream once every fourteen minutes, Jack. This is empirical fact. If we

20

did not dream, then we would drive ourselves into insanity. I believe that all mammals dream, in fact. It's nature's safety valve."

"No," Erthmun maintained. "I don't dream. I never dream." But this was not entirely true. He did dream. He dreamed variously that he was a clump of earth, a root, a worm, a rock. And because such things have no real intelligence or memory, when he woke, he had no recollection of these dreams.

He tired completely, to the point of exhaustion. This happened once a day, and it happened very quickly. He ate voraciously—rare meat (beef, lamb, poultry), green vegetables, carrots, potatoes, berries, fruit—read his evening paper, and then stripped, turned up the heat, and went to bed. Sleep usually overtook him within seconds.

He always woke with an erection. He was a very sexual man. He got an erection when he looked at an attractive woman. He got an erection when men he worked with talked about a previous evening's conquest. He got an erection when Patricia David walked away from him to go back to her desk, or walked in front of him on the way to the car. It was her rear end that he liked most.

He wasn't a virgin, but he had never had a sexual encounter that he felt was socially satisfying because he was prone to premature ejaculation. Often, he ejaculated before intercourse began. Ejaculation was a great joy for him, premature or not, but he had learned to understand and appreciate the needs of his partner, too. So, after apologies were made, he often helped his partner to achieve orgasm as well. This made him feel that his premature ejaculation was not as much of a problem as others apparently thought it was. Besides, wasn't it true that humans were the only species who carried on with intercourse for more than a couple of seconds? Look at dogs, cats, squirrels, rhinos, lions. Didn't they get the whole thing finished as quickly as possible? Many of these creatures did indeed engage in extended foreplay, it was true, but foreplay wasn't intercourse, and foreplay wasn't ejaculation.

This night, the night that the man in the bright blue parka was being autopsied, Erthmun's phone rang while he slept. He did not sleep through a ringing telephone, but he did not awaken at once either. Those who knew him understood that if they called him while he was sleeping, they would have to let his phone ring a couple of dozen times, and that, even after he answered it, he might not be completely available for rational conversation for several minutes.

"Erthmun," he said when he at last answered the telephone.

"Jack, this is Patricia. Are you awake?"

"Awake? No."

"When will you *be* awake?"

"How can I answer that?"

"Jack, wake up."

"I'm awake."

"No, you're not."

"I'm talking to you. I'm awake."

She sighed. This kind of somnolent logic was hard to counter. She said, "What are you doing now?"

"Now? Nothing."

"You're *talking* to me, Jack. I called you and you're talking to me. Now wake up. This is important."

"I am awake."

Another sigh. "Jack, we've got work to do."

"I am working."

"You're *sleeping*, for Christ's sake!"

"For Christ's sake! That can't be. How can that be?"
More somnolent logic.

"Jack, get up, get a drink of water, look out the window—"

"Get up, get a drink of water, look out the window. Who can do all that?"

And so it went. It took another fifteen minutes before Erthmun was actually awake and responding lucidly.

TEXT OF A REPORT WRITTEN BY OFFICER GORDON LOW SUBMITTED TO NEW YORK COUNTY SUPERIOR COURT ON THE INVESTIGATION OF A MURDER AT EAST 9TH STREET AND AVENUE B IN 1992

Detective Erthmun arrived on the crime scene at approximately 10:30 p.m. on the night of August 12. He did not appear to be drunk or under the influence of drugs. He said hello to this officer and to the other officers then on the scene, and did not look at the body immediately, but looked through the apartment very briefly. After he had done this, he went out on the balcony and stood on it for approximately fifteen minutes. This officer doesn't know what Detective Erthmun was doing on the balcony because the light was low there. Then Detective Erthmun came into the apartment but still did not look directly at the body, but asked this officer if there was anyone else in the apartment. I told the detective that there was no one else in the apartment, and then he shook my hand. He appeared to be trying to avoid looking at the body, and this officer asked the detective if something was wrong. Detective Erthmun said that everything was okay. Then he went and talked to the other uniformed officers who were on the scene. There were three other uniformed officers. They were officers Grady, Bord, and Winde. There was also another detective, but she was there in an unofficial capacity as a homicide trainee, and her name was Patricia David. She was standing in the dining area of the apartment.

This officer overheard Detective Erthmun ask one of the officers if the coroner had been called, and the other officer told Detective Erthmun that he was not empowered to do that but Detective Erthmun was empowered to do that. Detective Erthmun nodded his head, and this officer overheard him say that he knew that he was empowered to call the coroner and then he apologized for his confusion.

Detective Erthmun then turned his head so he could look at the victim's body. The victim's body was behind the detective at this point in time. The detective looked at the victim for approximately five minutes. The detective did not appear to move his body during this time. The detective's facial expression appeared to change during this time. It became an expression of anger. That is, his eyes narrowed and his lips grew tight. His hands became fists during this time, as well. This officer came forward and asked the detective if there was a problem, but the detective did not answer except to the extent that the detective repeated verbatim what this officer had said to him.

Then the detective bent over the murder victim so the detective's face was very close to the victim's face, who was on her back. The victim's eyes were open.

Then the detective appeared to this officer to look into the victim's eyes. Then the detective's mouth moved, as if he was talking, but this officer did not hear any words.

The detective's mouth movement continued for several minutes, and then the detective bent over further so that his ear was close to the victim's mouth, which was open. Then the detective stood up and he motioned to Detective David to come over, which she did.

At this point in time, Detective Erthmun said to Homicide Trainee David that the victim had told him that it was "unfortunate about failed relationships" and that the investigation of the crime should center on the victim's most recent boyfriend. Detective David seemed incredulous about this, although she said nothing directly to Detective Erthmun within this officer's hearing.

Chapter Five

A thousand deaths happened that day. Most of the deaths went unnoticed, except by those that killed and those that died. The city survived because of the dead; the dead made room for the living, and the children and grandchildren of the living.

Near the edge of the city, at the perimeter of a landfill, in a place where they would not be seen, two brothers laboriously dug a deep hole and then dumped the body of a middle-aged hooker into it.

In Harlem, a man barely in his twenties leaped from the top floor of his tenement house and died instantly when he hit the pavement, fifteen stories below.

On East Houston Street, near the Bowery, a sanitation engineer standing too far out in the street, waiting for his coworker to return with a load of garbage, was clipped by a passing taxi and sent sprawling headfirst into a street sign. He broke his neck.

In the Holland Tunnel, a woman on her way out of Manhattan to visit her daughter in New Jersey began swiping furiously at a spider on the inside of her windshield and hit another car head-on. A gasoline tanker, just behind her, jackknifed into the wreckage and exploded within seconds. The resulting inferno killed a dozen people, and sent another dozen to various hospitals in Manhattan.

In Greenwich Village, a four-year-old boy playing with his father's .38 pointed the weapon at his mother, said "Bang!" and pulled the trigger. The bullet lodged in his mother's lung; she died on the operating table four hours later.

These were the kinds of deaths that happened regularly in the city. And those who paid attention to them would merely shake their heads and cluck that accidents happened all the time, there was really nothing anybody could do about it, or they'd whisper that the Mafia had its hands into everything, or proclaim that they'd never have a gun in *their* house.

These were the kinds of deaths that people could deal with. In a sense, they were a form of entertainment.

The stairwell where the woman's body lay smelled of shit, urine, blood, hairspray, and chocolate. The combination of odors was wrenchingly odd, and Patricia David gave the body a cursory glance, made her apologies, and said she had to leave the building for a moment.

Erthmun said, "Sure, I understand," though in his heart he didn't, and bent over the body. He did not find the odors here as off-putting as Patricia did. He liked chocolate—he was all but addicted to it, in fact. And here, in the stairwell, the overpowering smell of the stuff came from the victim's open mouth, which had had a good half pound of dark chocolate jammed into it. Some of the chocolate had melted around the woman's lips, but most of it was still chunky.

Erthmun stood close to the body and stared at the chocolate. There were several uniformed cops nearby; he glanced at one of them and said, "What do you think this is? Hershey's?"

The cop shrugged. "Who knows?"

Erthmun turned back to the victim. "It's cheap chocolate," he said. "It's too sweet—you can smell that it's too sweet. It isn't Perugina or Godiva."

Patricia David reappeared. He glanced at her. "This is cheap chocolate," he said.

She nodded grimly.

Erthmun straightened a little, though he was still bent over the body. It was naked and it had been hacked up so completely that blood covered it like a body stocking. Even the long hair was covered with blood. Its natural color may have been blond, Erthmun thought, but it was covered with blood, and he couldn't be sure. The pretty, oval face, however, looked as if it had been meticulously cleaned off, and the very pale skin there, contrasted with the nearly total covering of blood on the body and hair, was jarring.

Erthmun said, to no one in particular, "She looks like a mime." He bent over the body again and stared into its open eyes, which were bright jade green. "Beautiful," he said. "I don't think I've ever seen eyes quite this color before."

"Those are contacts," Patricia told him.

He glanced quickly at her, then at the victim's eyes

again. "Are they?" he said, but it was a rhetorical question, and Patricia thought for a moment that Erthmun was toying with her, though that, she knew, would have been out of character for him. She knew him as a man to whom humor was not a necessity.

He asked, "What do you think did this?" He was still looking at the body.

"You mean the murder weapon?" Patricia said, and gave the body a quick once-over. "It wasn't an ax, or a hatchet. That's obvious. The wounds are too narrow."

"Too narrow," Erthmun said, and asked, without looking at Patricia, "Some kind of sword, then?"

She shrugged, began to answer, and Erthmun cut in, "Do you want to leave the building again?" He glanced around at her. She thought he looked genuinely concerned. She shook her head quickly.

He said, "I think you do."

"No. You're wrong." She gestured at the body. "Let's concentrate on what we're doing here, okay?"

"You're angry," Erthmun said. "Why are you angry?"

"Jack, please—"

"It wasn't a sword," he interrupted. "The wounds are all of a uniform length. See here." He pointed at a bright red gash on the woman's left arm. "That's what? Six inches?" He pointed at a similar gash on her right arm. "Six inches here, too." He pointed at her belly. "And here." He pointed first at her right thigh, then her left, both of which bore similar gashes of similar lengths. "And they're all the same depth, too." He was smiling now, and this made Patricia uncomfortable because she wasn't sure *why* he was smiling, and because he so seldom smiled.

Erthmun declared, "This is a very ritualistic thing. Someone has made this woman up with her own blood!" He straightened suddenly. His smile became a flat grin.

T. M. Wright

"Look at her! Look at her! She's been made up with her own blood! It's a religious thing! Some religious person has done this!" He stared at Patricia. His eyes were wide, his grin still flat. He looked like a madman. "A priest or a rabbi has done this!" he declared. "Or a shaman!"

Patricia said, "Jack, if this is supposed to be funny . . ."

"Supposed to be funny . . ." he said, repeating her words. He stooped over again, so his face was very close to the dead woman's. He stared into her bright jade green eyes and whispered hoarsely, "What's going on here?" He grabbed her hard by the shoulders.

"Jack?" Patricia shouted. "For Christ's sake . . ."

Erthmun whispered at the dead woman, "Tell me something, damnit!" He shook her by the shoulders. Her head flopped backward, forward, backward. Bits of chocolate flew from her mouth.

Patricia shouted, "Jack, are you nuts?"

Erthmun stood with the dead woman. He held her erect by the shoulders. Her arms were tight against her sides, because of his strong grip on her, and her knees were bent a little because her feet were touching the floor. Her head flopped left, right, backward.

Patricia shouted, "Put her *down*, Jack!"

". . . *down*, Jack!" Erthmun echoed. He shook the dead woman. "Talk to me!" he yelled. "*Talk* to me!" He was splattered with her coagulated blood, now, because her body had bumped against his chest. "Talk to me, talk to me, goddamnit, talk to me."

Patricia grabbed his arm. "Jack, put her down! What in the hell are you doing?"

"Talk to me!" Erthmun yelled into the dead woman's face. "Talk to me!"

Patricia pulled on his arm. It was no use. He was too strong. She glanced frantically at one of the uniformed

30

cops, who was looking on open-mouthed. "Help me, for God's sake!" she shouted.

The uniformed cop nodded, came forward quickly, grabbed Erthmun's left wrist.

Erthmun continued shouting at the dead woman, "*Talk to me, goddamnit! Why won't you talk to me?*"

Chapter Six

In his dream, he was a clump of earth. He was moist, and dark, and he had no memory, no consciousness, no name, and no age. He could not see, or hear, taste, touch, love, or hate. He could not become angry, or confused, he could not feel pain, or joy, loneliness, or fear, because he wasn't yet a living thing. He was a clump of earth.

Then he awoke in a strange place, and remembered nothing of his dream.

Patricia said to him, "Jack, you did a weird thing." A man stood next to her. Erthmun didn't recognize him. He was tall, strongly built; he wore a gray suit, a thin, black mustache, and his eyes were small. "Detective," he said, "your partner's right." His voice was steady and his tone probing and judgmental. "You did a very weird thing."

Erthmun said, "I don't remember, I don't remember." It was the truth.

Patricia said, "This is Mark Smalley, from Internal Affairs, Jack."

"I guessed as much," Erthmun said. He didn't like looking at the man. Something in his small, dark eyes prompted Erthmun's urge to violence and he saw himself, in his mind's eye, springing from the bed and attacking him.

Smalley said, "Do you know where you are, Detective?"

Erthmun looked around. The walls were beige, the windows narrow—wire mesh covered them—and the floor was composed of black and white linoleum squares. "I'm at Bellevue."

Smalley nodded. "That's right, Detective. You're in the psych ward at Bellevue. Do you have any idea why you're here?"

"No," Jack said. "I told you, I don't remember, I don't remember."

Patricia asked, "Do you remember the woman in the stairway?"

"No."

Smalley grinned. It was humorless, flat, and cold, and Erthmun, looking at it, wanted to rip the man's lips from his face. Smalley said, "Of course you do, Detective. A naked woman with chocolate stuffed in her mouth. Who could forget something like that?"

Jack shook his head. "For Christ's sake, why don't you stop being coy and simply tell me what it is I'm supposed to have done."

Patricia told him. When she was finished, he said, "Why in the hell would I do something like that? I've never done anything like that before."

"Yes," Patricia said, "I know."

33

"It's a fucking strange thing to do," Smalley said. "And that's why you're here."

Jack said. "So what does any of this have to do with Internal Affairs?"

Smalley grinned again. "We think you knew her, Jack."

In another part of the city, a woman awoke from dreams she too could not remember. She was a stunning woman, with hip-length brown hair, sky-blue eyes, and a face as exquisitely and preternaturally beautiful as anything that lived.

Like Erthmun, she slept naked, under a cocoon of blankets and quilts, but when she woke, she did not come back from sleep haltingly, as Erthmun did—she came back all at once, as if she had been walking, and had simply changed direction.

Blood stained her body this evening, and when she looked at herself in her mirror, and saw the blood, she grinned as if at the memory of something pleasurable. Then she got into her shower, washed the blood off, and soon had forgotten the blood, and the pleasure.

"Knew her," Erthmun said. "Knew who?"

"The woman with chocolate stuffed in her mouth," Smalley said.

Patricia asked, "*Did* you know her, Jack?"

Erthmun sighed. "Of course not. What in the hell makes you think I knew her?"

Smalley said, "Because you called her by name."

"By name," he echoed. "I did?"

Smalley nodded. "You called her Helen. That was her middle name. We think it's probably what her friends called her."

Erthmun shook his head in confusion. "I don't know anyone named Helen."

"We want to believe you, Detective," Smalley said. "And maybe we do, as far as it goes."

"Meaning?"

Smalley shook his head a little. "Shit, I don't know. Maybe I'm just trying to give you the benefit of the doubt. Maybe I'm trying to be magnanimous. They tell me I'm nothing if not magnanimous." He grinned, glanced quickly at Patricia, who was giving him a puzzled look, then looked at Erthmun again. "How in the hell can we believe you, Detective? You called the dead woman by name, for Christ's sake. You picked her up and shook her like a rag doll, and you called her 'Helen,' which was her name. And now you tell us that you don't remember doing it, and that you don't know anyone named Helen. Give me a break, man. I don't think *you're* stupid, and I know for a fact that *I'm* not."

Erthmun gave him a steady, unblinking gaze. "I didn't know her. If you claim that I said these things, then I must have said them. I have no reason to believe that either of you is lying. But I didn't know her."

"Noreen Helen Obermier," Smalley said.

After a moment's silence, Erthmun said, "Yes? And?"

"That was her name."

"I'll take your word for it."

"Why do I get the idea that you're not cooperating with this investigation, Detective?"

"Because it's in your nature to be suspicious," Erthmun answered.

"Damn right," Smalley shot back. "And I'm proud of it. It makes me good at what I do." He grinned again.

Erthmun looked away. His fists were clenched; he

closed his eyes. "Listen," he said, voice tight, "I'm tired. Why don't you both get out of here."

"For now," Smalley said, and left the room.

"Rest, Jack," Patricia said.

"Rest, Jack," Erthmun echoed her. He was released later that day.

When she had dressed herself, and had lingered at her mirror—because she was fascinated by what she saw reflected in it; she was a creature new to the earth, and most things fascinated her—she ate ravenously of fruit and meat and went out into the night.

She was a creature of the darkness. She loved darkness. She saw well in it; she saw, in fact, many things in darkness that were hidden to the eyes of others.

She walked with the grace, certainty, and stealth of a predator, which, to onlookers, was a sensual walk, alluring and fantastic. It was the walk of sex, which is the walk of power. Men turned to look at her, and women did, too, because she was unlike any human they had seen before.

Chapter Seven

When Mark Smalley interviewed Noreen Helen Obermier's friends and relatives, he could find no one who could connect her to Erthmun. This made Smalley confused and angry, because he was certain there was a connection. A man simply doesn't call a dead woman by name if he doesn't know her—Erthmun wasn't *psychic*, for Christ's sake!

And now he—Smalley—thought it would be smart to begin interviewing Erthmun's relatives. His sister, Sylvia Grant, lived on Staten Island, and though Smalley could telephone her, he decided it would be best to talk to her in person. He decided this because he was convinced that women could not easily lie to him face-to-face. It was clear that he intimidated them because he was tall, strong, and athletic-looking, quick with a one-liner, and not easily surprised. He thought that men often saw this winning combination as a challenge, but that women, even women cops, found his rock-hard sensuality, his probing intelligence, his wit, and his charm impossible to resist. And though they might try to lie to him, they always gave themselves away—a bat of the eye, a twitch of the hand, a blush, an awkward sideways glance. Sometimes they held his gaze too long, or not long enough. Sometimes, if they were dressed right, he could tell that they were lying because their nipples erected. He found this fascinating, and had wondered if it bore some parallel to lying and male erections. Perhaps all lying was somehow tied to sex. Perhaps all *wrongdoing* was tied to sex.

He did not telephone Sylvia Grant first. He had hoped to find her home, but if he didn't, then it was all right. He'd come back another day and catch her by surprise.

But she was home. She invited him into her house— after he told her who he was, and after she made him produce his badge to prove it—and led him into her spacious, well-appointed living room. He thought she didn't look at all like Erthmun—she was blond, thin, very tall— and he wondered if they were really brother and sister.

She said, when he was seated in a Queen Anne love seat that was too small and straight-backed for anyone's comfort, "Could I offer you a refreshment of some kind, Detective? Some tea, perhaps a glass of lemonade?"

He shook his head, said, "No, thanks, I won't be long. I only have a question or two."

"As you wish," she said, smiled graciously, and sat across from him in another Queen Anne love seat. "Is Jack in trouble?" she said, still smiling.

"No. There are merely some questions we'd like answered."

"And that's why you're here, of course." She was still

smiling. It pleased him. People who smiled too much were people who lied.

"Yes," he said, "that's why I'm here."

"You say you're with Internal Affairs, Mr. Smalley?"

"That's correct."

"And you're investigating Jack?"

He nodded. "Yes."

"Then he *is* in trouble." She was still smiling.

Smalley shook his head. Her continuous smiling was beginning to annoy him. "He's not in trouble, Mrs. Grant."

"But he may soon *be* in trouble, isn't that right?"

He ignored the question. "Could you tell me about Jack's friends? Particularly his girlfriends."

"He doesn't have any."

"He doesn't have any friends?"

"He doesn't have any girlfriends. Not at the moment anyway. Actually, I don't think he ever did."

Smalley cracked a quick smile. Her first lie. "That's a little hard to believe, Mrs. Grant. He's a grown man, after all—"

"I meant that he's never had any lasting relationships, Mr. Smalley. He's had one-night stands, of course. He isn't a choirboy."

"Of course he isn't. Who is?" said Smalley.

The phone rang. Sylvia Grant turned her body for a moment in its direction, and Smalley looked at her breasts. She was wearing a blue satin blouse, and her breasts were large, but she was clearly wearing a bra. He was disappointed. She turned back. He looked up quickly from her breasts to her face, and saw her smile go crooked for a moment because she had obviously caught him looking at her and had thought he was merely being lecherous.

"Excuse me, please," she said, and went to answer the telephone.

Erthmun could not remember the face of the dead woman. He could remember only the smell of the chocolate that filled her mouth. When he tried to remember her face, he saw the face of another woman instead—a face so exquisite it was nearly unreal, as if it were not a human face at all, but one that existed only in his imagination.

He was sitting on the edge of his bed. The day was nearly done, and he was ready for sleep. But he knew that he wouldn't sleep. He knew that he'd leave the apartment and that he would look for the woman his fantasies had shown him. Because he knew that, unlike him, her time was night.

Other than the hunter, that which moves at night is the prey of the hunter—the foolish and the unwary, who laugh and make noise to attract the hunter, who douse themselves with scent and powder so they can be easily discovered, who dress in clothes that reflect the light, and shoes that make them sway like worms, who drink themselves giddy, and so become defenseless.

These foolish and unwary were what the earth had given her. These prey were for her.

She shivered with excitement. She grew moist, flush, and warm, and she groaned deeply. Her voice was husky and sensual.

Around her in the cafe, people stared. Some were concerned because they thought she was in pain. Others knew well enough that she was not in pain, and they grinned.

One man said, "I didn't know there was a floor show," and his friend laughed.

But she heard no laughter, and saw no one staring, because the judgment of others had no meaning for her.

Erthmun's night vision was unusual. If an object were moving, then he saw it well, but if it were not, then it melted into the background of artificial light or shadow and he saw little except vague shapes in ill-defined shades of gray. Consequently, as he walked, cars moved past—against the backdrop of storefronts and apartment buildings, street signs and garbage cans—as if against the backdrop of a fog. He had never questioned this way of seeing because he so seldom went out at night, and because he had always assumed that everybody saw the way he saw. It was, after all, the best way to experience the world after dark. What was more important at night than that which was moving?

He walked quickly because he was cold. It was not a particularly cold night—in a city where winter winds often moved with skin-numbing force through the corridors between buildings—but that didn't matter to Erthmun. He was cold because night, simply enough, was a time for sleep. Night was when the body shut down and sent its precious heat to the internal organs so the brain could rest.

Night was a time only for predators, and their prey.

He muttered to himself as he walked. He didn't know that he was muttering. He didn't hear himself muttering. Often, during daylight, he had seen others in this city muttering to themselves and he had thought they were pathetic.

He muttered about his childhood, which was a mystery to him. He had concocted many fantasies about his childhood, not so much to solve the mystery as to push it aside, so he wouldn't have to deal with it.

41

He did not mutter loudly, as some in this city did. His muttering was little more than a whisper, and because there was a good deal of traffic on the avenue, no one walking nearby could hear him.

"The pine needles make a soft bed," he muttered. "I run here, and here, so there will be no mistake," he muttered.

He had his hands deep in his coat pockets, and though he was wearing gloves, his fingers were numb, and he would have found that they were useless if he had tried to use them. But he was not aware that they were numb.

A dog barked at him from an alleyway. It was a Yorkshire terrier, lost and confused, and it barked not as a warning, but as a plea—*Take me back to my owner*. But Erthmun took no notice of the dog.

"I climb the tree, you can't catch me," he muttered. "Good night, Moon," he muttered. "Good night, chair."

A woman came out of a cafe, saw him—the fixed stare, the quick, stiff gait, hands shoved hard into his coat pockets—and, as he passed close to her, she heard him muttering ("Mother, can we go home, now?"), and so she stepped away from him. She was a visitor to this city, and Erthmun frightened her—she thought he was just another of the thousands of crazy people she had been told walked the night streets of New York.

And as she stepped away, Erthmun turned his gaze to her and stopped walking. "What are you doing?" he asked.

"Nothing," she answered, her voice high pitched from fear. "I'm sorry."

Erthmun regarded her warily for a few moments. "You've got to be careful," he said. "Don't take people by surprise," he added curtly, and walked on.

Chapter Eight

When Erthmun woke the following morning, he remembered that he had gone out, but not why, or to where. He remembered *being* out, in the night. But he remembered it in the way that other people remembered dreams—like trying to hold onto a butterfly made of smoke.

And when the phone rang, he knew before answering that it would be his lieutenant and that he'd tell Erthmun there had been yet another murder, though Erthmun realized that he had no rational way of knowing all of this.

The lieutenant said, "Internal Affairs isn't suspending its investigation, Jack, but we really do need you down there," and he gave Erthmun the location of the latest murder—an apartment building on West 82nd Street. Erthmun was at the building a half hour later.

Patricia David, dressed well and wearing a trendy

brown hat, was waiting for him inside the front door. She smiled unsteadily and said, "We're calling these 'The Chocolate Murders.' " She looked a little queasy. "Brief, descriptive, catchy," she added. "It'll play well at the *Post*."

"Uh—" said Erthmun, who had wanted to say *Uh-huh*, but couldn't because of the smell here—once again, the overpowering smell of sweet, cheap chocolate—and the body—female, mid-twenties—awash in its own blood, except for the white and pretty face, eyes as transparently green as the leaves of an air fern.

"Again, contacts," Patricia said.

"Uhn—" said Erthmun, who was bending over the body and looking into its eyes. "This is not a coincidence," he said, without turning away from the body. "The killer puts these contacts in."

"That's very odd," Patricia said.

"Odd," Erthmun echoed her. "Everything's odd."

"There's been nothing similar before," Patricia said. "We've checked." She paused, then asked, "How do you know the killer puts the contacts in?"

"Helen," said Erthmun.

Patricia looked confusedly at him, but said nothing.

He turned and looked at her. "Did I say 'Helen'?"

"You did, yes."

"Yes. I don't know why. I don't believe this woman's name is Helen." He was feeling very confused and fuzzy-headed, as if he were in the first moments of an illness.

Patricia said, "No one knows what her name is, Jack. There's no ID. No clothes, anywhere. We assume she lived in the building. We're checking."

"She does," Jack said.

Patricia said, "You knew her?"

"Knew her? No. How could I?"

"Jack, you're making no sense."

"She lived here," he said. "That's why she died here. It makes perfect sense."

Patricia sighed and tried to think of some response.

Erthmun said, "We are born where we all must die. What could be clearer?"

"Are you kidding, Jack?" She knew that this wasn't likely. Erthmun laughed only occasionally, and he never made jokes. She asked, anyway, "Are you making a little joke?"

Her question confused and offended Erthmun. He looked at the body again. He centered on the eyes. He reached, touched one of them.

"For God's sake, Jack," Patricia said, "we already know that she's dead."

"I'm doing nothing," Jack said. "I'm touching her eyes. I need to touch them."

"Shit," said Patricia.

"Shit," echoed Erthmun. "I'm not going to remove the contacts."

"Don't touch them, Jack. If you're right—for God's sake, if you're right, and the killer put them in, they could hold his fingerprints."

"They don't."

She came forward, bent over, took Erthmun's arm. He yanked it away, miscalculated, jabbed his finger hard into the victim's eye, felt the eyeball pop.

"Good Lord," Patricia said.

"It's nothing," Erthmun said. "It's not important."

"Jack, stand away from the body!" Patricia ordered.

He stayed where he was, bent over the body, his gaze on its eyes.

"Jack, I'm telling you to stand away."

"I can't. How can I?"

"How *can* you? By God, you *will*!"

He looked at her. She had drawn her weapon, though she wasn't pointing it at him; she was holding it at her side. He glanced at the weapon, then into Patricia's eyes, which were the eyes of a cop, then at the popped eyeball of the victim. He stood abruptly and said, "I'm sorry. You're right."

"Step away from the body, Jack!"

He did it. Patricia came forward, put herself between him and the body, and called, "O'Connell, come in here."

A uniformed cop came in.

She said to him, "I'm ordering this detective to leave the crime scene. Will you see that he doesn't come back in here?"

The cop nodded once, uncomprehendingly. "Sure," he said.

"Jack," Patricia said, and nodded toward the door.

Erthmun nodded, too, and left with the uniformed cop.

Chapter Nine

Smalley said, "I've got a transcript of your conversation with Patricia David at the crime scene, Detective. Do you want to read it?"

They were in the interrogation room at the precinct house. Smalley was standing several feet in front of the table where Erthmun was seated.

"Read it?" Erthmun said. "No, I remember what I said." In his mind's eye, he saw himself reach far across the table and tear Smalley's throat out. The image was very satisfying, and he found himself closing his eyes, found himself *seeing* it happen, *felt* Smalley's blood wash over him, and when he opened his eyes, he discovered that his arm had risen from the tabletop, and that his fingers were wide. He lowered his arm abruptly, saw that Smalley was looking questioningly at it, and looked away.

After an uneasy silence, Smalley told him, clearly trying

for a tone of bravado, "Of course you remember what you said, Jack." He came to the table, leaned over it. "I talked with your sister. She has some very weird ideas about you."

"Does she?"

"For instance, that you've never had a long-term relationship with a woman. Is that true?"

"I've had as many relationships as you have," Erthmun said.

Smalley straightened, smiled. "I doubt that, Detective." His smile faded. "But that's not the question I asked, is it? I asked if you have ever had a long-term relationship with a woman."

Erthmun said. "Listen, am I a suspect in these killings?"

Smalley savored the moment before answering. "Yes," he said, and smiled again. "As far as I'm concerned, you are."

"And, as a suspect, am I being removed from active duty?"

"That's up to the captain. I'm recommending that you be put on unpaid leave."

"Am I going to be arrested?" Another smile.

"It's likely."

"On what evidence?"

"There is no direct evidence. You know that. We're talking to you because of your behavior at these crime scenes. I think you knew these women. Shit, I'm *positive* you knew these women."

"Prove it. You can't."

"Goddammit, you knew them and you killed them. That's what I believe. It's what I *know*!"

Erthmun stood, withdrew his .38, put it on the desk, followed that with his badge. He looked at Smalley, who glanced confusedly at the badge and the .38 for a moment, then, just as confusedly, into Erthmun's eyes. "What's this?" he said.

Erthmun left the room without answering.

He got into his bed before dark, while the pale light of late afternoon was on him. He could feel the light on his face. Usually, it was warm, and forgiving, and maternal. Now, it wasn't, and he didn't know why.

He was more exhausted than he had ever been. Surely, he thought, it was the kind of exhaustion that was like the quick approach of death, overwhelming and inescapable.

But sleep eluded him. Perhaps because it was still daylight, or perhaps because he was simply too exhausted to sleep (a complaint he had heard from others, but which he did not understand).

He lay with his eyes open under his cocoon of blankets. He lay stiff and tense, as if expecting some deadly surprise. This made him feel like an animal in hiding from predators. It was a feeling he could not remember having experienced before, and he didn't like it. It made him want to lash out at random noises—the radiators clicking, horns blaring, the rushing noise of the refrigerator springing to life.

After an hour, he threw his blankets off, went to his window, and looked out at the street below. Dusk, now, and the street lamps had winked on. People walked quickly, coat collars turned up, heads down, shoulders hunched. He guessed that it was cold beyond his window, and he wondered why he—naked—didn't feel it. He decided that his tension and anger were making him warm.

He saw his dim reflection in the window—square face, barrel chest, short, well-muscled thighs, and his great erection, too, which came to him whenever he was naked.

T. M. Wright

(This fact had caused him endless trouble in situations where he had found himself naked among other men, because erections equaled arousal, of course, and if he was with other naked men, then, ipso facto, it was they who were causing his arousal. But this was not so, and he had tried, as a teenager, to convince other young men that it wasn't so. "I'm simply . . . *ready*!" he declared, which was the truth, as he saw it, but it elicited gales of hooting laughter.)

His reflection in the window started a moment's impulse to violence, as it usually did, but the impulse dissipated almost at once.

No one this night looked up at him as he stood naked at his window. New Yorkers did not usually look up as they walked. They held their heads at a slightly downward angle and walked quickly, with purpose; it was a statement to any who might want to bother them—*Keep your distance!*

But Erthmun wasn't interested in this, and he wasn't interested in the briskly moving passersby four stories below, or in the glowering Manhattan sky. He was interested in the creature who had come to live in his city. The creature who killed with sweet and sick gusto, and who left her victims looking foolish.

She was there, in the night, where he was so unwilling to follow. She was there, in those buildings, with those people. She joked with them and laughed with them and slept with them. But she was not one with them.

She was one with *him.*

He lurched away from the window, as if he had been dealt a physical blow.

One with him? What was he thinking? He didn't even know her name. He had never seen her. He wasn't even certain that she *was* a she.

He sat on his bed, bent forward, cupped his hands on either side of his face.

He knew her. She was murderous and predatory, and she lived only to bring herself pleasure, and others pain.

And she came from the same place that he had come from.

Chapter Ten

"Is he a blood relative?" Mark Smalley asked Sylvia Grant.

"Is the answer to that question germane to your investigation?" she shot back.

Smalley shrugged, grinned. "Sure, it's germane."

"I don't see how."

"Can't you simply give me a straight answer?"

"Yes, certainly."

"Can I assume, then, that he is *not* a blood relative?"

"You may assume whatever you like, Mr. Smalley. I am obviously not in control of your assumptions." She smiled. It was comely and confrontational at the same time.

Smalley's grin became a smirk. "I should tell you that your responses reveal more than you might believe."

"I doubt, Mr. Smalley, that I am so open a book that

you can say from one moment to the next what I might or might not believe." She was still smiling. She had a cup of tea in front of her on a coffee table. She picked it up, brought it to her lips, tipped it very slightly—not enough, Smalley guessed, to drink—then put the cup down.

He was seated opposite her on the uncomfortable Queen Anne settee. He had perched himself on the edge of the settee, as if ready to leap from it at any second. He thought that it made people nervous to look like he was going to leap up at any second. It was one of several poses he employed. Sometimes, depending upon the person he was talking to, he chose to look very relaxed. He guessed that this made people believe he was a friend, or a confidant. But he had sensed that Sylvia Grant was very smart—nearly as smart as he was—and that such a pose wouldn't work. It was best, with smart people, simply to put them on edge, to appeal to their fear and paranoia, to play with their emotions. This dulled their intelligence and caused them to slip up.

He said, "Your brother looks nothing like you, Mrs. Grant. There seems to be absolutely no family resemblance. So my assumption is—"

"Again, Detective, your assumptions are of little consequence. Jack is indeed my brother, and I am his sister, and we do indeed share the same mother"—she hesitated—"and father. Now if that is the extent of your inquiry—"

"No, of course it isn't!" He heard the edge in his voice and it surprised him. He shook his head. "It's not nearly the extent of my inquiry, Mrs. Grant."

She nodded, gave him another comely and confrontational smile, delicately sipped her tea again. He looked into her cup as she set it on the coffee table. It was less than half full. He pursed his lips, annoyed, looked at her breasts, saw that she was again wearing a bra, looked into her eyes, saw that she was amused.

He leaped from the settee. "Goddamnit, you have simply *got* to be more cooperative with me!"

She smiled up at him. "When we were children, Mr. Smalley, I remember that Jack often volunteered to wash the dishes, especially in the winter. He never told me why he did this, but I guessed that he did it because the hot water felt good on his hands."

Smalley stared uncomprehendingly at her.

She continued. "When other children went sledding, Jack stayed inside and read a book, or played a game with our younger sister—checkers and Parcheesi were their favorites—or he listened to the radio. He didn't like TV. He's never liked it. He complains that it confuses him. He says that he can actually *see* the separate scanning lines, and so the picture itself is lost to him." She shrugged a little, reached for her teacup, touched it, went on. "It all sounds very fanciful, doesn't it?" She picked up the teacup, with the saucer, held it near her chin, and continued. "But in summer, and spring, and in the autumn, you couldn't keep him in the house. He'd stay out for hours and hours. Even in the pouring rain. Actually, he loved the rain. I don't believe that he loves it quite so much now." She smiled ruefully. "I suppose that's all a regrettable part of growing up." She sipped her tea; it made a slurping noise as it passed her lips, which jarred Smalley. She set the cup down. "So you see, we really did grow up together. I know him as well as anyone. He's my brother, after all."

Helen was watching a movie in a theater on 42nd Street. The movie was a sweeping, romantic saga laced with violence, and lust, pain and forgiveness, heartache, death, and renewal. She loved it. It spoke to her. It was a romance of the earth, a story about people who tilled the land and created children, who built dynasties and amassed great wealth and power, who sought to make of themselves, at any cost, something that the world would long remember. The movie's message was—*We are far more important than that which has created us!* It was a message with which she rabidly agreed. Isn't a great work of art far greater, she maintained, than the artist who creates it? And wasn't *she* a work of art? Wasn't she the earth's masterpiece! Wasn't she something unique, and fantastic! Wasn't she the only true predator in a world of prey!

Erthmun opened his apartment door and saw a cat in the long hallway. The cat sat facing him, and its large eyes were on him. The cat was licking its chops, as if it had just eaten something tasty. It was a very big gray cat, and Erthmun could hear it purring, even though it was at the end of the long hallway. *Big cat, big purr,* Erthmun thought.

A door opened near the cat and a young woman dressed in a blue satin robe came partway into the hall, bent over, and scooped the cat up. As she straightened, she saw Erthmun and nodded and smiled at him. He nodded back.

"Hello, Mr. Erthmun," she said.

"Hello," he said. He looked quickly down at himself, uncertain that he wasn't naked. He saw that he, too, was wearing a blue robe.

The woman said, "We're both wearing blue robes."

Erthmun nodded. He felt an erection starting. The woman was tall, brunette, and her mouth went a little crooked when she smiled, as if she were remembering some delicious secret. Erthmun said, referring to their blue robes, "We are, aren't we."

She nodded. She stroked the cat's ears as they talked. The cat's purring was very loud. He was so large that his rear end hung to below her waist, and his tail to her knees. Erthmun didn't believe that he had ever before seen such a large cat.

He said, "That's an awfully big cat."

"He's a Maine coon cat," said the young woman, and gave him one of her crooked smiles; he loved her smile—it fired up his erection.

He saw her glance at his crotch; she smiled once more. "It was good talking to you, Mr. Erthmun," she said. "Perhaps we can talk again."

"Talk again," Erthmun echoed her. "Yes." But she had already disappeared into her apartment.

In his own apartment, Erthmun thought about mounting the woman in the blue robe. She could even hold her big cat while he did it, he decided. He would mount her from behind, while she cradled the big cat in her arms. He would bend her over the bed and mount her from behind. He'd lift her robe up and enter her, while she cradled her cat in her arms. She would smile her crooked smile, and her big cat would purr while he pushed himself into her. He'd put his hands on her ass while he pushed into her, and he'd knead one cheek of her ass while she smiled her crooked smile.

He ejaculated as these thoughts came to him. And when his erection subsided, and as the pleasure of his ejaculation slowly left him, he looked down at his stained blue robe, and he felt suddenly, completely, and terribly alone.

* * *

Patricia David stared at the body splayed out in the bottom of the empty Dumpster on East 75th Street and said to the detective with her—a heavyset, jowly and, as legend had it, deadly serious middle-aged man named McBride, "This is a copycat killing."

"Is it?" said McBride. "How can you tell?"

"Look at the wounds." She played her flashlight along the length of the naked body. "It's like someone went after her with a lawnmower, for Christ's sake. There's no finesse here."

McBride harrumphed his agreement.

"This is not a good thing," Patricia said.

"It's a terrible thing," said McBride.

"I mean that we have a copycat killer," Patricia said. "One killer was awful, but two is really lousy."

McBride gave her a disapproving look.

"You don't agree?" Patricia said.

"With what?"

"That two killers is really lousy."

"I don't think 'lousy' is the word I'd use under these circumstances."

"Oh," Patricia said.

"I think 'tragic' is more the word I'd use."

"Sure, it fits."

"This young woman"—he nodded at the corpse—"was someone's daughter, someone's sweetheart, someone's mother, perhaps."

"Conceded."

"And she has been reduced to . . . this." He looked at the body. "You know, she looks like . . . her face looks like the face of a girl I took to a dance, once. I think it was a dance. It might have been a movie." He glanced confusedly at Patricia, then at the body again. "I think *was* a movie. *Breakheart Pass*, I think. With Charles

Bronson." He glanced at Patricia again, held his hand out for the flashlight; she gave it to him. He shone the light on the corpse's face. "Jesus, she's the spitting image of that girl. Her name was Brenda. Pretty little thing." He held the light on the corpse's face for a long while, without speaking.

"And?" Patricia said.

"And not a whole hell of a lot," said McBride. "This isn't Brenda. It couldn't be. Brenda's my age now."

"Of course," said Patricia.

"But she could be Brenda's daughter. I don't think she *is* Brenda's daughter. But she could be." He shone the flashlight down the length of the body. "Jeez, I hate to see this sort of thing. Don't you hate to see this sort of thing? It's so . . . disrespectful."

"At the very least," said Patricia.

"I mean, she could be somebody's *mother,* for God's sake. Or somebody's sister."

"Yes," Patricia said.

"And now here she is. In a Dumpster! No one deserves to end up in a Dumpster, wouldn't you agree?"

Patricia said nothing. She guessed that his question was rhetorical.

He looked at her. "Well, don't you?"

She nodded quickly. "Yes. I agree. It's a horrible place to end up."

"Damn right. I mean, it's not like she's a transient or something. Good Lord, she could be somebody's *mother.*"

Chapter Eleven

The man thought, *I am powerful, and I am in control.*

He had photographs. He'd developed them himself in a rented darkroom, and they were spread out in front of him on his kitchen table.

He lived in one room and shared a bathroom with nine other tenants on the second floor of his building. The building was on 123rd Street, and it was rambling, nasty, and decrepit.

The man thought he was a very good photographer. He had used his new flash attachment well; he had illuminated the woman's body without causing harsh reflections, and without making her loom out of the dark background like a phantom. He had many talents, and photography was only one of them.

Murder, he guessed, was another. This first ambitious effort, at any rate, indicated that he had much potential.

T. M. Wright

And it was unfortunate that the *Post* had referred to him as a "copycat." When a man embarks on a new endeavor, he has to start *somewhere*. Why not on a path that has led another to glory? Later, he could make his own path.

He loved his photographs. They were the best he'd ever done because they were *real*. No poses, no artifice. Just reality—hard, cold, and pungent!

A knock came at his door and he snapped his gaze to it. No one had ever knocked at his door. He paid his rent on time and stayed away from the others who lived in the building, so who could be knocking? Certainly not the police. He was too smart for them. And they wouldn't knock anyway.

Another knock—soft, but insistent.

"Who's there?" he called.

"Who's there, indeed," he heard. It was a woman's voice.

This was wonderful. Fortuitous. Karmic. A woman at his door!

He stood, glanced at his photographs, thought briefly of hiding them, decided that the woman at his door would be impressed with them, went to the door, opened it quickly.

She was beautiful. Beyond beautiful. Sky-blue eyes and hip-length auburn hair and a body that was the promise of pleasure. "Do you know me?" she said.

"No," he said, grinning obscenely. "Not the way I'd like to."

"And you are?"

"Roger," he said.

"Well, then, Roger," she said, and moved past him, into his room, "I have something for you."

He watched her move, loved the way she moved, thought she would look good to his lens, and to his

60

weapon, and then to his bawdy instrument.

She was turned away from him. She was perfectly configured, he thought. Perfectly wrought and conceived. He said, "Oh, what?"

And she turned as quickly as a snake and plunged her hand deep into his gut, into his colon, and snarled, "Oblivion!"

Chapter Twelve

Thirty-seven Years Earlier
Early August in the Adirondack Mountains
Near the House on Four Mile Creek

This is good here, the woman thought in so many words. She was inclined to such thoughts. She was a poet, and her work had been published in several university journals and small literary reviews. She had even had a nibble of interest from a New York City book publisher, though she had been giving the whole idea of book publication more than a few second thoughts because she wasn't sure that she was quite ready. She did not believe that her work was yet mannered enough. It tended, as well, toward the darkly romantic, and it was filled with unfortunate angst, worry, and despair. She needed to cultivate a lighter attitude, although poetry, she maintained, should not be about love; it should be about hope, which was so much more than love. It was more than sex, too, of course, which was, itself, so much less than love or hope.

She smiled as these thoughts came to her on this warm and sunlit afternoon. She smiled because she could not remember having had such fanciful thoughts before—perhaps she could work them into a poem before long. She smiled, too, because the birds were gaily chattering at her, and because the squirrels were gamboling playfully among the oaks and tulip trees, and because the honeybees were busily foraging among the wildflowers.

It was surely a poet's day!

She was happy there was no one else about. Happy that Thomas had found this secluded place for them to raise their three young daughters. As a family, they could choose when to engage in social relationships, and they could choose when to employ solitude, which was what she had chosen for herself today. She thought that she would like to lie down in the tall, pale green grass. It was something she had never done before, though she had seen it depicted in paintings. She had always been a little leery of doing it herself because meadows such as this were alive with insects and spiders. But she thought that should be of no consequence to her. Insects and spiders were, after all, a part of the natural and benevolent world to which Thomas had brought her and the children. He might not be a kind and benevolent man himself, but Thomas Erthmun was thoughtful enough to put his wife and daughters in a kind and benevolent place.

Out of the corner of her eye, she saw movement in a line of trees not far off, as if someone were running. She turned her head quickly, but saw nothing. She sighed. Who could be here? It was miles to another house, and besides, their land was posted. Perhaps she had seen a deer, or a fox. Yes, of course. There was no doubt of it. She had seen a deer or a fox. It made her glad, and she smiled again.

But she did not lie down in the weeds right away. She kept her eyes on the line of trees where she had seen movement until, at last, a chipmunk appeared on the side of a great oak and she sighed again and thought, *Well, that is what I saw. A chipmunk.* And she lay down in the tall weeds, adjusted herself so her head was comfortably on a clump of earth, spread her arms wide, closed her eyes, and let the warm sunlight play on her face. This was wonderful, she thought. This was heaven. Alone with the works of nature. Alone with what God had wrought. Somewhere in this experience there was a poem.

She heard movement in the weeds nearby. Her eyes popped open. She thought of calling out, "Who's there?" But she kept silence. Who *could* be there? Who would disturb this perfect and poetic moment, these minutes stolen from eternity, this time that she had given to her soul so it could breathe? But still, she turned her head a little and looked in the direction where she had heard movement. She saw the tops of oak and tulip trees, a coagulated mass of pale green grasses, a praying mantis moving on the earth close to her face. She listened. After a minute, she closed her eyes again and let the sunlight play on her skin, and let her soul breathe.

She was dressed well, in a long, flowing, earth-colored skirt and a green cotton long-sleeved blouse that had no pockets, and which billowed nicely around her breasts, and hugged her waist. Her hair was red, and she wore it long. Thomas had told her often that she was an attractive woman, and she knew that it was true, but she did not want to cultivate this attractiveness because that would be superficial.

Sleep had never come with difficulty to her, and it did not come with difficulty now. The sun was warm, a leisurely breeze was stirring the tall, pale green grasses, and she was alone in the meadow, except for her soul, which could soar on the wings of this glorious day.

So she slept.

And dreamed.

And, in her dream, she saw the face of an angel above her. It was a dark and perfect face, and its eyes were sky-blue, and enormous passion was in its mouth.

And then she felt her own passion responding, felt it swelling up from within her, heard the moans that came from her own mouth, and felt, too quickly, too quickly, the inrush of seed and love and man.

And she awoke breathing very hard, and saw that her earth-colored skirt was around her waist, and that her panties were torn, and her legs wide, and that the insides of her thighs were chaffed and wet. And she heard something moving swiftly off through the sunlit weeds.

And when she turned her head to look, she saw flowing dark hair, and a naked back.

And she screamed.

Chapter Thirteen

Patricia David had never visited Erthmun at his apartment in the West Village. She had never needed to—she'd always assumed that their relationship was strictly professional. She had suspected, in fact, that she didn't like him very much. She respected him as a cop, but he was often humorless, distant, off-putting, at times even rude. He was clearly a man who valued his privacy, and she had always been more than happy to give it to him.

So she was a little perplexed as to why she was ringing his buzzer and waiting for some response from him through the building's intercom. She could have telephoned. She had no reason to believe—now that their professional relationship had been put on hold—that he needed to see her any more than she thought she needed to see him.

She rang the buzzer for a third time. Shit, it was obvious that he wasn't home. She reached behind her, found the knob for the outside door.

"Yes?" she heard through the intercom. She hesitated, let go of the knob, pressed the talk button. "Jack?" she said tentatively.

"Yes."

"It's me. Patricia."

Silence.

"Jack?"

"I'm here. What is it?"

She sighed. "I don't know. I was a little . . . concerned."

"Concerned. Do you want to come up?"

"Not if I'm disturbing you. Am I dis—"

The inner door clicked; she grabbed the knob, opened the door, heard, "You know the apartment number?"

She stretched her arm back for the talk button and called, "Yes. It's how I buzzed you in the first place."

"Oh, of course," Erthmun said.

He had wrapped himself in a green quilt to answer his door. She thought that he was shivering a little beneath it, and that he did not look rested or happy. He even seemed to be having trouble keeping his eyes open.

"You were asleep, Jack?" Patricia said from outside the door. "I'm sorry." She glanced at her watch, saw that it was barely 8:00 p.m., gave him a look of concern. "Are you ill?"

He shook his head. "Ill? No, it's all right." His voice was hoarse. "Come in." He backed unsteadily away from the door.

She looked past him, into the apartment, first. It was dark, except for light filtering in from beyond the windows. She said, "Could you turn a light on, Jack?"

He nodded and flipped a switch next to the doorway.

T. M. Wright

A low-wattage overhead copper fixture bathed the room in a soft yellowish light. She saw a threadbare, red couch under the windows, a white enamel dining table and two white wooden chairs, a small refrigerator; a black clock radio stood on top of the refrigerator.

Jack took another step back. "Are you coming in?" he said; he sounded peeved.

But she thought she wasn't sure if she was coming in. Perhaps this had been a mistake. Jesus, the man lived like a hermit, and from his tone and demeanor, she was the last person he wanted to see tonight.

"Patricia, please," he coaxed. "I'm glad you're here."

"You are?"

He managed a lopsided smile.

She stepped into the apartment. He closed the door. She stood quietly for a moment, then said, "This is very Spartan, isn't it?"

"It's my taste," Jack said; he was standing behind her, at the door. "No TV?" she said, because she was an avid TV watcher. She glanced around at him.

"No TV," he said, and managed another smile. She thought he was doing more smiling now than he had ever done during their shifts together. "Why don't I put some clothes on, Patricia." He went to his bed, where he'd draped a pair of jeans and a gray sweatshirt over the footboard, scooped them up, went into his little bathroom, and reappeared moments later. He smiled again; it was a good and comforting smile, she thought, though she did not feel comforted by it, and wasn't sure why. "Okay," he said, "what can I do for you?"

She shrugged. "Nothing, really." She looked around for a chair, saw that there was only the threadbare couch and white wooden dining chairs. She gestured at them. "Can I sit down, Jack?"

"Can you sit down?" Another smile; he seemed amused. "Why wouldn't I let you sit down, Patricia?"

She shrugged again. She realized how nervous she looked, and it embarrassed her—they'd worked together for over a year, after all. She nodded, went to one of the dining chairs, pulled it out, sat on it.

"You could sit on the couch, Patricia," Jack said.

"No, no. This is good. I've always liked sitting in kitchens."

"I don't have a kitchen."

"Sure, well, this is a kitchen," she said, meaning the dining table and chairs, the refrigerator, the little gas stove.

He sat across the table from her, smiled again his good and comforting smile, and she thought she was beginning to feel at least a little comforted by it. "It's pleasant to see you, Patricia," he said. "I'm glad you came."

"I should have called first," she said.

He shook his head, then smiled again. "Do you want something? Some coffee, a beer, maybe some tea?"

"Thanks, no. I'm not staying long—"

"Why?"

"Why?" The question took her aback.

Erthmun said, "You can stay as long as you'd like." He reached across the table a bit, as if to touch her hand, though his reach didn't extend far enough. His fingers fluttered for a moment in the air between them; then he laid his hand flat on the white enamel tabletop.

Patricia lowered her gaze because his gaze was so . . . expectant. "Jack, I'm sorry . . . did you believe that I—"

"Did I hope that you were coming on to me?" Another smile. "Perhaps."

She shook her head, gaze still averted. "I was concerned about you, Jack. Only concerned. And I thought you might like an update." She heard a little tremor in her voice, as if she were lying; it surprised her.

"An update," Jack said.

"On these murders."

He nodded a little. "On these murders. Yes. I'd like an update."

She wasn't sure if she believed him. She said, "Actually, there's not a whole hell of a lot to report." Again, she heard a tremor in her voice. "You know about the copycat—"

"I read the papers."

"Then you know that he was murdered?"

"Yes."

She took a breath. "I probably shouldn't be telling you this, Jack, since you're not involved with the investigation anymore—" She hesitated as if uncertain how to continue.

"Go on," Jack coaxed.

She nodded stiffly. "He had the same things done to him that the killer did to the women."

Erthmun didn't miss a beat: "You mean the chocolate in the mouth, et cetera?"

Patricia tried to gauge his demeanor; his tone seemed oddly flat. "Yes," she said.

He nodded a little, his dark eyes closed as if he were in thought. He said nothing for a long moment:

"Jack?" she said.

He opened his eyes. She saw something indefinable in them—a strange combination of desperation, panic, memory. He said, "Then his killer was the same person who killed the two women."

"Yes. The killer was making a statement, I think. Putting the copycat in his place." She felt a little smile creep onto her lips.

"Putting the copycat in his place." He paused. "Yes, that's obvious, isn't it."

"The green contacts, too," Patricia said.

"Of course," Jack said. He sounded suddenly disconnected from the conversation.

Patricia pushed on. "And as for the overall investigation, we have just about zip, I'm afraid. No prints, no weapon—"

Jack cut in. "I would have been glad, Patricia, if you *had* been coming on to me. But since you weren't, and aren't—that's okay." He leaned far over the table and touched her hand.

She looked silently at his hand.

He said, "Am I making you uncomfortable?"

She lifted her gaze to his and nodded a little.

"Why?" he said.

Why? she wondered. For God's sake, he had to ask *Why?* "Perhaps this was a mistake, Jack." She stood.

"It wasn't," he said, and smiled up at her from his end of the table. "Please, sit down. I really do have no expectations at all in this situation."

She thought about this, decided he was sincere, realized that she really didn't know what her own expectations were tonight. At last, she sat down again, sighed, and said, "Tell me how Internal Affairs is treating you, Jack."

"I'd rather not."

"I understand."

"It's unpleasant," he said. "It's business. They're treating me poorly."

"Smalley seems like a real asshole," Patricia said.

"He's a limited man doing a tough job," Erthmun said. He sat back in his chair, smiled again—clearly to get on to another topic—and said, "I'm going to have a beer. Have one with me, okay?"

71

She nodded. "Sure."

He stood, went to his refrigerator, poked around in it, came back to the table with two bottles, asked if she needed a glass.

"No," she said.

He sat across from her again. "I want to tell you something significant," he said.

This made her smile. It was so formal.

"Significant?" she said.

He wrapped his hand tightly around his beer bottle, looked earnestly at her for a moment, then turned his head to look out the window. She noticed, for the first time, an odd smell in the place. It wasn't unpleasant. It was evocative of . . . the earth, she thought, and she realized that she had smelled it before, at other times, while she and Jack had worked together. But it was less distinct, then.

He said, "I am not the person I appear to be."

Her immediate inclination was to say, *Who is?* But this would be trite, she decided, even insulting. Clearly, Jack thought that his pronouncement was indeed significant, so she said nothing.

He went on. "I would say, in other words, that I don't know who I am."

"Sort of like a mid-life crisis?" Patricia offered.

"Sort of like a mid-life crisis?" He grinned and shook his head. "No. It's too soon for that."

She grinned back, embarrassed.

"Shit, Patricia, I'm only thirty-seven years old. Do I look older?"

"No, no. You look thirty-seven."

Another grin. "Not thirty-six or thirty-eight?"

She chuckled.

He said, "Do you remember much of your childhood, Patricia?"

"Yes. I had a good childhood. I'm a little surprised when other people complain about their unhappy childhoods. Mine wasn't unhappy. Mine was okay. I remember most of it, I think. I remember milking a cow when I was . . . two years old."

"You grew up on a farm?"

"No. I was a city brat. But my grandparents lived on a farm and we visited them a lot. They were great. They used to sing us French folk songs and my grandfather played caroms with us till our fingers hurt—"

"Caroms?"

"Sure. You never played caroms?"

"I don't remember playing any games when I was a kid, Patricia."

This announcement surprised her. "All kids play games, Jack. It doesn't matter who they are or who their parents are. All kids play games. The kids in Harlem have the fire hydrants turned on in the summer and they run around in the water. That's a game."

"I remember running, yes," Erthmun said. "I remember running everywhere." He leaned over the table and lowered his head, so his gaze was on the lip of his beer bottle. "Jesus, I could run like a fucking jackrabbit. Jesus!" He grinned. "I don't *look* like I could run like a jackrabbit, do I? But I could. I remember it."

Patricia reached far across the table and touched his hand. She wanted to say something comforting.

He went on, looking at her. "I had four sisters, did you know that?"

She shook her head. "No, I didn't."

He nodded, lowered his gaze again. "One died shortly after I was born."

73

"I'm sorry."

"She disappeared, actually. She was six years old. She went out to play . . . she went to a place that my mother had told her to stay away from, and no one ever saw her again." He closed his eyes and shook his head, as if the memory gave him pain, although, Patricia guessed, he couldn't have remembered the incident. "They found her clothes. Her shorts and her shirt and sneakers. I remember that my mother told me to stay away from the same place when I was three or four. I don't think I obeyed her. I can't remember. I think I went there once or twice. I think I actually went there looking for my sister. The sister I'd never met." He glanced out the window, then into Patricia's eyes again. "I've seen pictures of her. She was a cute little thing."

"She looked like you, Jack?"

He shook his head. "No. None of my sisters looks like me. They're all tall and blond and gray-eyed."

"Very pretty, then."

"Very." He grinned at her.

She saw her faux pas. "Jeez, I didn't mean that the way it sounded, Jack. You're a very attractive man."

"A very attractive man," Jack echoed her. "I'm built like a fire hydrant."

"Yes, but you're an attractive fire hydrant. I mean that."

He nodded, said they were getting off the subject, to which Patricia said, "I didn't know we were on a particular subject."

"Yes," he said. "We are. Me. Fascinating subject." Then he smiled again, and she realized, at last, what all his smiling and grinning should have already told her.

"My God, Jack, this *is* some kind of crisis you're going through, isn't it?"

"Crisis?" he said, and seemed to think about the word for a moment. "Yes," he said, still smiling.

"This is a personal crisis for you, isn't it?" she said.

"It's that and a lot more," he said. "And I'm sorry I've trapped you in it."

"Trapped me in it? I don't feel trapped."

"But you are, Patricia."

It sounded like a threat, though Patricia was certain he hadn't meant it that way. She said, "I don't know what you mean, Jack," and felt a nervous grin play on her mouth. She took a sip of beer, heard it pass noisily down her throat, chuckled a little, embarrassed, and set the bottle down hard on the tabletop.

Erthmun said, "Do I scare you?"

"Scare me?" she chirped.

"I do, don't I?"

"No. Why should you?" She gave him a big, broad smile.

"I shouldn't," he said. "But I think I do. I'm . . . unpredictable."

She said nothing. He was right, but she didn't want to tell him so.

He said, "I scare myself these days." He stopped talking; he looked perplexed.

"And?" Patricia coaxed after a few moments.

"It's like . . . Do you know about the tumors some people get . . . they get tumors, say, in their groin or in their armpit, and when the doctors take them out, these tumors are the remnants of the person's twin? Have you heard of that? Jesus, it's ghastly, isn't it!"

Patricia didn't know what to say. She took another noisy sip of her beer. She wanted to leave the apartment, but had no idea how to do it without hurting his feelings. He was right, she realized. She really *was* trapped.

He went on. "It's like I have one of those twins inside me, Patricia. But it isn't a twin *per se*. It's not a clot of fetal matter that might once have been my brother." He grinned oddly. "It's part of *me*." He paused, as if for thought, and continued. "It's what *completes* me." He seemed to think about this, too, then sighed. He looked hopelessly at sea. "Do you have any idea what I'm talking about, Patricia?"

She didn't. She said, "I think so, Jack. I'm not sure." She took another noisy sip of her beer.

"Listen, I'm sorry," he said. "This all sounds very, very strange, doesn't it? I'm really sorry. But there's something else, too. This thing inside me, this . . . *me* inside me . . . Jesus, it's"—he pointed stiffly at the window—"*out there*, too! And it's not just one, or two or three, it's . . . dozens. Hundreds!"

She nodded quickly. "Yes, out there," she said. "I understand," she finished; it was a lie.

He looked hard at her, slowly lowered his arm, wrapped his hand tightly around his beer bottle. "This could have been a romantic evening for us, Patricia," he said.

Chapter Fourteen

The city bus moved leadenly through the deep, new snow. Beyond its windows, the Manhattan streets were white and gray streaked with flashes of yellow—the city's taxis moving about in the storm with the agility of rabbits.

The woman who called herself Helen sat rigidly in a seat near the back of the bus, where the bus's heater blew hot air on her legs and feet and warmed her enough that she could breathe.

The woman wasn't frightened, though she could not move. She was a creature caught up in a battle for survival, because she had chanced into the hands of her killer—the storm, the snow, the bitter cold.

She did not give time to regret or self-recrimination. She felt the awful pain that the frigid night air gave her, but she did not cry out, or weep. In her short time on the earth, she had never cried out or wept because of pain.

* * *

Patricia had gotten up to leave Erthmun's apartment. The act surprised her. She didn't believe, rationally, that she was afraid of the man. He puzzled her, she thought, but surely he didn't frighten her.

She had gotten halfway to the door when he'd called, "Don't go out there, Patricia. Please stay." If she had listened to his words alone, she would have assumed it was a sexual invitation. But his tone seemed to be one of urgency, as if it were desperately important for her to remain in the apartment with him.

She looked back at him and said, "Why?"

"Because I want you to stay here. With me."

"I can't."

"This isn't a come-on. Do you think it's a come-on?"

"No."

"Yes, you do. Of course you do. What else would it be? But it isn't. I really do want you to stay. An hour or two. We'll have something to eat. I'll make us some food. I have lots of food here. I have steak, I have some steak. I could cook it. You must be hungry."

She stared at him a few moments and it came to her what was wrapped up in all this babble—he was trying to protect her!

The woman who called herself Helen did not try to understand why this cold night was so different for her than other cold nights. She did not say to herself, *It's because this is the coldest night of the year,* or *The wind-chill factor is low,* or *It's a combination of the wind and the snow and the cold.* These facts meant nothing to her. And her pain meant next to nothing to her—it was merely an obstacle to overcome.

The bus was empty, except for herself and the bus

driver, and he was taking the bus back to the bus barn because his shift was done. He hadn't yet noticed her, but he did now, and he called, "You gotta get off the bus, lady." He pulled over to the curb and opened the rear doors.

She said nothing. She didn't look at him. The blast of cold air did not make her wince, but it drove her pain deeper, and made her muscles tense. And it started in her as well, an instinct, a capacity, and a power that she had used often since coming to this city, though not in a way that could draw much attention to her.

The driver said again, "You gotta get off the bus, lady." He looked at her in the rearview mirror, saw that she wasn't looking back at him, muttered, "Shit," thought, *She's drunk, dammit!* stood, and started walking back to her. "Come on, lady," he said. "Don't make life difficult for the both of us." He stopped walking. She had looked up at him, had leveled her gaze on him. "Jesus Christ!" he whispered.

"Jesus Christ!" she whispered, and her voice was *his* voice.

He started backing away from her, tried to keep his eyes on her, but couldn't because she wasn't there. Then she *was* there. Then she wasn't. She was a part of the bus seat, a part of the advertising placard overhead—Bacardi rum—a part of the dark floor, a part of the rear window and the blowing snow, the headlights, the neon, the street lamps, the wind, the black sky. But she was teeth as well, and breasts, hips, sky-blue eyes, and dark pubic hair. She was a naked phantom, and she was a living woman, dressed garishly for an evening in cheap hotels. She was a part of the dark floor, the neon, the blowing snow, and the black sky.

The bus driver fell backward in his desperation to get

away from her. He muttered little pleading obscenities at her, saw her coalesce with the air itself, saw her reappear—teeth and hands and breasts and pubic hair.

Then she was upon him.

Patricia said, "Jack, does all of this have anything to do with the woman you called Helen?"

"Helen? Yes," he answered, "it does. She exists. There is at least a Helen."

She gave him a puzzled look. *At least a Helen?* She said, "You know this woman?"

"Know this woman? I don't think so. I've never met her. I've never met any of them."

Patricia sighed. *I've never met any of them?* What was that supposed to mean? Jesus, the man was falling apart before her eyes. She came back and stood behind her chair at the white enamel table. "What in heaven's name are you talking about, Jack? Is this all in the nature of . . . intuition, premonition, precognition? You're not making a hell of a lot of sense."

He looked at her a moment, looked out the window, looked at her again, said, "I don't know what any of that is, really." He noticed for the first time that a storm had begun.

Patricia said, "You mean you don't know the definitions of—"

He gave her a weary smile. "Sit down, Patricia."

She hesitated, then sat down. He said, "You can't go anywhere anyway. Look at it out there."

She looked, scowled. "Shit," she muttered.

"So you see, you've got to stay."

"Yes," she said.

"Yes," he said. "I'm glad."

* * *

Helen did not eat all of the bus driver. But she ate some of him. The tender parts. His palms, his cheeks, his stomach, his thighs. He was a very overweight man, and the fat did her good. It gave her warmth and strength.

And when she was done with him, she left the bus through the rear doors that he had opened for her, and she moved quickly through the snow-covered streets. No one saw her, and no one looked. There were few out and about on the streets of Manhattan this winter night, except the taxis, and if their drivers looked in Helen's direction, they would have seen only a change in the pattern of the blowing snow, little else, and they would have thought nothing of it.

"Can I have another beer?" Patricia asked. "If I'm staying, there's no real reason to remain sober."

Jack said, "I don't really know what that means," and smiled, got up, got another beer from the refrigerator, brought it back to her. She looked at the label, told him he had good taste in beer.

"I like beer," he said. "I like to *eat,* in fact."

Patricia said, "You mentioned something about a steak." She was beginning to feel more comfortable with him. Maybe it was the alcohol, though she didn't make much of an effort to analyze it. She trusted her instincts, though they seemed to be running in opposite directions tonight.

He nodded, went back to the refrigerator, withdrew two T-bones, took them to his little counter, and turned his gas broiler on to preheat. He said, as he took the steaks from their Styrofoam containers, "I'm hungry, too. I don't usually eat at this time of the night. I'm usually asleep."

This had not seemed like a rebuke to Patricia, but she said anyway, "If I'm keeping you—"

"I'll sleep another night," he cut in, smiling.

She thought that his smile had changed. There was nothing of crisis in it now. It seemed to signal that he was genuinely pleased to have her there with him, and this made her feel good.

She stood, joined him at the counter, said, "Is there something I can do?"

"Do?" he said. "Yes, you can eat what I make for you."

"I will," she said. Then. "Tell me what you meant about Helen."

"I don't know what I meant. It was a hunch, I think." He got a bottle of seasoning from a drawer. "Do you want some of this on yours?"

"No. I like it plain. And rare."

"A woman after my own heart."

"About Helen?" Patricia said.

"Not much," he said. "I don't know." He grinned oddly at her. "What's in a name, after all?"

The woman loved being a part of this city. She loved the buildings and the lights and the odor of diesel fuel. During the summer just passed—her first summer—she had loved going into the parks at night and stripping naked, and running, and running, and running. She loved running at night through the streets, weaving like a quirky breeze through the little knots of people, and then tossing her strange and coarse laughter back at them.

Memories meant little to her now. She remembered the name she had taken—Helen—because she loved the sound of it, and she remembered the building where she spent her days, because it was a place where no one else spent time, and so it was a place of protection.

And she remembered her birth especially, because it was a time of enormous pain and incredible pleasure.

And she remembered coming here, to this city. Remembered being drawn to it by the heady mixture of smells, by the noise, by the feel of the air and the ever-present promise of pleasure.

She slept now. She was a night hunter, her hunting was done, and so it was time to sleep. The sounds and smells of the city were distant in this place, distant enough, at least, that they did not draw her. And this early morning, the sounds of the storm covered them, too.

She curled up in her cocoon of quilts and blankets, and she dreamed only of being a clump of earth, a rock, a root. She did not remember these dreams because such things as clumps of earth, rocks, and roots have no memory.

Chapter Fifteen

Thirty-eight Years Earlier
Summer in the Adirondacks

Cecile Erthmun had the words ready, and she could see that Thomas—who had just come out of the bathroom and was rubbing his face with a black towel—was looking expectantly at her, as if he knew she had something to say, but the words that came out of her were not the words she so needed to say.

"Bacon this morning, Thomas?" she said.

He looked silently at her a moment, as if trying to decide if she was being somehow dishonest, then nodded, and went back into the bathroom.

She threw her blanket off, swung her feet to the floor, heard herself call out, *Thomas, I was raped!* But she knew that she had said nothing.

She stood.

Thomas reappeared. He was a very tall man; his face was angular and his eyes intense and authoritarian. He went to a closet, opened it, rummaged in it a moment, found a white shirt, put it on. As he buttoned it, he said, "I'm going to be gone for two weeks, Cecile."

"Two weeks?" The idea frightened her—she and the girls alone at the house for two weeks! How could he let that happen? "That long?" she said.

He nodded again. "Breakfast?" he coaxed.

She nodded back, but stayed where she was, seated on the edge of the bed in her yellow, floor-length, cotton nightgown. He gave her a questioning smile. She looked away briefly, looked back, smiled a little, stood.

"Is something wrong?" he asked.

She didn't answer at once. She went around the bed, found her slippers, put them on.

"Cecile, I asked you a question."

She went to a clothes tree near the bedroom door, got her green robe, put it on, looked back at him, sighed, nodded.

He said, "Is that a yes?"

She nodded again. "I think . . ." She paused. "I had some . . . difficulty yesterday, Thomas."

"Did you?" His tone betrayed no concern.

She nodded. "Thomas, I think that we should . . . leave here."

"Leave here? Leave this house?" He was clearly astonished.

She nodded a little, in pretended uncertainty.

He said, "Why in heaven's name should we leave? I have no intention of leaving."

She heard herself yell at him, *For God's sake, Thomas,*

I was raped! But she knew, again, that she had said nothing.

He repeated, "I have no intention of leaving this house, Cecile. I brought you and the girls here for a reason. The cities are turning into muck and mire. We have had this discussion. Why should I leave this house?"

She stared at him. He was so intransigent. Why had she ever married him?

He said, "Home schooling is best for the girls, as we have agreed. And you can write your poetry here. I can think of nothing more fitting for a woman such as you than to be ensconced in her country house writing poetry. It's fitting that this is something a woman should do. And we need have no worry about the filth of the cities infecting us."

I was raped! she heard herself whisper, and wondered if the words had actually passed her lips.

"What was that?" Thomas said.

She thought that he had heard her say something, and that he was asking her to repeat it. She shook her head. "Nothing," she said.

"More than *nothing*," he said, and moved quickly past her, into the hall. She saw him look left, right. "Damnit," he whispered. He looked back into the bedroom. "Well, didn't you see it?" he snapped.

"See what?"

"Someone ran past this doorway."

"One of the girls—"

"Not one of the girls! It was male."

"My God!" Cecile breathed.

Thomas went to the railing that looked out on the first floor of the house.

"Thomas?" Cecile said.

He waved his hand behind him. "Quiet. I'm listening."

"To what?"

"Shut up, Cecile!"

She fell silent.

The house had been built so its facade faced east, and the rising sun. A huge open area stood at the front of the house; a tall, multi-paned window had been built above the front door. It was not quite 6:15, and the sun was rising now, casting yellow light through the tall window, into the house, and onto the landing, where Thomas stood. A stationary, horizontal shadow was also cast through the window; this was from the limb of a huge oak tree just inside the perimeter of the stylized picket fence.

As Thomas stood at the landing, a shadow moved on top of the horizontal shadow. "Oh, yes," Thomas whispered.

"What is it?" Cecile said.

"Your damned cat!" Thomas said, and turned to face her. "See there?" He pointed. The shadow of a cat moving on the limb was on the floor of the landing, and on the railing. "It was your damned cat!" Thomas repeated.

Cecile shook her head quickly.

"But it was," Thomas assured her. "It was the cat."

It wasn't the fucking cat! Cecile heard herself say, but realized, again, that she had said nothing.

"Mystery solved," Thomas declared. "No mystery whatever." He looked questioningly at her. "Breakfast?" he coaxed once more.

Chapter Sixteen

Patricia David thought that her night with Jack Erthmun had been incredible. She thought that she was a reasonably attractive woman—she exercised, usually ate the right foods, wore nice clothes, kept up with current events. Men were *attracted* to her, for Christ's sake. She got asked out by strangers at least three or four times a week. So why in the hell had Jack Erthmun let her sleep on his bed—while he slept on the couch—without making a move? What had the evening actually meant? It was clear that he was attracted to her, and she had to admit, however reluctantly, that she was attracted to him.

Her new partner, McBride, apparently caught on to her perplexity, because he said, from his desk, "Something wrong?"

She had just come into the squad room; she was forty-five minutes late. She shook her head too quickly, muttered, "No. Nothing," heard the peevish tone in her voice, and hoped that McBride hadn't heard it, too. She didn't want him asking a lot of questions.

He shrugged. "Okay." He handed a Polaroid snapshot across the desk. "I hope you haven't eaten yet."

She took the photograph. Her stomach lurched. "Jesus," she said, "this guy looks like he's been *cannibalized*!"

"He was," said McBride. "They found him early this morning. He was a bus driver. They found him in his bus."

Patricia said, staring open-mouthed at the Polaroid, "You mean, someone actually *ate* him?"

McBride nodded. "Not all of him, though. Just the juicy parts. His hands, you know. The fleshy parts of his hands, and his gut. His genitals, too."

"Yes," said Patricia. "I see."

"It's not without precedent, of course. Even in this country. People get eaten a lot more than you might like to think, and I'm not talking only about Jeffrey Dahmer. Sometimes we pull transients and homeless people out of some of these abandoned buildings and you'd swear that it wasn't only rats that had been eating them. Of course, no one looks too closely into these deaths. I mean, who cares, right?"

Patricia didn't answer. She handed the Polaroid back. "I assume he's at the morgue."

McBride nodded.

Chapter Seventeen

Thirty-six Years Earlier
In the House on Four Mile Creek

This is how Cecile Erthmun wanted to begin her admonition to her six-year-old daughter, Rebecca: "If I've told you once, I've told you a *thousand* times..." But she didn't say that because her mother had said the same thing to her, a thousand times, and she wasn't about to repeat her mother's mistakes.

Rebecca looked expectantly at Cecile Erthmun. Rebecca was a child who could guilelessly defuse anger with just such a look; it said, *I am listening to you because you love me, and because I love you.*

Cecile Erthmun asked, "Do you remember what I said about that place?"

Rebecca nodded, her pretty rosebud mouth open a little, as if she did not really understand the purpose of her mother's question, and her gray eyes locked on her mother's dark brown eyes, because her mother's eyes were, of course, the source of all love and caring.

"Good, then," said Cecile Erthmun. "Good." She leaned over and gave her daughter a hug. Rebecca very much enjoyed these hugs because her mother smelled like freshly washed clothes and sweet perspiration. Cecile sat on her haunches, took her daughter by the shoulders, and added, "So you know that it is not a good place to play?"

Rebecca nodded a little, as if unconvinced.

"And you're going to stay right here. In the yard. Isn't that right?"

Another slight nod. "Yes."

Cecile hugged her again. "I know you are, sweetheart," she said as she hugged. She heard the infant, Jack, crying from the other room. "I've got to see to your brother now. I'm sure one of your sisters will be out to play with you as soon as they're done with their chores."

Rebecca did not respond to this. It wasn't awfully important to her that her sisters come out and play. Their games weren't very much fun—hide and seek around the tall bushes that were everywhere near the house, leapfrog (which she wasn't big enough for), Simon Says, and tree-climbing, sometimes (though she wasn't big enough for that either).

But she had other playmates. And they were quicker, and smarter, and they knew lots of tricks. They could run as fast as birds could fly, and they could say things to her sweetly, the way her mama did, or angrily, like her father, and they could giggle like her sisters, and disappear, poof! too—she'd seen it!

They were everywhere. Not just in the place her mother had told her to stay away from. They were in the trees that her sisters climbed, and in the bushes where her sisters played hide and seek, and around the yard where they played Simon Says, and they were in the house, too.

They were everywhere.

They were wonderful!

Chapter Eighteen

Erthmun asked his reflection, "What in hell is this? Who in the hell are you?" He saw his lips form the words, and heard the words come back to him from the enamel and the glass, from the hard, white plaster walls and the gray tile floor.

He told himself that he was being foolish. He said to his reflection, "You're a fool." He saw his lips move, and heard the words come back to him from all the hard surfaces in the little room. "You're a fool," he said again.

He was looking into a small mirror, mounted at head height above the sink, and he was naked. He couldn't see himself completely in the mirror unless he leaned toward it and looked down. He did this, and studied his body in the mirror. It seemed foreshortened. Fat. He thought that his penis had disappeared into the fat below his belly.

What was there to look at? A little dark pink nubbin, like the head of a turtle.

He leaned back from the mirror, looked at his face, said, "My face." He leaned forward again and looked very closely at the eyes reflected in the glass. They were brown and black, rimmed by folds of dark pink skin.

He thought that he should be able to see himself in his eyes, in the irises. But he saw only darkness. He pushed his forehead and the bridge of his nose hard against the glass for a better look. He felt the cold enamel sink on his belly and his penis. He felt the cold mirror against his forehead and the bridge of his nose. He tried to find himself in his irises, but saw nothing in them but darkness. The cold enamel sink against his penis had given him an erection. This made him angry, and he shouted an obscenity that came back to him a hundred times from all the hard surfaces in the little room. He felt his hands tighten around the edge of the sink, felt himself push his forehead harder into the mirror, until it cracked and he saw a half-dozen eyes in it.

He pushed his forehead into the cracked mirror, until the shards themselves cracked, so there were two-dozen or more eyes looking back at him. The eyes were brown, and they were rimmed by folds of dark pink skin.

His mother was clearly surprised to see him, and her smooth, round face lit up with enthusiasm and happiness. For the first time, he noticed that strands of gray had crept into her red hair. It had been too long since he had last seen her.

"Jack," she said, and leaned up a little to hug him. They did not hug for very long—their hugs had always been brief—and when they stopped, he said, "I need to talk to you."

She nodded enthusiastically, said, "Of course," led him into her small, white Cape Cod, and sat him down on a massive blue cloth couch. There were two cats sleeping on the back of the couch, and when Erthmun sat down they opened their eyes a moment, blinked at him, blinked again, and, together, slunk off the couch. They threw him backward glances full of fear and mistrust as they made their way out of the room and into the kitchen.

His mother sat beside him and said she was going to make him something to eat, that she'd only be a moment. She said that he looked skinny and that he clearly had not been feeding himself properly.

"No. I'm not hungry," he told her.

"When you were a boy," she said with a smile, "you were forever hungry."

"We need to talk," he said.

"Yes," she said, "I can see that." She stopped smiling and looked concerned.

A long silence followed, while she waited politely and respectfully for him to speak. At last, he said, "I don't know what I want to say."

She told him that of course he knew what he wanted to say.

He said, "I should come here more often. I'd like to come and see you more often."

"Would you?" she said.

He nodded vigorously. "I would, yes."

"Then why don't you?"

"Work," he answered at once.

"Of course," she said. "I understand."

He said, "I didn't know you had cats."

"I do, yes, I do," she said. "I've had them since the summer. You weren't here in the summer, were you, Jackie? I didn't have them the last time you were here. I got them in the summer, and I named them Oriskanie and Powhattan. Those are good names for cats, don't you think?"

"They are, yes," he said.

"You seem . . . distracted, son," she said. "I can tell these things about my children. You especially."

He said, "I have some questions."

"Yes," she said, and put her hands comfortingly on his, which were resting on his knees.

He looked at her hands on his. They were not as smooth as her face, and they felt cold against his skin. They were heavily veined and the skin was gray-blue. He thought, looking at them, that the veins were like the branches of an old tree that reaches into the sky. The comparison appealed to him and he supposed that if this were some other day, he'd share it with her, because she'd enjoy it, too.

He said, his gaze still on her hands, and quickly, as if the words had been piling up for years, "I don't believe that the man I called Father was the man who was my father. I don't think I ever believed it." He looked into her eyes, saw something like panic in them, and said, "Tell me if I'm wrong, Mother."

She quickly looked away, took her hands from his, stood, leaned over the couch, as if to steady herself. He could see that she was shaking. "Of course he was your father, Jackie," she said. "I wasn't a promiscuous woman. Did you think I was promiscuous?"

"Promiscuous? No, I didn't think that."

"Your father wasn't easy to get along with, but he was the only man I ever slept with. I never slept with any man but him. Why would I? I'm not promiscuous." She was crying softly now.

He stood, put his hands on her shoulders, said, "I'm sorry."

She shook her head. "No. I understand."

"Do you?"

"Of course. You don't even look like your sisters. But that's all . . . genetics. Who knows what's going to pop out of the mix? Who knows? You throw in a little bit of this and a little bit of . . . that . . ." Her voice was quaking.

He nodded. He wanted desperately to leave, because he knew that he had made her very uncomfortable, and because he knew that she was lying. *You're lying,* he heard himself say, then was thankful when he realized he hadn't actually said it.

She asked, "Was that the answer you wanted, Jackie?" She attempted a smile that would put an end to the conversation.

He nodded. "Yes, it was. Thank you."

She touched his hand and told him that she needed to prepare him some food. He said yes, he'd like that, and added that it had been a long time, too long, since they had eaten together. But they ate in a near silence that was punctuated by quick, nervous smiles, and an occasional "This is good," from him, and from her, "Have you been to visit any of your sisters?" to which he shook his head, and made no explanations.

The cats slunk about the scene as if they were used to begging from the table but were wary of the stranger who had come to visit.

When Erthmun left, he said to his mother, at the door, "We should do this more often."

She said, smiling, "Yes, we should," and they briefly hugged one another.

* * *

That evening, he could not sleep because his Uncle Jack's words came back to him again and again:

"It's like this," Uncle Jack said. "You can't see them if you're actually looking at them. You won't see them that way. That would be too easy, wouldn't it? You can see them only if you're *not* looking at them."

Lila said, "What do they look like, Uncle Jack?"

"They look like you"—he touched her nose gently—"and you"—he touched Sylvia's nose—"and especially *you,* Jack."

Lila, asked, "And where do they come from, Uncle Jack?"

"Well, Lila," Uncle Jack said, "where does *anything* come from? Where do the plants come from, and the cows, and the fish in the sea?"

"I don't know," Lila said, clearly perplexed.

"From heaven," Sylvia offered.

"From heaven," Erthmun said.

And Uncle Jack declared, "Why from *here,* of course. From the earth itself."

"From the earth itself," Erthmun said.

"The earth can make whatever it wants to make," said Uncle Jack.

Chapter Nineteen

The woman who called herself Helen had gotten invited to a party in a high-rise near Central Park. The man who had invited her was wealthy and he looked upon her as another acquisition. Helen did not understand this, and it would have meant nothing to her if she did. What interested her was being among the people who lived in this city and making herself one of them. This was important to her because she was a social creature and so she needed the companionship of creatures who, in many ways, were like her.

She was also an almost entirely reactive being. She did not have the capacity or patience for rumination; she did have the capacity, however, to read people and their intentions toward her as quickly as others read street signs. This was a defense mechanism, and it was as well developed in her as in any of her brothers and sisters.

She had also conformed almost completely to the etiquette and demeanor required of her in this gathering. It was an ability that was not the result so much of intelligence as adaptive response. It was chameleon-like. She absorbed the manner in which other females at this gathering acted and reacted, then she *became* an amalgam of what she had absorbed. No one noticed that this was what she was doing, of course, though a few at the gathering thought she was odd. One woman said quietly to another, "It's a good thing she's so drop-dead gorgeous," and the woman to whom she was speaking nodded her agreement, though neither of them could have said, in so many words, what exactly they were talking about.

"Helen, yes," Helen said to a self-consciously dapper man in his mid-thirties who had come to the gathering alone but didn't want to go home alone.

"Like Helen of Troy," he said, thinking that she would know the reference instantly—*"The face that launched a thousand ships!"*—and so would realize that he had given her a high compliment.

Helen said, "Helen of Troy, yes," which sounded to the dapper man as if she were merely repeating what he had said.

He pressed on. "You're one of Martin's angels?" Martin was the man who had invited Helen; "angels" was a euphemism for the women he made available to his closest male friends.

Helen said, "Martin brought me here," and coquettishly sipped her drink. It was a Manhattan and the taste did not appeal to her, but she had seen others at the gathering drinking similar drinks and they had looked as if they were enjoying them, so she was able to conjure up the same look of enjoyment.

She continued, "I'm an angel of Martin," and gave the

dapper man a coquettish smile. This was unfortunate because coquettish smiles did not mix well with her naturally predatory and overtly sensual appearance, and so her attempt at coquettishness came off as archly dishonest, which almost caused the dapper man to go and hunt elsewhere for his evening's conquest. But he decided to stick with Helen because he thought that she really was a knockout, and so what if she was a bit strange.

"Have you known him long?" the dapper man asked.

"Only insofar as one knows anyone," said Helen.

"I see," said the dapper man, because her comment had not really been an answer to his question.

Helen reached out with one long, exquisite finger and stroked the man's lapel. "I like this fabric," she said.

"Thanks," the dapper man said—he was becoming increasingly uncomfortable.

She stared him in the eye and smiled coquettishly again. She was wearing a black dress with bare shoulders. She wore no jewelry because it felt harsh to her skin, but she had seen many other women wearing jewelry and had decided, in her way, that it was a thing she should do as well. She said, "If you're turned on, I listen well."

"Huh?" said the dapper man.

Helen didn't realize that she was making no sense, although she did easily pick up on the dapper man's confusion. She was also picking up on the fact that his initial attraction to her was dimming. This was not a good thing. She needed this man. She wanted to take the evening with him. She cast about within the consciousness that passed, in her brain, for intelligence, and soon decided what her next move should be.

She said, "I'm not available," and turned away, so her back was to the dapper man.

He stared at her back for a moment—it looked tanned

and smooth and exquisite—then tapped her lightly on the shoulder. This act surprised her. At this gathering, she was not prepared for surprises. Her eyes wide, she wheeled about as quickly as the swishing of a cat's tail and raked her fingers across his cheek. Blood flowed at once. His mouth fell open. He touched the scratches on his cheek, and saw the blood on his fingers. He looked confusedly into Helen's eyes, but saw nothing there that he had expected—anger, astonishment, apology, pending explanation. He saw that her eyes still were wide, and that her jaw was set, as if she were going to strike again. He backed away from her a step, and mumbled, "I'm sorry," though he had no idea what he was sorry for. He backed up another step, saw that Helen's eyes still were on him, that they still were wide, and that her stance was the stance of an animal waiting to strike—tense, anticipatory. Then, responding to some deep inner voice that told him that this preternaturally beautiful woman was a strange creature indeed, he turned and ran from the room.

But Helen had no idea that she had blundered. Even when two dozen pairs of eyes turned accusingly or questioningly or with surprise on her, and even when Martin himself came over and demanded to know what had happened—"Jesus Christ, do you know who that *is*?"—her thoughts still were on the dapper man himself, and upon the fact that he had aroused in her the same need that had been aroused the previous evening.

She salivated.

A muted growling sound started in her throat.

Smalley had come to Erthmun's apartment to tell him that Internal Affairs would probably call off their investigation, and that Erthmun would be reinstated to active duty in a couple of days.

Erthmun said, "You woke me up." He was standing in his blue robe at the open door to his apartment.

"Yes, I can tell," Smalley said, without a tone of apology; hell, it wasn't even 9:00 P.M.—what was this guy doing asleep?

Erthmun started to close the door; Smalley reached out and stiff-armed it. "Don't you want to know *why* we're calling off the investigation?"

"Not particularly," Erthmun answered.

"Shit, that's disappointing," Smalley said.

"I'm sure it is," Erthmun said. "Let go of the fucking door."

Smalley said, "We're calling off the investigation because of lack of evidence. Which doesn't mean the evidence doesn't exist." He quickly added, "Why do you think this perp stuffs chocolate in the mouths of the victims?"

"Suddenly you're a homicide detective?" Erthmun asked.

"I'm just curious."

"I don't know why the killer stuffs chocolate into the mouths of his victims," Erthmun said, and pushed hard on the door, which Smalley was still stiff-arming. "Back off," Erthmun said.

Smalley let go of the door.

Chapter Twenty

The Following Evening
Near the House on Four Mile Creek

The woman said to her male companion, "Do you know what my father used to say about winters up here?"

Her companion looked expectantly at her, but said nothing.

She continued. "He said they were cold enough to steal the breath from a dead man." She smiled. "I always liked that. I'm not sure what it means, but I like it."

Her companion said, "I think I know what it means. And it's true."

The woman took a long, deep breath. Her companion looked on, in awe; he knew that if he took such a breath in this frigid air, he'd end up doubled over with a fit of coughing.

The woman declared, "It's so bracing, don't you think, Hal?"

"Bracing, sure," Hal said.

The woman—her name was Denise—grinned at him. "This isn't your cup of tea, is it?"

"Of course it is," Hal claimed. "I'm the first to admit that we can't spend our lives wrapped up tight and warm within the cocoons that we call cities." He smiled, pleased with his metaphor.

"Agreed," said Denise. She glanced at her watch; it was closing in on 5:30 p.m. Soon, it would be dark, and the small lean-to where they had planned to spend the night was still a good distance off. She hadn't expected Hal to be so slow. Jesus, he jogged every day.

"Problem?" he said.

Denise glanced at the overcast gray sky. "Not really. I don't know. It doesn't . . . feel right here." They were in an open area fringed by evergreens, oaks, and tulip trees. The snow was knee deep and heavy, which made walking very difficult.

" 'Doesn't feel right'?" Hal said. "Could you explain that?" His sudden apprehension was obvious.

She chuckled. "Only that I think we've got a little weather on the way and that we should pick up the pace if we expect—"

"Weather? You mean a storm?"

She shrugged. "Possibly. A small storm." She took her radio from Hal's backpack; it was tuned to a weather channel in Old Forge, half a hundred miles south. She turned up the volume. Nothing. She cursed, shook the radio, turned it off, then on again. Still nothing. "Hal, did you put new batteries in this thing?"

He looked sheepishly at her and started to speak, but she cut in, "You didn't, did you?" She could hear the anger in her voice, but decided it was all right—he deserved it.

He said, "Actually, yes, I did."

"*New* batteries?"

Another sheepish look. "Have you checked the price on new batteries, Denise? Jesus, they're a couple of bucks. So, I figured—"

"This isn't a new battery?"

"Sure it is. You know those batteries in the drawer in the dining room? I used one of them. I even checked it on the battery tester first—"

"Dammit!" Denise whispered.

"I fucked up?" Hal asked.

She put the radio to her ear, turned the volume all the way up, heard nothing, sighed. "No, Hal, you didn't fuck up. It's all right."

"But we're in deep shit?"

"Not waist-deep. Not yet." She gave him a quick grin, as if for reassurance. "Listen, I know this snow is difficult to slog through, and I know you really hate being out here, but do you think that if we put our snowshoes on we could do a couple of miles before it gets too dark?"

"How many is a couple?"

"Three. Maybe four."

"That's not a couple. That's *several*."

"Okay, okay. Several miles. Can you do it?"

"Shit, Denise," he said, "I jog every day."

His leg cramps began twenty minutes later, when the light gray overcast had turned dark gray and a lazy snowfall had begun. He sat on a tree stump and massaged his thigh. "This is a very different kind of muscle action I'm employing here than when I jog," he explained.

They were in a sparse grove of evergreens. Beyond it,

to the east, the land sloped severely into pitch darkness; to the west, a few rust-colored remnants of dusk remained. There were no hazy reflections of city lights anywhere on the dark cloud cover, no distant noises of cars or airplanes. The air was as still and cold and quiet as stone.

Denise realized all at once that she wasn't absolutely certain of their location. She asked for the compass, which Hal kept in his jacket pocket. He fished it out and gave it to her. She checked it, looked at the dark gray overcast and the lazy snowfall, checked the compass again, gave it back to him, and grinned nervously.

He said, "Are we waist-deep in shit now, Denise?"

Her grin quivered. "Mid-calf, I'd say."

He stood, leaned over, massaged his thigh some more, and said, "A week from now, we're going to look back on this and say, 'Now that was a night to remember.' "

She gave him a quick, quivering grin.

He said, "We *are,* aren't we?"

She said nothing.

"Denise?" he coaxed, and noticed, then, that her gaze wasn't on him, but beyond him. He turned his head, looked.

She said, "Hal, I think that's a goddamned house."

He didn't see it. "Where?" he said.

"What do you mean 'Where?' Right there."

He turned around, so his back was to her, moved forward a few paces, then stepped to his right. The snowfall had picked up; a quirky breeze had started. He thought he was thankful for it, thankful for the whisper it made on the snow and in the trees. He had never been comfortable with silence.

He saw the house, then, though not much of it—a steeply pitched roof, part of the top floor. It was too dark now for him to say what kind of windows there were. "Do you think someone lives in it?" he asked.

"How would I know?" Denise answered.

"It doesn't matter, does it?"

"Goddamn right."

"I want you to admit one thing to me," Hal said.

"Oh, yeah? What?" Denise said.

"I want you to admit that you've fucked up. I want to hear you say, 'Hal, I've fucked up. It's a first, but I've done it.' Can you say that?"

They were standing in deep snow inside the remains of a picket fence. It was very stylized; each picket was flattened at its point, and, just beneath that, much fatter and rounder than normal picket fences. Denise had said that she liked this design quite a lot, and Hal had claimed that he could fashion similar pickets for their own fence, should they decide at some point to build one.

They were not far from the house itself, which was large, gray with age, sturdy-looking, and clearly empty. Denise said, "Do you require that I confess to having fucked up, darling?"

"Sure, I do," he said.

She admitted that she had, and it made him happy.

Then she said, gesturing to indicate the area inside the fence, "They liked bushes."

"Those are forsythia," Hal declared.

"I know that," she said.

"Well, then, that makes two of us."

She looked apologetically at him, then at the house, which, oddly, looked less forbidding from this vantage point—inside the friendly picket fence—than it had when they had first seen it. "Are we going inside?" she asked.

"Yes," he said. "I'm cold."

Chapter Twenty-one

Helen heard the music of living things, which, in this place, was at once dissonant, like the raucous noises of blue jays, and melodic—the wet and powerful noises of sex, which are the noises that scream into the ear of eternity. And she heard the whispers that come from sleep, and the cries and the shouting that leaped from the minds of those who dreamed. And she heard the music that *was* music to other ears, too—Mozart, George Harrison, Marianne Faithfull, John Prine, Samuel Barber—because these were the sounds that living things made to put themselves in harmony with the earth.

Helen's life was music, which was sex, which was food, which was music, and sex, and food, which was one thing, which was Helen.

The dapper man, wrapped only in a towel, and peeking around the open door to his apartment, said, "My God, how did you get in here?" because the building was very secure, of course. There were smells wafting out from within the apartment; they were the commixture of beef, mushrooms, cheese, and red wine, and they got Helen's saliva flowing again. And there was Hank Williams on the CD player, because the dapper man loved Hank Williams, though he played him only when he was alone.

How she got into the building was of little concern to Helen. She did what was necessary. It had been necessary for her to get into the building, so she had gotten in.

She said now, "I need you!"

"You *need* me?" The dapper man was astonished, confused. He touched the fresh bandages on his cheek, and repeated, "You *need* me?" and added, "For what?"

Helen did not recognize such questions. She barely recognized questions as questions. They indicated uncertainty, which was not a part of her existence.

She said, "You!" then swept past him, and shredded his stomach with her graceful fingers.

And when she was inside, and had turned to face him, he had begun to double over from the pain she had inflicted, and his gaze was rising questioningly to meet hers, to find some answer in her sky-blue eyes. *Why do you want to hurt me?* his gaze said.

But there were no answers in her eyes, and no questions in them either. There was simply need, hunger, and certainty.

"It's very dark," Hal said.

"That's because there aren't any lights," Denise said.

"Do you think this is safe?"

"What do you mean? The floor? Are you asking if the floor is safe? It feels safe." She lifted one foot and brought it down softly; it made a slight whumping noise. "See, safe enough." She thought that she was babbling, trying to find solace in the sound of her own voice. But solace from what?

Hal said, "There should be lights."

"And room service, too," Denise said.

"Okay, so what do we do now? Spread our sleeping bags out here?"

"No." She bent over and held her hand near the bottom of the front door; "See," she said. "Feel that draft? Jesus, we'll be popsicles by morning."

"I thought our sleeping bags were rated at twenty below."

"I really think that our best bet is to find some inner room and sleep there," Denise said.

"Inner room where? Down here? Upstairs?"

"I don't think it matters."

"Maybe there's a fireplace. I mean, there *has* to be a fireplace."

"I'm sure there's a fireplace." She looked at him; his face was only an elongated oval a little paler than the darkness in the house. "But I'm just as sure we shouldn't use it. I'd say that birds have been building nests in the chimney for a couple of decades. We might light a fire and fill the whole damned place with smoke."

"Oh, sure," Hal said, sounding chastened. "You're right. That was stupid."

She looked at him, again. Her eyes were beginning to adjust to the low light. She could see his features swimming on the creamy oval that was his face. "Am I a bitch?" she said.

And he answered, too quickly, she thought, "No. You're not a bitch."

She sighed. "I treat you badly sometimes, don't I?"

"No more than I deserve," he said. "Why are you suddenly assuming your 'true confessions' mode?"

This surprised her. " 'True confessions' mode? What's that? I'm just trying to be honest—I'm just trying to be fair."

"I understand that's what you're doing. But why here, and now?"

It was a good question, she thought. "Because I'm a . . . fair and honest person," she said.

A tall window, covered by the sad remains of a lace curtain, stood near the front door. Remarkably, all the glass was intact, and, judging from the motionless air in the house, all the window glass on the entire first floor was probably intact as well. Denise stepped over to the window, peered out, said, "You know what, it doesn't look too bad out there, Hal."

"Meaning?"

She straightened. "I think the snow has stopped."

"You're not suggesting we go and look for the damned lean-to in the dark, are you?"

She shook her head briskly. "Of course not. I was simply making an observation."

A brief and incoherent whisper crept out of the darkness in the house and made them fall silent for a moment.

Denise said, "What was that?"

Hal said, "I don't know. Nothing important."

She glanced at him. "Nothing important?" She smiled. "What would have made it important?"

"I don't know," he said again.

Another whisper crept out of the darkness in the house. But it was not incoherent. It was a sentence; "The damned lean-to in the dark."

Hal said, "It's a fucking echo."

Denise said. "It would have to be a very weird echo, Hal."

They heard birdsong, then. It was extended, tremulous, beautiful; it filled the dark house. And when it was done, Hal said, "A bird."

"Yes, a bird," Denise whispered, as if in awe.

"Yes," they heard from within the bowels of the house, "a bird."

"Nothing important," said the voice of the house.

They fell silent. The house fell silent. After several minutes, Hal said, "These phenomena must be repeatable."

Denise looked at him and forced a grin. "Huh?"

He said again, with emphasis now, "These phenomena must be repeatable. It's a respected tenet of science. In the face of unexplainable events, those events must demonstrate repeatability. Take the Search for Extraterrestrial Intelligence, for instance. Do you know what that is?"

"Of course I do."

"Okay. In the past thirty years of *that* endeavor, there have been numerous instances of strange radio transmissions from sources beyond our solar system. But none of these radio transmissions has . . ." He paused and finished, "Sorry, I'm babbling."

"It's all right," she said.

"And there's something else, too. I've got to pee."

"So do I," she said.

"And I think what I'm going to do"—he reached behind him and pulled a flashlight from his backpack; it was something he should have done before they stepped into the house, he realized—"is find the downstairs bathroom."

"You're kidding."

"Kidding?" He turned the flashlight on and shone it in Denise's eyes. She squinted because of the light and told him he was being an asshole, but he was happy to see her face. "Why would I be kidding?" he said, and shone the flashlight briefly up the stairs in front of them, and to the left, into a huge, open room. There was no furniture in the room, but there was a thick layer of dust on the floor, and the footprints of bare feet in the dust.

"Look there," he said.

"Yes, I see," Denise said. "Kids come in here and play. It's fun. I used to do it myself when I was a kid—go into an old house and play."

"Kids from where, for God's sake?" he said. "We're twenty miles from any kids."

Denise thought about this question a moment, then said, "I don't know."

The footprints in the dust were fresh because the hardwood floor was visible beneath them. Denise pointed this out, and Hal told her she didn't need to point it out, but then he said, "They're small footprints. They're just kid's footprints, like you said."

And another whisper wafted out of the bowels of the house. It was followed by birdsong, and by the chortling of toads, and the twittering of crickets, as if they were in a meadow in summer.

Denise, said, "What the hell *is* that?"

"Only what it sounds like," Hal said.

"Jesus," Denise said, "I don't know *what* it sounds like." After a moment, she added, "We should leave, Hal. I get an awful feeling here." But there were no whispers in the house now, and no chortling of toads, no echoes. A creeper of wind had snuck in from somewhere and had obliterated the footprints in the dust. Hal pointed out that the footprints weren't that fresh, after all, *look at them*. And Denise said that maybe he was right. What choice did they have, really? The night had thrust them into a life-and-death situation, and they had to make the most of it.

"Yes," Hal agreed glumly. "We do."

Denise cupped her hands around her mouth. "Hello," she shouted.

"Hello," they heard from within the house.

"Hello," she called again. "Is anyone there?"

"Is anyone there?" the voices of the house replied.

Then Hal said, "I don't think we're alone here," and shone his flashlight about frantically. Its yellow beam caught what looked like insects speeding through the cold air.

"Insects," Denise said.

Hal let the flashlight beam settle on a far wall—white plaster, orange wainscoting. A naked form—stomach, pubic hair, teeth, breasts, sky-blue eyes—stepped quickly and gracefully into the light, then was gone.

"Jesus Christ," Denise whispered.

Another naked form appeared in the light, and was gone. Then another, gone, And another. Gone. And then they were like insects moving through the light, and Denise whispered, "I'm sorry. God, I'm so sorry."

Because these, they knew, were the *others* in the house. They were on the stairs in front of them, and in the big room where the footprints had been. They were close enough to touch, and no more visible than shadows on a starlit night.

But they were *real*, and they moved with purpose, and grace, and terrible certainty.

Chapter Twenty-two

Erthmun thought that he should be asleep, but he couldn't sleep because he had a joke to tell, and no one to tell it to. It was a joke of his own devising and he thought it was very funny. It was his first joke, the only joke he had ever devised, and he was desperate to share it, but there was no one available to share it with. He had tried calling Patricia David, but had gotten only her answering machine. He'd tried calling the squad room, but there was no one there tonight whom he saw regularly on the day shift, and he felt very self-conscious at the idea of telling his first joke to a stranger. He'd even tried calling his sister, Lila, but she wasn't home either.

So he sat on the edge of his bed and he said to himself, "I have a wonderful joke but no one to share it with." It was pathetic, he thought. *He* was pathetic. For God's sake, everyone should have someone they could tell a joke to on a moment's notice.

And, for the second time in a week, he felt very lonely, and very alone.

The woman in the hall, he thought. The woman with the big cat. Maybe *she'd* like to hear his joke. She had a kind of bond with him, after all. They'd had an encounter in the hall. She had stolen a glance at his erection beneath his blue robe, and he had fantasized bending her over the bed. Surely that was a bond of sorts.

He went to his door, opened it, stepped into the hallway, stopped. Where did she live? he wondered. Which apartment? He looked left, right. Hadn't her big gray cat been at the end of the hall to his left? Sure. Left.

But maybe right.

He looked to his right, tried to visualize the cat at the end of the hallway there. But he could visualize nothing. He looked to his left again, tried to visualize the cat there. Still nothing.

Shit.

He decided that he'd knock on doors. She lived on the same damned floor—he knew that much about her anyway.

He looked down at himself, thinking he might be naked. He saw that he wasn't. He was wearing blue jeans, a white shirt, red socks. He grinned. Why would he have to actually *look* at himself to find out if he was naked? That was foolish.

He went to a door in the hallway to his left and knocked. The door was number 4C, and no one answered his knock. He knocked again, said, "Hello?" but still no one answered. He decided that no one was home, went to Apartment 4D, knocked there.

A tall, thin man sporting a trendy handlebar mustache answered his knock almost at once. The man looked upset and Erthmun guessed that he was upset at being interrupted while doing something personal.

"I'm sorry," Erthmun said, "wrong apartment," because he was not about to tell his joke to someone who was clearly upset with him, and someone who was, besides, a complete stranger.

The man silently closed his door.

Erthmun went to Apartment 4E and knocked. The woman he had seen a week earlier answered his knock within moments. She was cradling her big gray cat in her arms and she was dressed in the same blue robe in which Erthmun had first seen her. She smiled ingratiatingly and said, "Mr. Erthmun, how pleasant to see you." She was stroking her cat, and as she spoke, her stroking action quickened, as if, Erthmun guessed, his appearance at her door actually *had* given her pleasure.

He beamed what he hoped was an ingratiating smile and asked, "Do you have time for a joke?"

"A joke?" She looked suddenly perplexed.

He nodded vigorously; her look of perplexity became a look of concern. "Yes," he said, "I made up a joke." He smiled ingratiatingly again. "What's your name? I think I should know your name."

"My name?" She had stopped stroking her big, gray cat.

Erthmun said, "My name's Jack."

She said, "Cindy," and put her hand on the open door, as if getting ready to close it.

He nodded, as if accepting the fact of her name, and hurried on. "May I come in to tell you my joke, Cindy?"

She shook her head. "No, I don't think so." It took a moment for her rejection to sink in. He backed away from the door, felt suddenly, and inexplicably, embarrassed, said, "Sorry. My mistake," and went quickly back to his apartment.

He sat quietly on the edge of his bed for a long while, then he called Patricia David's number again, but without success. He tried his sister Lila's number again, too, but without success. He tried his mother's number; it was busy.

He got off his bed, went to his window, put his hands flat on the windowsill, locked his arms, and said, into the myriad lights of Manhattan, "There was a man who was waiting for his wife to have quadruplets. The man knew that his wife was going to have quadruplets because the doctor had performed an ultrasound exam. While he waited for his wife to have quadruplets, the man tried to devise some names. Maxwell, Hiram, George, Terry, Bud. But he liked none of these names, and he thought that he had better wait for the moment that the quadruplets were born before trying to devise names. Then he was called into the delivery room, where he watched as his wife gave birth first to one son, then another, then another, and still another. He smiled and said to the doctors present, and pointing at the babies, 'That's Ted, that's Fred, that's Ed, and that's Ned.' Then he thought about this, realized what he had done and proclaimed, 'My, how rhyme flies when you're having sons.' " Erthmun smiled. It was a good joke. *My, how rhyme flies when you're having sons.* A pun. His first joke had been a play on words. Didn't that say much about him and about his . . . humanity? Didn't that *prove* something?

The woman was blue-eyed and auburn-haired, and she had been told more than once that this was a stunning combination. She had also been asked more than once

119

where it came from—some topsy-turvy intermingling of genes, a Swedish father and a Mediterranean mother? She had grown tired of such questions, and now, when they were asked, she became surly and uncommunicative. She didn't know why. She was not normally surly and uncommunicative. She was normally vivacious and outgoing. In the past month, she had even bought green contact lenses to ward off the questions, but they felt harsh on her eyes, so she did not often wear them.

Her name was Greta, and she was twenty-seven years old. She was a copywriter for an advertising firm on 42nd Street, and she lived in a studio apartment near Central Park. The apartment's only window looked out on the park, in fact, and Greta had spent many nights and days staring out that window at the park, because the view called up her formative years on her parent's farm in northern Pennsylvania, when her second story window looked out on a very similar landscape.

On several of the nights that she'd looked out at the park she had seen Helen. It did not occur to her that she was seeing anything unusual; she supposed that she was seeing some odd movement of air and leaves and snow, something that only for the briefest moment became a naked human form and then instantly coalesced into air again, roadway, tree trunk, street lamp, dust, heat; and so, Greta supposed that she was seeing nothing, not even a brief fantasy.

This night, she saw no dust, and there was no heat. Snow covered the park, except for the roadways, which were used often during the day, and they were dark and narrow. The snow tangled in tree limbs, dipped like a garland over the tops of bridges, held fast and fat to the tops of benches.

Greta could see all of this and much more from her

studio apartment. She paid well for the view; she had even given up one meal a day for it, and this was a great sacrifice because eating, and eating well, was one of the great pleasures of her life.

She thought that she liked her view of the park most at night because she could easily work her childhood landscape into it. There were no blue-suited joggers at night, and few yellow taxis, or people sledding or skiing. Occasionally, a horse-drawn hansom cab crossed her field of view, and she especially enjoyed this because she had owned a horse on her parents' farm in Pennsylvania.

It had never occurred to her to go into the park at night. She thought of herself as a sensible woman and she knew that, even in winter, the park was not a safe place, especially at night.

But she supposed that, this night, it would be all right simply to go to the edges of the park and peer in. What could be wrong with that? There were people walking on Central Park West. She would be one of them, and she would peer into the park, and what she would see there, up close, would feed the nostalgic fantasy she had indulged in so often at her window.

She thought that she would have to be impulsive about this because if she wasn't impulsive, then she would decide not to do it, and so would probably never do it. She thought that she had to cultivate her impulsiveness, that the city was squashing it, somehow, that, as a child, her every act had seemed impulsive, capricious, and whimsical. She had not come here to have the child inside her squashed by this big and impersonal place.

She got into her green leather coat, which covered her to mid calf, put on her brown leather gloves, and her slip-on boots, studied herself in the full-length mirror near the door, decided she looked good, but needed her hat, got it

out of the closet, put it on—it was a stylish red beret—
and left her apartment.

She was on the street within a minute and trying to
decide whether to cross at the light, a block away, or wait
for traffic to clear and then jaywalk. She'd been ticketed
for jaywalking, and it had been an unpleasant experience
in a city that was, she thought, no stranger to unpleasant
experiences.

Shit, she thought, who was going to see her jaywalk
here, at night? She waited for the traffic to clear, crossed
Central Park West to the sidewalk, hesitated a few feet
from a tall wrought iron fence, then crossed to the fence
itself. She put her hands on the bars and felt the cold of
the black iron through her leather gloves.

She put her face between the bars and peered into the
park, but saw little. There were tall, snow-covered bushes
in front of her, and she could see a triangle of snow-
covered grass between them. She let go of the fence,
stepped back. This was all very disappointing. She'd have
to find some other place where she could peer into the
park.

She went back to the sidewalk, saw a young couple
walking toward her, felt suddenly foolish and self-
conscious, and began walking quickly away from them.
Why was she doing this? she asked herself as she walked.
She had no answer. She was acting under an impulse that
was unknown to her.

She walked faster.

After a minute, she looked behind her and saw that the
young couple was gone and that the sidewalk was empty.
Five blocks south, she could see that traffic was moving
slowly on Columbus Circle. She found it astonishing that
she had walked so far in so short a time.

She looked toward the park. There was no wrought-iron fence here, only a waist-high stone fence. She thought she could easily climb it, which was an idea that appealed to her because it involved another impulsive act whose origin was shrouded in the mysteries of her subconscious.

But she did not act at once. She ruminated upon the idea for several moments. She tossed the pros and cons about in her head. She asked herself, *What if there is someone just beyond that stone fence, and he's waiting for a fool like me to venture into the Park?* And she answered herself, *What* fool, *indeed, would be waiting there at night, in the frigid cold?* It was a good question.

At last, she crossed the little strip of snow-covered grass to the fence, hesitated only a moment, put a leg up on the fence, and climbed over it, into the park.

She smiled. This, she thought, was much better, though the deep snow here was very cold on her bare calves, and was already beginning to make its way down her slip-on boots.

She saw much. Paths winding like a tangled Mobius strip through the park, snow tumbling through the dark sky, birds shivering in their pitiful spaces, the wretched homeless making the most of their cardboard shelters in the park's secluded areas, ice on the lake cracking under the weight of cold and atmosphere.

She thought she had never seen so much with such startling clarity.

She thought she had stumbled upon some great hidden talent.

She heard movement nearby.

Her breathing stopped.

Who's there? her brain demanded.

A shadow appeared not far away. It was a little darker than the snow, and it was tall. It moved toward her with deliberation. In a man's voice, it said, "You're a damned fool!"

Go away! her brain screamed.

"A damned fool!"

"I have Mace!" her mouth screamed.

"Use it, then!"

She took a very quick glance behind her at the stone fence. It was right there, at her heels; she needed only sit on it, tumble backward, do a little reverse somersault back into the city's spaces, out of the park.

"Use it!" the man demanded again.

But she did not do a reverse somersault.

And the man came quickly at her.

Chapter Twenty-three

"You look pretty much like shit, Jack," Patricia David said. Erthmun was seated at his desk, opposite hers; it was the first day of his reinstatement.

"Uh-huh," Erthmun said. "I wish I felt as good as I looked."

"Maybe you should go home. What is it—the flu?"

"The flu? Who knows?"

She told him that the mayor's nephew had been murdered two nights earlier and that they might be assigned the case. He said, "The mayor's nephew?" and Patricia gave him the man's name.

"I am not one of the mayor's fans," Erthmun said, and Patricia told him that the remark was a non sequitur; "What does it matter if you're not one of the mayor's fans?" she asked.

He said that he didn't know what difference it made,

then asked, "Do you want to hear a joke, Patricia?"

She smiled at him across her desk. "A joke? This is a first."

"It's not a good joke. But it's mine."

Patricia was a little surprised at how earnest he seemed, and at how urgently he needed to tell his joke. She said, "Sure. Tell me your joke."

He told it to her. He delivered it haltingly, as if he were devising it all over again, and when he was done, Patricia looked blankly at him and said, "I don't get it."

He sighed. "I told you it was a bad joke. Let's go to work."

"No, no. Please. Explain it. 'How rhyme flies when your having sons.' I think that I *should* get it, Jack, but I don't, and it makes me feel stupid. I don't like to feel stupid the first thing in the morning."

"You're kidding, right?" Jack said.

She smiled.

"Right?" he said again.

"Yes," she admitted. "I am. I mean, one bad joke deserves another, right?" She passed an 8x10 photograph across the desk to him. "This is the mayor's late nephew," she said. "As you can see, Jack, he's been cannibalized. It's not in the papers, yet, but it appears to be working into something of a trend."

Dog walking was a very pleasant early morning occupation, the old man thought. If the dog was well trained, as his as, then it was not strenuous exercise, but it *was* exercise. It wasn't dangerous either, because people stayed away from big dogs on stout leashes, and so he—the old man—could content himself with whatever daydream was current.

He was walking in Central Park, on a path that wasn't

often used because it wound into a thick stand of trees. He had used this route often, however, and no one had ever bothered him because of his dog, whose name was Friday. The dog was as gentle as a baby's laugh, but looked very fierce and wolf-like.

The old man's head moved a lot as he walked, not because of a nervous condition, but because he liked to see what was going on around him. Usually, on these walks, there was very little to see that he had not seen a thousand times before, but he looked anyway because he liked catching a glimpse of the occasional squirrel or chipmunk or cardinal, and because he was interested in more than simply the narrow dirt path and his dog's rear end beneath its upturned white tail.

The bright morning sunlight reflected off the new snow and into the old man's eyes, which made him squint. When he walked into shadow, out of the bright sunlight, and no longer needed to squint, the world around him darkened, then brightened slowly, and images shimmered.

He thought at first, seeing this way, that the man sitting up against a tree not far off the path was wearing a rust-colored jogger's uniform, but then the old man's eyes adjusted and he saw that the man sitting against the tree was naked, and that he was covered with blood. He saw also that the man's mouth was wide open and that something dark had been stuffed into it. The old man could smell the stuff—he was not far off.

He stopped walking, whispered a curse, realized what he was looking at. Friday tugged very hard at the leash in his frantic efforts to get at the man sitting against the tree. The smells were so delightful—blood, chocolate.

"Damnit, dog!" the old man shouted. But it was no use. Friday was simply too strong for him.

* * *

She was blue-eyed and auburn-haired, her name was Greta, and she had been having strange and confusing lapses of memory in the past couple of months. She remembered leaving her apartment the previous evening on some odd mission to discover Central Park at night, but remembered nothing concrete beyond shutting her door behind her.

And now there was a rust-colored residue in her bathtub, her beautiful green leather coat was missing, and her boots were smeared with blood. And as she peered out her studio apartment window at Central Park five stories below, she could see flashing lights. She knew that they were cop cars. She knew, also, that they were there, in the park, because of something *she* had done.

She was fascinated.

A memory came to her all at once. It was a memory from her childhood, and it bore a wonderful mixture of pleasure and pain; she saw the face of a young boy in it. He had dark eyes and tousled red hair, and she thought that she had heard him running toward her through tall grasses. Then he was simply . . . *there,* looking down at her. She thought that, in her memory, she could hear a stream moving close by. And she could smell the tangy odor of the earth, and could see the face of a doll lying in her lap. It was a very strange face. It had no eyes, only crumpled pieces of brightly colored paper where the eyes should have been, and mud had been stuffed in the mouth.

"Why'd you do that?" she remembered the boy asking.

Then the memory was gone, and try as she might— because it gave her so much delicious pleasure and pain— she could not get it back.

* * *

Patricia David, driving, exclaimed, "Jack, you look positively *bilious*," and then gave him a worried grin.

He leaned forward a little, adjusted the rearview mirror so he could see his reflection, and sat back without saying anything.

Patricia said, "I think I should take you home."

"Home," he said, and it sounded to Patricia like a question, though she guessed that it wasn't.

She said, "I think you should rest, Jack." She stopped at a red light. "Shit, why don't I turn here, go back down Lexington, and take you home."

"Home?" Jack said, and this time Patricia recognized that it *was* a question.

"Home, yes," she said. "To your little apartment."

"Apartment," he said.

The light changed; Patricia made a left on her way to Lexington, made a quick stop for a lanky, hollow-faced jaywalking man in an army coat and blue knit cap, swore beneath her breath, then got going again when the man had crossed. She said, "Apartment, yes. Home. The place you live. The place you hang your hat. The place where you eat and do all your little personal things."

"No," he said.

"No? No what?" She grinned at him again. He was huddled against the door, legs up, knees together, arms across his chest. His eyes were all but closed, and his mouth was shut tightly. He looked cold.

She said, "Are you cold, Jack?"

"Yes," he whispered.

"Do you want me to turn the heater up?"

"Heater up? Yes."

"Jack, Christ"—she turned the heater up—"I'm worried about you. Maybe instead of taking you home I should take you to the hospital."

"Hospital. No," he whispered.

She pulled over so she was double-parked in front of a deli called Sam's. She put the car in park, leaned over the seat, laid the back of her hand gently against Jack's forehead, and held it there a moment, surprised that Jack was making no protest. She withdrew her hand. "You don't seem to have a fever, Jack."

"No," he managed. "I'm just damned cold."

"I turned the heat up."

He said nothing.

"Do you want me to turn it up more?"

"Turn it up more? No. Thanks. Just take me . . . to my apartment."

"Right away," she said.

Chapter Twenty-four

Thirty-four Years Earlier
In the House on Four Mile Creek

Thomas Erthmun maintained that fear from his children was more important than love, because love was a fuzzy, undependable emotion. He was saying, "Jack, if you don't obey your mother, then it will be a very hard night for you when I return, do you understand?"

Jack's three-year-old eyes looked up at the man and Jack thought, not for the first time, that the man was bigger than trees, or mountains, and scarier than anything, and he wasn't easy to fool either, because he seemed to know everything that Jack thought, as if he had thought it, too. Jack nodded, wide-eyed, open-mouthed, and said, "Yes, Daddy."

The man said, "Of course you do, son," and then

leaned over and briefly kissed his wife, who was holding Jack, which provided the boy a whiff of the man's after-shave, and of the man's recently eaten breakfast—oat-meal, a generous slice of ham, a glass of orange juice and a cup of coffee—and then Jack felt the man lay a hand gently on his cheek. Jack winced in anticipation.

Jack's mother said, "Have a safe journey, Thomas."

"I will," the man said.

And he lifted his hand and pinched Jack's cheek hard enough that it hurt. Then he said, smiling, "And if you do not obey your mother, son, then that will be the least of your pain, do you understand?"

"Understand?" Jack echoed. "Yes, Daddy." He knew enough not to touch his throbbing cheek; that would show weakness. He felt his mother back a step away from her husband, who turned quickly, and was out the door a moment later.

Jack looked at his mother. He read several emotions in her, some of which he felt himself—fear, gratitude that the man was gone—but loneliness, too, which Jack had yet to feel. There was another emotion in her that Jack didn't understand; he sensed only that it made his mother look at herself as if in a mirror and see a stranger there.

He sensed, also, that she was going to set him down and tell him to go outside and play. He did not want this. He loved being close to her, loved being held by her, loved following her about the house as she tended to chores, loved her voice, even when she was scolding him, loved her eyes on him, her smell, her whispers, her smiles.

And then she set him down, despite his protests, leaned over, kissed him gently on the cheek that his father had pinched, and told him he could go and play.

Jack looked pleadingly up at her.

"Go ahead," she coaxed.

"I don't want to," Jack said.

"It's a beautiful day, Jackie. The sun is warm. Go outside and play." An edge of impatience had crept into her voice, and he knew that if he didn't do as she'd asked, the air around her would grow dark, and he would hardly recognize her as his mother.

"Okay, I will," he said, and there was the hint of defiance in his voice. He went to the front door, glanced back, saw that she was smiling, but knew it was the kind of smile that accompanied her need to be free of him. So he went out to the yard, where his sisters were playing hide and seek among the hydrangeas.

He saw his oldest sister, Jocelyn, first. She had taken up a position behind a very tall hydrangea near the picket fence that Uncle Jack had built. When she saw her brother, she put her finger to her lips to tell him not to give her position away to his other sisters, who were nowhere in sight.

He only looked at her.

She made pushing motions with her hand to tell him to go away.

This was all right; he had no need to play with his sisters—he preferred playing alone. But, at that moment, he most wanted to be with his mother, in the house. He wanted her to kiss his cheek again, where his father had pinched it, and he wanted to follow her around and smell her sweet smell and watch her do all the things that she did during the day. But he knew that she didn't want him in the house with her, and it was something he understood and accepted, in his child-like way. But he didn't know what else to do.

Jocelyn made pushing motions at him again, and added, in a whisper, "Go away, Jackie."

Lila appeared then. She was younger than Jocelyn by a

year and a half, but she was taller, and prettier, and Jack liked her better because she usually listened to him when he talked to her.

He looked blankly again at Jocelyn, and then wandered from the yard, past the ornate picket fence, and into the tall fields beyond.

These fields were alive with honeybees and warm sunlight. They smelled of wet earth, which was a smell that excited Jack and gave him an odd and pleasurable feeling he hoped his father didn't know about—he seemed to know about so many things.

And, quickly enough, he was beyond the noises of his sisters at play, beyond the smells of the house, beyond his view of the house itself, and he knew all at once that he had gone far from his mother.

He ran.

No one in his family had ever seen him run. If they had, they would have been astonished. They would have said, "How can such a little fireplug run like that?" He had told Lila how much he liked to run, and he'd asked her to come out in the fields and run with him, but she told him that although she'd like to, it was not a thing that young girls did, and he had read regret in her.

This morning, he ran for hours. The tall grasses passed him by as a whir of green and brown. Insects tried to hop out of his way, but he trampled many underfoot, and others hopped headlong into him.

He laughed as he ran. And as he ran, he could hear the laughter of others. It came from the high hills that surrounded these fields, and it came from the trees, too, from the tall grasses, from the earth itself. It came from everywhere.

Then, at noon, he was finished running and out of

breath, at last, so he made his way back to his house and sat at the dining room table—which was one of his favorite places to be—and ate a hearty lunch of meat and fruit.

Chapter Twenty-five

Helen saw the snow and knew that it was temporary.

Months earlier, she had seen birds flying south and she had known that their leave-taking was temporary.

She had watched daylight come, and had known that it was temporary, too.

She'd seen clouds covering the sun, people walking stiffly against wind and cold, ice forming on the lake in the park, butterflies emerging from their cocoons in summer, and she had known that it was all temporary.

Just as she knew that she was temporary.

She could not give voice to this fact—it was real, *she* was real, and now the time was coming when she would not be real. It was all right, because the earth—which was her mother and her father—was not temporary. The earth was eternal, so she was eternal.

She could feel her own disintegration starting. It was like a flower blooming deep inside her.

It was exhilarating.

The two young people had once assumed that they were immune to homelessness, that their jobs and their place in society were secure, that such awful things as homelessness happened only to other people. They had even had long discussions about the kind of society that would actually accept homelessness. The man had postulated that if a label—"the homeless"—is assigned to a group of people, it gave them a kind of awful validity, which meant that others in society could pity them, but didn't really have to help them. Their label was "the homeless," just as others were "the sick," or "the rich," or "the working poor."

But then one unfortunate and unforeseen event piled on top of another, and, in a few months, the young couple found themselves penniless and on the street. They had no family to turn to, no place to go, and no prospects for improvement, except in the eyes of the New York County Social Services Department, which deemed them "employable" and denied them benefits.

It was a great comfort to them that they had each other. They also thought, at first, that it was probably fortunate this thing had happened to them in a city like New York, where there were a number of places they could find shelter from the winter nights. There were Salvation Army missions, places underground—they had heard many stories about what lay beneath Grand Central station; *Beauty and the Beast* had been one of their favorite TV shows—and countless abandoned buildings within a few minutes walk. Certainly, with all that to choose from, they could find a safe place to spend their nights.

He was tall and lanky, and he had quickly begun to look unhealthy—"Gaunt," his wife told him—after they had found themselves on the street. He wore a blue knit cap that had been given to him by a beloved aunt, now dead, and an army coat that offered him more protection from the cold than any other coat he had owned. He had caught glimpses of himself in shop windows, and had thought each time that he really did look like the archetypal homeless man, which made him abysmally sad.

This day, he and his wife had decided to leave Manhattan. They thought they could walk across the George Washington Bridge and make their way downstate, through Delaware, eventually, then into Maryland, and finally back to South Carolina, which was where they both had been born. They had no real plan about what to do for food and shelter; they knew only that the city had worked its grim magic on them, that there really was no safe place to spend their nights, and that if they wanted to put their lives back on track, their first step was to leave Manhattan. It was a desperate idea, they realized, but it was their only idea.

Erthmun sat huddled in a trench coat and two blankets at his white enamel table, near the open window. He had turned the heat to maximum, and he could hear the radiators clicking as hot water raced into them.

A cold breeze was blowing on him from the open window, but it touched just his face, the only part of his body that was exposed. The idea that he should close the window was never far from his mind, and he wasn't sure, either, why he had opened it in the first place. He realized that, in the past few weeks, he had become an enigma, not only to Patricia David, Mark Smalley, and the woman down the hall, but to himself. It was painful not to know the reasons for the things he did. It made his future, his present, and even his past, seem uncertain and treacherous.

He wished that he had kept a photo album. He thought that it would have thousands of photographs in it, and they would show not only him, but all the people in his life, from the moment of his birth. They would show his sisters, his mother, and his dead father. They would show all the women he had slept with, and all the murder victims whose eyes or wounds or lives he had looked into—the woman in Central Park who'd had her throat slashed and her red wig stolen, the woman in Harlem whose husband had shot her first with a handgun, then with a shotgun, and, finally, had put an arrow through her heart, all in an effort, he said, "to destroy the evil that settled in her" when she joined a weight-loss club. The man on 42nd Street who had simply been beaten to death for his wallet. The family in Queens who had been variously shot, drowned, and stabbed, and then incinerated by a perpetrator who had never been caught. And a thousand other victims, some unique, most mundane, culminating in the women who'd had cheap chocolate stuffed in their mouths and their faces cleansed.

And all the photographs in his personal photo album would be in black and white because that was the way he saw scenes from his past—in black and white.

Except for his birth.

Which was a world of color, pain, and pleasure.

His phone rang.

He let it ring until it stopped.

"Damnit!" Patricia David whispered. Where the hell was he? She'd dropped him at his apartment only an hour and a half earlier, and he had seemed to want only to go to bed and get warm. She tried his number again, let it ring nearly two dozen times, hung up. She wished he had a goddamned answering machine, like everyone else.

She decided that she'd have to go back to his apartment. He was probably asleep, and it wasn't hard to imagine that in his condition he could sleep through a ringing telephone.

She looked at McBride, who was standing at a file cabinet nearby and was obviously waiting for her to acknowledge him. "I'm going to Erthmun's apartment," she said.

"You can't," McBride told her. "The lieutenant says he needs us both on this, like now!"

"It's too bad," Patricia said as she stood and shrugged into her coat.

"Is that what I tell the lieutenant?"

"Sure. Tell him it's too bad. Use those words exactly." And she walked briskly past McBride and out of the squad room.

Erthmun saw his face in his memory. It was in shades of black and white, too. Round and jowly, dark-eyed, thick-lipped, heavy-lidded, and prematurely aged. He thought that age had become a reality when the person on the outside mirrored the person on the inside. He hoped that it wasn't the face that other people saw. He hoped it was a kind of quirky Dorian Gray portrait that only he could see.

It occurred to him all at once that he had done a lot of sitting at this window, had watched a lot of people passing by. Thousands, maybe. Thousands of victims, and thousands of passersby.

He became aware that something strange was happening inside him. As if some anonymous thing deep within his biology were bursting or blossoming slowly. This frightened him. He thought it foretold his death, and he did not want to die. He thought again about his Uncle Jack and his last words. "Oh, shit!"—such lazy and damnable resignation in the face of death. He—Jack Erthmun—wasn't going to die that way. He would fight Death, he would spit it in the eye and blind it so it wouldn't recognize him. No one was going to shovel him into a rectangle of earth without a lot of kicking and screaming!

So what, he wondered, was he doing at this open window, wrapped up in his cocoon of blankets, waiting for that anonymous thing inside him to burst? It was almost as if he were *offering* himself to it.

In his mind's eye, he saw himself throwing the blankets off, slamming the window shut, and giving death a real fight, if only with *action* and *movement* and *noise*.

But it was a fantasy. He did not move from his cocoon of blankets, the cold breeze pushed hard against his face, and he felt the thing inside him blossoming, as if it were about to slowly consume his internal organs from the inside and leave him nothing but a shell of skin and hair, jowls and heavy eyelids.

And suddenly he found that this was a gratifying and pleasant thing he was doing. It spoke of some great inevitability that he had long denied, and, with that denial, he pushed back—as if he had lived his entire life tottering on one leg, afraid to fall. What right did he have to spit into the eyes of eternity?

Helen didn't know how long she had, and it didn't matter. A week. A month. An hour. She would be what she was until she came apart, then the flies and the burying beetles could have her. She had made food of the living. Soon she would be food *for* the living, and that irony wasn't something she easily understood. She was breasts, hair, gut, teeth, palate, heart, legs, and hunger.

She was hungry now.

And so she would eat.

Chapter Twenty-six

The young homeless couple was peering in a shop window at TV sets. They were both thinking that it would be nice if they had even just one room to live in and that room had a TV set in it. They wouldn't even need a remote control. The TV set could have an old fashioned rotary dial; they wouldn't mind at all getting up from the bed or their chairs to change channels. And it didn't need to be a color set, either, and it didn't need to be hooked up to cable. Three channels would be fine. *Two* channels would be fine.

They were on West 161st Street and they had been on their way out of the city, on their way to the George Washington Bridge, then to New Jersey, then Delaware—on their way to South Carolina, eventually—and they had begged enough money to enjoy a breakfast of fried eggs, toast, and coffee, which had been the best eggs, toast, and

143

coffee they'd ever eaten. They had stopped to look in the shop window because, since childhood, they had been addicted to television.

The young man said, "See, I told you. Reruns of *Let's Make a Deal*. Look at that. Jesus, Monty Hall's giving away a twenty-five-year-old Dodge."

His wife said, "It wasn't twenty-five years old, then. It was new."

"Yeah," he said. "I guess."

This conversation had been designed to give them each a little comfort because it was one they had had in their pre-homeless days. But now it only punctuated their desperation, and so they quickly moved on.

It had been a couple of hours since breakfast, and both of them were starting to grow hungry again. After a few days of homelessness, they had tried to ignore hunger pangs, but with little success.

"It's not such a bad face, is it?" Erthmun whispered to Patricia David, who was bending over him and was looking very concerned.

"It's a beautiful face, Jack," she said.

"It doesn't look like the face of a toad?"

"It's a beautiful face," Patricia repeated. "Jack, can you get up?" She glanced at the open window. "I'm going to close that," she said.

"No, don't!" Erthmun protested.

She hesitated only a moment, then stepped over to the window and slammed it shut. Erthmun looked confusedly at it, as if uncertain why he had opened it in the first place.

Patricia put her hands under his arms. "C'mon, Jack, we've got to get you out of here and to a hospital. You may be suffering from hypothermia."

"I've got . . . a joke," Jack whispered.

"A joke? Sure. Tell it to me on the way to the hospital."

"No. Let me tell it to you now."

She still had her hands under his arms. She thought he felt very cold beneath his heavy jacket. She let go of his arms, straightened, looked down at him. She could see only the back of his head. "If I let you tell me the joke," she asked, "will you let me take you to a hospital?"

"To a hospital? Yes," he whispered.

"Okay. Tell me the joke."

"It's another word joke, another pun," he whispered, and turned his head a little so he could see her out of the corner of his eye.

"Yes. Good," she said. "A pun. Tell it to me."

He turned his head back, fell silent a moment, said, "I don't remember it. It had to do with classical music."

"Classical music?"

"Yes."

"But you don't remember it?"

"Don't remember it? Yes. I don't remember it."

"Does that mean you'll cooperate with me now?"

He nodded. "Yes."

"Good." She put her hands under his arms again to help him up.

He shook his head. 'No. I remember the joke."

"Jack, for Christ's sake, this really is not the time for jokes."

"It is," he whispered. "Of course it is." He turned his head and looked pleadingly at her. "Who tells jokes, Patricia?"

"Huh?"

"*People* tell jokes. *People* tell jokes! Let me tell you mine. Then I'll go wherever you want me to go."

145

T. M. Wright

* * *

Before their homelessness, the young couple had read both the *New York Times* and the *Post* religiously. It had seemed to be a necessary part of living in society. They had both kept up with politics and social issues, and they had read the comics and sports pages, too. He had liked baseball and football. She had liked tennis and auto racing.

They no longer read newspapers. It didn't seem necessary because they didn't feel that they were a part of society anymore. They felt that society had rejected them, had spit them out.

If they had continued reading newspapers, they would have seen news about the second massive storm in less than a week that was heading through New York State, driven by fierce arctic winds. So, when the temperature dropped precipitously, and the winds picked up, and the snow started, and when the young man's trick knee began to ache, it was their first hint that they were in trouble, that their plan to make it to the George Washington Bridge today would have to be postponed. That they'd have to find some kind of shelter quickly.

They were on West 161st Street. The Hudson River was not far to the west. To the east, a row of sad brownstones stood empty. This, they decided, was their salvation.

"Here's the joke," Erthmun declared. He had begun to shiver. It wasn't continuous—it came and went—and Patricia didn't know if this was a good sign or a bad sign.

"Yes, the joke," Patricia coaxed. "Go ahead." She was still standing behind him. Snow was pelting the window with a random tap-tap-tap.

Erthmun sighed, shivered. "Classical music," he said.

"Do you know about classical music?" He was slurring his words now, and Patricia thought this was a bad sign.

"Yes, I do," she said, though it was a lie. She wanted to get him moving.

"Yes," he said, repeated, "Classical music," and added quickly, "What did the . . ." He stopped.

"What did the . . . what?" Patricia coaxed.

"What did the . . . shape-shifting classical composer . . ." He stopped. He was slurring his words badly now. Patricia could hardly understand him.

"What did the shape-shifting classical composer . . . what?" she coaxed.

"What did the shape-shifting classical composer say?"

"I don't know."

"He said this: He said, 'I'm . . .'" Erthmun shivered, shook. "He said, 'I'm Haydn now, but I'll be Bach later.' "

Patricia laughed quickly.

"I'm Haydn now, but I'll be Bach later," Erthmun repeated.

Patricia said, "It's funny, Jack. Can we go now?"

"Funny?" Jack pleaded. "Is it?"

She said, "Jack, I can't understand you. You're slurring your words."

"Is it funny?" he repeated, emphasizing each word.

She understood him. She said, "It is, Jack. It's funny. Didn't I laugh?"

He shivered again.

"Didn't I laugh?" Patricia repeated.

"Yes," Erthmun said.

"So we can go now?"

"Go now? Yes," Jack managed.

T. M. Wright

*   *   *

Breaking into one of the abandoned brownstones hadn't been as easy as the homeless couple had imagined. They had chosen one whose door still was planked shut because the others, they decided, were probably filled with druggies and other homeless people. But getting the plank off the door was no easy matter. The young man had thought he could simply pull it loose by hand, but it had been nailed into the oak door frame with huge nails, and though he and his wife both tried, they soon realized that pulling the plank loose without some kind of lever would be impossible.

He told her to wait on the steps of the brownstone while he went looking for something with which to pry the plank loose. The snow, by then, had begun curling around them like a cloud, and the wind was painfully cold, so she agreed to wait for him in a little sheltered area to the right of the front door.

He looked in the storm for quite a while; at last, he found an abandoned car whose trunk wasn't latched securely. He located a tire iron in the trunk—this was a providential find, he decided—made his way through the storm back to the brownstone, and pried the plank loose from the front door. It was a chore that made his hands ache from exposure to the cold wind and his arms ache from the effort, so when he was done, he cursed into the storm and threw the tire iron away in anger.

The inside of the brownstone was a place of devastation. A stairway that had once led to the second floor was gone. A homemade wooden ladder stood in its place. Much of the first floor was missing, revealing a basement full of litter and yellow dust. Above, snow was making its way through what could only have been a hole in the roof, down a short hallway, and then over the landing.

The young woman said, "This is an awful place."
Her husband agreed.

They decided that as soon as possible, they would leave. But for now, it was their only shelter.

They climbed the homemade ladder to the second floor.

Chapter Twenty-seven

Erthmun dreamed of running. He dreamed that the tall golden grasses moving past him, as he ran, coalesced into one monolithic golden form because he was running so fast. He dreamed that the sun raced him through the day, and that he outran the noises of insects and birds, and he saw other insects, and other birds, in a blur, trying in vain to flutter out of his way. But he was Death, and he was Life, and nothing could get out of his way, and nothing could stop him.

It was a wonderful dream, and he did not wake from it at once.

Patricia David said, "He's smiling."

The doctor standing with her at Erthmun's bedside said, "A dream."

"I know," said Patricia David. "I assume that's a good sign."

The doctor shook her head a little. "It's a dream, that's all."

In the empty brownstone on West 161st Street, the young homeless couple had busied themselves with talk of architecture because they were trying to ignore their hunger pangs, their desperation, and the storm that had worked into an urban fury beyond the tall windows. Most of these windows were cracked, though none on the second floor were broken, and some had been covered with plywood that, oddly, still smelled of glue and formaldehyde, and still bore a fresh, orange cast.

The young man had said, "They don't make houses like this anymore."

The young woman had agreed, and then announced that it was a Federal-style house, to which the young man chortled and said that of course it wasn't a Federal-style house, it was a Late Victorian house.

There were four rooms on the second floor. They were of a uniform size—large enough for a double bed and a couple of dressers, though the rooms were empty now— and each had a small closet with a closed door. The young couple had not looked into any of the closets because their curiosity was not at peak today, and because they did not imagine there was anything in these closets that they wanted to see, or that would be useful to them.

There was also a bathroom, sans fixtures, except for a water-stained oak medicine cabinet with a cracked mirror. All the walls had been done in a bold, blue-flower print wallpaper that was remarkably well preserved, though water-stained, too, and the floors were hardwood,

151

covered with a fine gray dust, which was undisturbed; the young couple had accepted that this was a good sign.

They were huddled together in a room that was protected from the direct onslaught of the wind and so was a few degrees warmer than the other rooms. The young man said, "It usually doesn't get this cold in New York."

"But it gets real hot in the summer," the young woman said.

"I wish it was summer now," said the young man.

They fell silent after that, and they maintained silence for quite a while. They did not want to believe that the storm was intensifying, although it was obvious from the whining noise the storm made against the window glass. They didn't want to admit, either, that the day was ending, that the pale light in the house was beginning to fade. Cold, darkness, and hunger in such a place as this was not what they had planned for themselves a year earlier. They had planned babies, mortgages, car payments, barbecues on balconies that overlooked Central Park.

Erthmun's dream of running ended and became a dream of disease. He saw the earth beneath his feet rise up in great globular pustules that ran with putrefaction and partly coagulated blood. This blood clogged the mouths of living things around him—insects, animals, birds, people at play—and made them gasp for air and fall dead. Then they became globular pustules that ran with putrefaction and coagulates that clogged open mouths; these open mouths appeared from the earth around him, from within mounds of fallen leaves and punctured mushrooms and flower petals. These open mouths became open eyes that were sky-blue, and they quickly became clouded with coagulates. Then there were faces in the earth, open rose-

bud mouths and open sky-blue eyes, and noses clogged with coagulates and clumps of earth.

Then the earth was alive with dark creatures that ran naked through golden grass and mounted one another and laughed and ate and ate and ate, and mounted one another, and mounted one another, and watched the air change and the living things sleep, and dream, and die, and then they died, too.

And the earth was a place of disease and cold and death. And Erthmun himself was running naked in this place. His bare feet plunged into hip-deep snow, and he leaped as if he were weightless through it. Then the snow caught him, held him, clogged his mouth, his nose, clouded his eyes, became warm, became clumps of wet, warm earth, became great globular pustules that spouted partly coagulated blood and putrefaction, and then there were mouths in the putrefaction, mouths spitting out the coagulates, mouths screaming, mouths crying, "I am human! I am human!"

"My God!" breathed Patricia David.

"Mr. Erthmun," said the doctor who had been standing by the bedside with her; the doctor was shaking Jack, now, trying to rouse him. "Wake up, Mr. Erthmun! Wake up!"

"Jack?" Patricia whispered.

The young woman whose name was Greta felt delicious, real, alive. She felt as if she could jump from her fifth floor window, land unscathed in the park, and then run for hours and hours without losing breath. She thought that she had once actually done just that sort of thing, but in a different place. Not her childhood home in Pennsylvania, but some other home. She tried to remember it. She saw trees and hills in her mind's eye, and the name of the place itself tickled and teased her memory but stayed just out of reach.

Five stories below, at Columbus Circle, she could see that some of the police cars were leaving. She thought again that she was somehow responsible for what they had been doing in the park, but when she tried to recall exactly how she could have been responsible, she got only a sense of quick desperation, then a feeling of orgasmic satisfaction. It was very stimulating, so she tried to tweak the memory often as she sat at her window. If she had cared to look, she would have seen her dim reflection in the window glass, would have seen her quivering smile come and go as if in time with her inhales and exhales. And, not for the first time, she would have wondered just what sort of creature she was.

Chapter Twenty-eight

Ten thousand living things had made a home of the brownstone on West 161st Street. Jumping spiders, silverfish, German brown cockroaches, termites, fleas, mice, rats, lice. And two human beings removed from their place in society by unfortunate events.

There was another in the brownstone, too. She had been displaced and destroyed by humans in times past, and then had been remade the same as she had been, much the way the earth remakes a carrot, or a head of lettuce, or a burying beetle.

The young homeless woman said that she was depressed, and her husband said that he was depressed, too, but who could blame them? Christ, here they were, in a shitty abandoned brownstone in a shitty part of New York City, on a shitty day when they couldn't go anywhere even if they had wanted to, and it was goddamned

cold, besides, and they were both goddamned hungry—
Gee, wouldn't a steak be nice . . .

"Enough!" cried the young woman.

"Sorry," said her husband.

"Enough," she said again, more quietly, with resolve.
"I have had enough. I'm not depressed, or sad, or any of
that shit. I have just *had enough*!"

"I understand."

"I don't *want* you to understand. I don't want anything. I don't want a steak, or a TV, or a fucking bus
ticket to South Carolina, or any of that stuff. I don't even
want a bed to sleep in, or a nice pillow, or a fucking pet
hamster! None of that stuff means anything because you
lose it all anyway. It all gets taken away from you. You
try to hold on to it, and it all gets taken away. Jesus!—I
have just had *enough*!"

"I know. I'm sorry."

She didn't look at him. It would have been difficult for
him to see her if she had looked at him, because the light
had grown very dim in the room. Its two tall windows
had been boarded over with plywood, and the only light
was a rectangle of soft, blue-green phosphorescence at the
doorway; this was light that the storm had let in from the
city around them, and it was so dim that they could not
see it unless they looked obliquely at it, the same way
they might have seen a very dim star on a clear night.

"I don't like you feeling this way," the young man said.

His wife said nothing.

"Things will work out, you'll see. We'll just stay here
tonight, and tomorrow we'll go and . . . hell, we can get
some day jobs, and we can stay here for a *couple* of
nights, if we need to, as long as we're trying to save
money—"

"Shut up!" whispered the young woman.

"Yeah, sure, I'm sorry," said the young man.

He put his arm around her. She did not protest this, nor did she lean into him for warmth, or affection. He said, "Don't give up."

But she said nothing.

The other creatures sharing the brownstone with them were not interested in much besides warmth, except for the termites who, en masse, generated their own heat within the wood in the house as they made an extended meal of the place. The cockroaches congregated in another part of the building, where there was plenty to eat, and the jumping spiders—there were four of them in the house—spent their time huddled in corners, legs tight around their little dark bodies, their senses alert to the errant fly or spider mite or flea. It was a brutal existence for everything in the house. Lives ended and lives began cyclically, just as in the universe beyond the house, in the earth itself, in the plant life that sprang from the earth, in the insects that fed on the plant life, and in the birds that fed on the insects.

"Listen," said the young man. "I know you don't want me to talk to you. I know you want me to shut up. But is it all right if I just . . . talk? You don't have to listen."

His wife said nothing. She was tense under his arm. He could feel her breathing, though the noises of the storm covered the sounds of her breathing.

"Okay," said the young man. "I'll talk." And he did. He kept his eyes on her and he talked to her for a long, long while. He told her about how he was going to get them out of their crummy situation. He told her that he was going to go back to college and get a teaching certificate and get a job at a high school. He told her that he'd teach shop, or gym, and then he'd get tenured, so they couldn't fire him, which would mean that their future would be pretty secure, and they could have kids.

And when he stopped talking for a moment, and looked away from her—his eyes had adjusted to the dim light and he could see her profile; it was gray against the darkness—and looked at the blue-green phosphorescence that was the doorway, he saw that someone was standing in it, hunched over, hands on the doorjamb, legs wide.

And he screamed.

Erthmun said, "I don't know." He closed his eyes, looked as if he were in pain.

The doctor said, "Mr. Erthmun, perhaps it's best if you sleep."

"I've *been* asleep, damnit!" He opened his eyes. He sighed, looked at the doctor. "I've been asleep," he repeated. "I don't need to sleep." He closed his eyes again, opened them, looked first at Patricia, then at the doctor. "What is this place?" he asked.

"You're in a hospital, Jack," Patricia told him.

"You're suffering from hypothermia," the doctor said.

"Hypothermia," Erthmun echoed.

"You're going to be all right," Patricia told him. "You need to rest."

"What is this place?" he asked again.

"A hospital."

"Hospital," Erthmun echoed. "Hypothermia." He closed his eyes, opened them, stared at the ceiling. "I dreamed," he whispered, as if to no one in particular. "I never dream. But I dreamed."

"Mr. Erthmun, it was a nightmare," the doctor said. "But you're awake now."

"I don't have nightmares," Erthmun said. "I don't dream."

"We all dream," said the doctor.

"I don't know," said Erthmun, and his eyes were still on the ceiling.

"What don't you know, Jack?" Patricia asked.

He said nothing.

"Jack?" she coaxed.

He said nothing.

Chapter Twenty-nine

And when he was done screaming, the young homeless man saw that the thing standing in the doorway had vanished, and he could feel that his wife was clinging to him so tightly that it hurt.

After several minutes, he said, "I saw something."

His wife said nothing. She still clung to him. He put his hand comfortingly on hers. "I saw something," he repeated. "I screamed because I saw something." He played back the moment, saw again in his mind's eye the thing standing in the rectangle of soft blue-green phosphorescence that was the doorway. He continued. "I thought I saw something." He nodded to indicate the doorway. "There." He paused. "But maybe I didn't." He patted his wife's hand, thought it was a stupid gesture under the circumstances, and said, "It's all right. There's no one in the house but us. How would they get in? They couldn't get in." He paused. "We're the only ones here."

His wife clung silently to him.

Greta liked chocolate. She thought that she had always liked chocolate. She thought she remembered stuffing gobs of it in her mouth when she was a child and telling her mother—who she remembered had looked on with an odd mixture of horror and rebuke—"It's better than mud," which she thought made her mother's look of horror and rebuke become one of perplexity.

Greta was eating chocolate now. It wasn't cheap chocolate. It wasn't mud. It wasn't Hershey's, or Nestle's Crunch. It was lovely chocolate. Godiva. Perugina. Chocolate that was sex and sensuality. Chocolate that was life itself. Chocolate that filled her soul. Chocolate that made her moist, and made her eyes close, and made her senses quiver.

Greta was surprised at this new creature that had emerged from within the Greta she had known for so long. And she was delighted, too. This Greta would not sit longingly for hours at her window and do nothing. This Greta had enough life in her to do what that other Greta was afraid to do.

Breathe!

Be!

The doctor said to Patricia David, "He clearly is experiencing some disorientation. It's not unusual in cases of hypothermia. But he's no longer in any danger. I'd say it was fortunate that you got him here as soon as you did; otherwise this whole scenario might have played out very differently."

Erthmun was asleep. He was on his back and he was breathing very lightly. Patricia had supposed that he was a man who snored. But he didn't snore. He slept as silently as stone.

Patricia said, "So you think he'll be able to go home in a day or two?"

"There's no reason that he can't go home tomorrow," the doctor said.

"Tomorrow? That's good."

"We'll just keep him here tonight as a precautionary measure, and he can go home tomorrow."

In the brownstone on West 161st Street, the young homeless man felt trapped by the storm, by his homelessness, and by the sudden, silent, and motionless panic of his wife. He felt trapped, too, by the thing that had appeared so briefly, and now, he knew, waited for him somewhere beyond the tall rectangle of soft, blue-green phosphorescence that was the doorway.

He said to his wife, "C'mon, babe, we've got to get out." He had said the same words to her a half-dozen times in the past fifteen minutes, but with no response. She continued clinging to him; she was still hurting his arm with her incredibly strong grip, and he imagined that he'd have finger-shaped bruises on that arm before long.

He said now, "What are we going to do, babe?"

She said nothing.

"If we don't get out of here, this is it," he said.

Silence.

Beyond the house, the storm droned on. He thought it sounded like laughter.

Chapter Thirty

These weren't dreams. How could they be dreams? He could smell the tangy odor of wet earth, freshly washed clothes, his father's aftershave, a breakfast just eaten.

How could this be a dream? Because his mother was here, too, and his sisters, and his house, although it existed only as a dark, windowless box at the horizon, and the golden grasses swaying like flowers, and the insects that tried to get out of his way—the crickets, the mantises, the gaily colored garden spiders retreating deep into their webs.

And the others.

Those who shadowed him, and ran with him, who made the most of their time, just as he was doing, who made the most of what the earth had given them, just as he was doing.

His mother would have been amazed if she had seen

him run like this. His father, too. And his sisters. All amazed. *Look at that little fireplug run!* they would have said. *Who would have known he could run like that?*

Who?

Only the others.

The ones who shadowed him and ran with him and mimicked his laughter, and felt his joy.

They were the only ones who existed here. There were no murder victims in this place, in these high hills and golden fields. There were no men with wounds and mouths agape. There were no women who had been made to look foolish.

There was only the dark, windowless box that was his house, far off, at the horizon. Only the golden grasses.

Only the others.

And him.

And the other child. The one he had found playing with a doll at a stream far from the house; the one who told him her name was Greta, and whom he had found spooning mud into the mouth of her doll.

"Why are you doing that?" he asked.

"Doing that?" echoed the girl. "It's chocolate. I like chocolate. My doll likes chocolate."

"I like chocolate, too," he said.

"Chocolate, too," she echoed. "And do you like my doll's eyes?"

"Doll's eyes," he said, and looked closely at it; it was a naked, plastic doll—its eyes had been plucked out and crumpled bright green paper put in their place.

He asked, "Why'd you do that?"

"Do that?" she echoed. "I like green. Don't you like green? I like chocolate and I like things that are green."

"I like green," he said.

"I like green," she echoed.

*   *   *

"This is what I'm going to do, babe," said the young homeless man to his wife. "I'm going to leave you here"—she clung even more tightly to him—"I'm going to leave you here, and I'm going to go just over there"—he nodded at the doorway—"and then I'll come right back." She continued clinging to him. He took hold of her hand, tried to pry her fingers free. He pleaded, "You've got to let go of me, babe." He pulled hard on her fingers, hoped he wasn't hurting her, got her hand free for a moment, let go of it; she grabbed his arm again, even tighter.

"Babe," he said, "this is stupid. We don't want to die here, do we?"

Nothing.

"Do we?" he said again.

Nothing.

He lurched away from her, suddenly. It was for her own good, he told himself. At this point, she was her own worst enemy. Better a little pain now than death later.

He stood unsteadily, because his legs had gone to sleep, wobbled a bit, looked down at her. She was a yellowish mass near his feet. He thought she was looking up at him. "I'm going over there," he said, and moved his arm a little to indicate the doorway.

She said nothing.

"Okay?" he said.

Nothing.

He thought that he needed a weapon. But what was there? The room was empty.

Something in the closet, maybe. Where was it? He looked about. He saw a dark rectangle against the far wall. Surely that was the closet door.

"I'm going over there," he said. "I'm going to go and look in the closet."

"No," she whispered.

He was happy that she'd spoken at last. "I have to," he said.

"Why?" she said.

"I need some kind of weapon. I have to look in the closet."

"Don't!" she said.

"I have to," he said again. He thought that he was becoming angry with her.

She said nothing.

He crossed slowly to the dark rectangle he supposed was the closet door. He hoped that as he drew closer to it, he would be able to see it better. But that didn't happen. It was in a darker area of the room, well away from the bedroom door and the soft blue-green phosphorescence, and as he drew closer, the dark rectangle merely became darker, and monolithic. When he was close to it, he reached into the area where the doorknob should have been. His fingers touched cold wood. He lowered his hand a little. His fingers touched colder metal. He probed the metal, found a small hole in it, whispered, "Shit." No doorknob.

"Don't!" he heard from behind him.

"I have to," he said yet again.

"Don't!" he heard.

"It's all right, babe," he said.

"Don't!" he heard.

He began to speak, and heard, from the middle of the dark room, in his own voice, "It's all right, babe."

He whirled about.

He saw the dark oval of a face near his, the darker ovals of eyes on him, the oval of a mouth wide open.

Chapter Thirty-one

Then it was gone. And he saw that his wife was standing between him and the doorway.

She said, her voice shaking and weak, "What was it?"

He said nothing. He had backed reflexively away and now was standing with his rear end to the closet door and his legs quivering. He thought that he had peed his pants.

"What was it?" his wife said again. "Dammit, what *was* that thing?" Her voice had become stronger, firmer.

The young man said, "I . . . don't know."

"You don't know?" she shrieked. "You don't fucking *know*?" She came quickly forward. "For Christ's sake, why *don't* you know? Why in the hell *don't* you know?" She was standing directly in front of him now. "You bring me here, you bring me here to this goddamned place and you don't fucking know what *lives* here? That's fucking stupid! *You're* fucking stupid!" She put her hands flat on his chest and pushed against him, but he went nowhere because he was standing against the closet door. She shrieked at him, "I'm going to *die* here, for Christ's sake, and you don't know *why*? Why *don't* you know, why *don't* you know?" She pummeled his chest with her fists. "It's up to you to *know*! You're my *husband*, you *have* to know! You *have* to know!"

He let her pummel him. She wasn't hurting him much, and he thought he deserved whatever pain she could inflict. Because she *was* going to die, it was obvious. And so was he. What could they do about it? They were trapped, by the storm, by their homelessness, by the thing that shared this place with them, by hunger.

In the House on Four Mile Creek
The Same Moment

They were like termites in the house. They huddled together in corners in its many rooms. And if a person had been listening to them, that person would have heard what sounded like a deep purring noise—throats responding to the quivering that kept them warm, that produced heat, and kept them alive in this place where huddling together was the only way to contain heat.

Occasionally, amid this purring, a listener might have heard words, too. The voice of a male, and the voice of a female. A listener would have heard, "Do you think this is safe?" and "Okay, so what do we do now? Spread our sleeping bags out here?" and "Maybe there's a fireplace," and, "Inner room where?"

In this month, under this desperation, these creatures had no idea what such words meant. They had heard the words, and they were repeating them. They repeated much. They loved the sounds they heard. They repeated the sounds of animals, too, and insects, and birds. In summer, a listener might be walking in a meadow and hear what he supposed were only the many and varied sounds of the meadow. And, after a fashion, he would be right.

But this month, under this desperation, these creatures quivered for warmth, and sounds came from them involuntarily, like the grunting of bears on a lazy stroll. And the twittering of insects, too, the raucous cries of blue jays, a human conversation born of fear and impending panic.

Under their desperation, these naked forms knew nothing of time and everything of cold, which was death. And so they huddled together in the corners in all the rooms of the big house, and the noises that came from the house were like the noises of meadows, and conversations, sleeping cats, and strolling bears.

The homeless man's wife had done what the man thought was a very stupid thing, though he couldn't blame her for it. She had run from him, out of the room, into the hallway, and then, in the dark, had blundered over the place where the stairs should have been. Now she lay groaning somewhere below him; the young man wasn't sure if she was on the first floor, or beneath that, in the cellar—he could see her only dimly. And he was trying to imagine how he would reach her, because, in her fall, she had knocked the homemade ladder over.

He called to her, "Are you all right?" but she only groaned in response, and he tried to convince himself that this was a good sign, really—at least she could groan—and he repeated, "Are you all right?" though he knew that she wasn't. How could she be? She'd fallen . . . what?—fifteen, twenty feet in the pitch dark, in the cold, and God only knows what she might have fallen *on,* or what bones she might have broken. He imagined her lying in pain and in terrified resignation about her own death, and it tore him apart because he loved her, and because he had loved the life they had once planned to live.

"I'm coming down there, babe," he called. And he knew that this was true. He really *was* going down there, to where she lay. He simply didn't know, at that moment, how he was going to do it.

When Erthmun woke he saw black and white floor tiles, beige walls, shadowless fluorescent light, and he smelled antiseptic, blood, freshly cooked eggs, and he heard people talking at a distance—"Look what Karen brought you, darling. Isn't it sweet?" and, from another place, "He says it's not a problem and that we have nothing to worry about."

Erthmun sighed. No high hills and golden grasses in this place. No crickets hopping out of his way.

This was the place of the grinning dead.

Chapter Thirty-two

Morning in Manhattan

It had been a bad night for the homeless man. What could he do? It was too dark to find his way down to his wife, who had groaned for hours, and now was silent. He could see her, though not clearly because the storm was stealing sunlight from the morning. He saw her as if through a fog. He saw that she was on her back in the cellar and that her arms and legs were spread wide. He couldn't see her face. He wasn't sure that he wanted to see it.

And the storm had lashed the brownstone all night, too, which had been maddening for a couple of reasons, not the least of which was the fact that he hadn't been able to *hear* anything beyond his wife's groaning—which had been as loud as a scream, and was clearly the result of terrible pain. But he hadn't been able to hear anything else, hadn't been able to hear if something were moving toward him from within one of the bedrooms. So he had sat with his all-but-blind gaze on the second-floor interior of the brownstone, and had listened to the screams of the storm and the screaming groans of his wife, and he had prayed for morning.

The doctor said, "He checked out, Miss David."

"When?" Patricia asked.

"About a half hour ago, I think."

"Just like that?"

"Of course. We have no right to keep him here."

"Do you know where he went?"

"My assumption is that he went home."

"Thanks," Patricia said, and hung up.

Erthmun was like many New Yorkers; he didn't own a car. It was too much of a hassle to keep one parked and secure. You paid as much a month to park a car in a secure parking garage as many outside the city paid for a mortgage. And if you parked on the street—assuming you could find an empty parking space—the chances were more than even that you'd wake in the morning and find that the car had been stripped of everything except its gas tank and brake pedal. So, at work, he used his unmarked police car, which he turned in at the end of his shift, and took a bus home, or walked.

This morning, there were no buses, only a few taxis, and even fewer private cars moving on the streets of Manhattan. The snow was knee-deep on many of the side streets, and on the main streets—Broadway, Lexington, Fifth Avenue, Madison—plows were trying gamely to bring the city back to some semblance of normalcy. But it was impossible because storms of this magnitude were a once-in-a-decade occurrence here, and no one knew how to deal with them properly. The city had come to a standstill.

He found a little deli called Marty's on 32nd Street. It was empty, except for the owner, who was standing behind the counter in a white T-shirt and white apron, looking glumly at the storm beyond his windows. Erthmun went into the deli. "Jesus, mister," the owner said to him, "what the hell are you doin' out there?"

Erthmun sat at the counter. It was a highly polished pale green, and squeaky clean; there were ketchup bottles and little metal baskets filled with Equal packets placed neatly every couple of feet on it. "Dying, I think," Erthmun said. He folded his hands in front of him, noted their reflection in the countertop, saw that they were shaking.

The owner of the deli smiled and said, "Ain't we all, huh?"

Erthmun nodded.

"Ain't we all dyin'?" the owner said, and then announced that he was Marty himself, and extended his hand. Erthmun stared at it a moment, then lifted his own quivering hand and shook Marty's. "Tell me you ain't a cop," Marty said.

Erthmun said, "I'm a cop."

"I know cops," Marty said, grinning. He had a round face and big, oval dark eyes, and his grin was pleasant and nonjudgmental. "I been servin' cops here for twenty-five years, huh. Coffee?"

Erthmun said, "Coffee? Yes."

Marty gave him a concerned look. "You okay?"

"I'm okay."

"You don't seem okay. Maybe you need more than coffee, huh?"

"No, just coffee." Erthmun could feel that he was shaking now. He thought that in the very recent past he had felt the same way that he was feeling at that moment, and that it had not boded well for him. He added, "Have I been in here before, Marty?"

"I don't think so," Marty said, and put a big, cream-colored mug full of pitch-black coffee in front of Erthmun. "But who can say? What, you don't remember?"

Erthmun shook his head, sipped his coffee, spilled some on the counter because his hands were shaking. Marty mopped up the spill immediately with a towel.

Erthmun sipped his coffee again. He thought that he was being very noisy about it, and he apologized.

Marty said. "Every morning I got fifty noisy sippers in here. It's like music." He grinned again.

Erthmun said, "I'm being stalked, I'm being hunted."

Marty said nothing.

Erthmun sipped his coffee.

Marty said, as if concerned, "Who's stalking you?"

Erthmun said, "It could be anyone." He realized that he was shaking badly now, and that it was affecting his speech. He thought that he sounded like a fool, but these were such important things to say. "It could be you. It could be anyone. It could be Helen."

"It ain't me," Marty said.

"It could be Helen," Erthmun repeated. "Do you know her?"

"Who?"

"Helen."

"No, I don't know no Helen."

"Who does? Who does? She's like . . . a puff of . . . smoke, Marty. Smoke. She's like smoke. Do you know her?"

"No," Marty said again.

"Who knows her?" Erthmun said. "I don't."

"Sure," said Marty; he was getting nervous.

"She could be you, or me, or anyone," Erthmun said. "But she isn't. She isn't. She's . . . Helen. And she does what she does!"

"Sure," Marty repeated.

"She eats," Erthmun said. "We all eat."

"Sure we do. We eat," Marty said.

"I don't know," Erthmun said. "I met someone once. A long, long time ago, in another place. But she wasn't Helen. Only Helen is Helen. Helen isn't me, or you."

"Maybe you'd like your coffee warmed up?" Marty asked.

"But she could be you and you wouldn't know it," Erthmun said.

"You're shakin' real bad, mister," Marty said. "I can't understand what you're sayin'."

"You don't need to," Erthmun said. He set his cup down hard, so more coffee sloshed onto the counter. Marty did not step forward to clean it up.

"Jesus!" Erthmun shouted.

Marty lurched.

"It could be you, it could be you!" Erthmun shouted. "Why did I come in here?" The energy of his sudden anger was overcoming the fact that he was cold and shaking, and his words were easier to understand now. "Did you *invite* me in here?"

"You came in here all on your own," Marty said.

"Did I? Why would I do that?"

"I guess to get some coffee," Marty said.

"Are you *human*?" Erthmun shouted. "Are you *human*?"

"Sure I'm human."

"But do you *know*? Can you prove it? No. Who knows? Can you reach back and pull yourself out of your

175

mother's womb and say, *This is me, and I'm human*? No. Who can? No one. Do you realize that there are dead women with chocolate stuffed in their mouths in this city right now as we speak? Think of it, think of it. Chocolate in their mouths! Naked, dead women with chocolate in their mouths, and no one knows why! Do *you* know why? No. No one knows! These are *previous* women!"

"Sure," said Marty. He was backing away as Erthmun ranted.

Erthmun said, "Women who are no more than soil, no more than the earth itself, women who are like plastic dolls, women who will never taste the chocolate that fills their mouths!"

"Sure," said Marty.

"And what do you know, Marty? Can you reach into your mother's womb, can you go back in time and reach into your mother's womb and say, *Yes, this is me, and this is my father, who fucked my mother one night, who fucked her sweetly and said he loved her when he was done, and put his seed into her, and it was that seed that made me*? And can you say, *And this is my mother, whose womb I'm in*? You can't say any of that. You can't say any of it!"

Erthmun stood suddenly. Marty lurched. There was a small handgun beneath the counter not far from him.

Erthmun said, "It is these women who are stalking me!"

"Sure," said Marty, bent over, and put his hand on the gun beneath the counter.

"What's that?" Erthmun said. "What are you doing?"

"Nothing," said Marty.

"Good," said Erthmun.

*　　*　　*

At that moment, Patricia was trying to telephone him from her cellular phone. She was in her car and the car was stuck in snow near the corner of Lexington and 37th Street. There were other cars stuck around her; most had been abandoned, but a few drivers were furiously trying to get their cars moving.

She let Erthmun's number ring a couple of dozen times.

The homeless man could see well enough now, and he thought that was wife was dead. He could see her eyes, and they were closed. He could see her mouth, and he thought that it was open a little. He didn't think that her chest was moving at all. She lay directly beneath him, in the cellar, and her legs and arms were splayed out.

He hoped that she wasn't dead. He thought that he actually loved her and that he didn't want to lose her like this.

He wondered if he could jump from here to the first floor. It was only a little farther, he guessed, than if he stood with his arm straight up. It wasn't twenty feet, as he had first thought. It was fifteen feet, tops—not a whole bunch more than the distance from a basketball hoop to the ground. He could jump it. He could do it, and when he had done it, it would be done, and he wouldn't have to think about it anymore. It would be behind him. He'd be on the first floor, and he'd be able to tell if his wife was dead. And if she wasn't . . . What then? What was he going to do then? Carry her somewhere? Carry her to a hospital? Go and call an ambulance? How would he pay for it, because for sure they'd want him to pay for it. He didn't even know the address here. *A brownstone on West 161st Street*—is that what he'd say? *And how are you going to pay for this ambulance?* they'd say. He'd have no answer.

He stared at his wife. He hoped to see that her chest was moving a little, that her lips were spluttering—though, if they were, he realized, he wouldn't be able to see it from here—or that her eyes would open.

He wanted her to live.

He wanted them both to live.

Christ, he was hungry!

Chapter Thirty-three

Morning at the House on Four Mile Creek

Sunlight fell on some of the creatures huddled in a corner in that house. It was like a salve, a healing potion. They had watched it creep across the floor toward them as morning started. They had known what it was, and that its very touch brought wonderful pleasure and warmth. But they didn't move to greet it. No one got up from the naked heap and moved across the floor to greet it. This would have taken heat away from the others and would have brought cold and pain to the individual who did it. Better to wait for the sunlight together, as one.

The sunlight touched a few of them at the feet, though not all of them; and when this happened, all groaned in pleasure because all could feel the sunlight through the ones that it touched.

He was still bent over, still had his hand on the butt of the gun. He could see the other man's eyes on him, and he could read no threat or danger in them. But the man was so odd with his talk of naked women and chocolate and stalkers. The man was crazy, sure, and crazy people did crazy things, unless they were stopped.

Erthmun said, "I don't have a gun. Did you believe that I had a gun?"

Marty said, "I want you just to leave, okay?"

"I'm cold," Erthmun told him.

Marty gripped the gun, straightened with it in his hand, but kept it pointed at the floor.

Erthmun said, "Would you shoot another human being?"

"I don't know if I ever would shoot anybody," Marty said.

"I'm another human being," Erthmun said. "I'm another human being," he repeated. "And I'm cold. I need to be here."

"I don't think you can stay in my delicatessen," Marty said; his words alone would have indicated uncertainty, but his tone was firm. "I have the gun and I don't know what I would do with it. I think that you should go to the hospital."

Erthmun pointed stiffly to indicate the street and the storm. He said, his voice quaking again, "Do you see that?"

"I see it," Marty said.

"If I leave here, that storm will kill me," Erthmun said.

Marty shook his head. "No. Not in this city. There are places for you to go. So I want you to leave and go to one of those places. Go to Penn Station. It's not far. It's warm. Go there."

Erthmun stared at the man for a long moment. These words went through Erthmun's head; *What's happening to me? What do I know? Why am I here, in this city, in this restaurant? Why does that man have a gun in his hand? What does he want to do with it? What am I? What am I?*

As quietly and as gracefully as a moth opening its wings, Helen had stepped out of the near-dark in the cellar of the brownstone on West 161st Street, and now she stood naked and incredible in the dim morning light, dark hair streaming down her back, her sky-blue eyes fixed on the homeless man above her, on the second floor, as if she were mentally weighing his worth to her. And he stared back in awe, because he knew that this was the incredible creature that had haunted him the previous evening.

Under other circumstances, the homeless man would have thought, "She's naked, she's a woman—she's vulnerable." But these were not such circumstances. This creature was no more vulnerable than the storm that still lashed the house. No more vulnerable than Death itself.

So he stared silently at her. His gaze did not move more than once from her eyes to her body, which was as exquisite as any female body he had seen.

And, still as if assessing his worth to her, she stared silently back. And after not too long, she bent quickly over the body of the homeless man's wife, ripped open the woman's gray wool jacket, tore at the blue sweater beneath, and the pink blouse beneath that, and shoved her hand far into the woman's stomach. Then she devoured what she pulled out of that stomach—the woman's small intestine, part of the woman's liver, a kidney—while the homeless man watched silently from above.

181

"Who the fuck moves that quickly?" Erthmun snarled.
"Who?"

Marty's mouth was open and the nose of his own gun
was stuck into it. Erthmun was holding the gun, and he
had bent Marty backward over one of his stoves—which
had not been lit. Erthmun was holding the neck of
Marty's white shirt tightly in one hand.

A dollop of drool fell from Erthmun's mouth to
Marty's neck, which caused Marty to make a little
squeaking noise.

"What's that!" Erthmun demanded. "Did you say
something to me?"

Marty shook his head a little. He did not want to annoy
this man. Marty had seen him move at a speed at which
no man should be able to move. He thought, upon awed
reflection, that the man had even become invisible for a
moment because he was moving so fast.

"Do you know this?" Erthmun snarled. "Do you know
this?"

Again, Marty shook his head a little.

"Do you know this?" Erthmun repeated, and Marty
got the fleeting impression that Erthmun had no idea that
he was asking a question, that the words were simply an
echo. Marty shook his head again. Another dollop of
drool fell to his neck; he tried to ignore it.

Erthmun said, "I don't *want* to kill you. I don't *want*
to kill you." Short pause. "But maybe I *need* to!"

"You don't!" Marty whispered.

"Maybe I do! How do you know what I have to do?
How do you know what I'm compelled to do? You don't
know me. Who knows me? You don't!"

Marty said nothing.

Erthmun cocked the gun. "Maybe I *do* want to kill you!

Maybe there's no maybe at all about anything I do. I do what I do because I feel good when I do it. And so I do what I do to feel good, because it's part of being alive. Feeling good is part of being alive. I feel good. You feel good. We do what we do and we feel good. That makes sense. Doesn't that make sense?"

Nothing.

"Answer me, goddamnit! Answer me!"

"Yes," Marty whispered.

"Do you know me? How can you know me? Who knows me?"

Marty shook his head in terrified confusion.

Erthmun took the gun from the man's mouth, pointed it at the ceiling, fired, fired again, again. Marty's body lurched with each shot.

Erthmun tossed the gun far across the deli. He held his hand up, fingers wide, for Marty to see. "I don't need that," he said. "I have these!"

Chapter Thirty-four

Helen had finished. She was drenched in the blood of the homeless woman, whose eyes had opened in the past few minutes; the woman's husband had dimly noted this from his perch above, and, as dimly, he had ascribed it to some errant reaction of nerves. It did not occur to him for long that his wife had been alive through her own devouring. The idea was monstrous; no one could continue living in the human community, or could go on believing in an ordered and sane universe, and accept that such a thing had happened to one who is loved.

Helen had finished, had consumed her last meal, had known her last great pleasure.

And now she was dying.

The homeless man did not know this. He saw her move off—with more clumsiness than the quiet grace with which she had made her appearance—into the near dark on the first floor of the brownstone. Her hip-length auburn hair was the last he saw of her. And as he stared at his disemboweled wife, the fleeting idea came to him—as a combination of abstraction and words—that surely he and his wife would never have children now, not only because she was dead, but because her ovaries and uterus had been ingested by the naked woman, and that was a fact that would never change.

And he realized this, too: He realized that he had never been hungrier.

"My mother," Erthmun declared—he was still holding Marty bent backward over one of his stoves—"writes poetry! Isn't that civilized? What more civilized thing is there than fucking poetry?"

"Uhn—" Marty groaned.

"It's very bad poetry," Erthmun said. "But still it's civilized because *she* is civilized. My mother is a very civilized woman. And because *she's* civilized, so am I!"

"Yes," Marty managed.

"But poets can kill, and have," Erthmun declared. "Poets bring us more pain than whole armies of armed men!"

Marty said nothing.

"I'm not a poet," Erthmun said. His tone had softened. He spoke in what could almost pass for a quiet and conversational tone now, except that there was much tension in it. "I'm a cop. I investigate murder. That is what I do and it is what society expects of me, so I do it happily, and well. I get money for it, and a place to live. I write nothing, I create nothing. And I have never killed." He cocked his head, continued. "Perhaps I should begin. I think there's something very deep inside me that wants me to. It feels deprived, neglected, left out . . . of the human equation. Do you have that same feeling"—short pause—"Marty?"

"No," said Marty.

"I think you do. I think you may be lying."

"No," said Marty.

Erthmun felt the man's terror, panic, and desperation. He could see a life in it, and pain—Marty's life, and Marty's pain. It made him soften his grip on Marty's shirt collar. Marty stayed put. The terror, panic, and desperation passed. Erthmun's grip strengthened again, and he said, "You're talking to me, aren't you, my friend."

"No," said Marty.

"But you are. You're telling me all about yourself. You're telling me you want to live, and you're telling me about your children, you're telling me that you don't want me to hurt you, and you're telling me that you don't like pain. Shit, that's nothing new. Who likes pain?"

"I'm not saying nothing," said Marty.

"I can *hear* it, my friend. I can hear you speak."

"No," said Marty.

"And the big question is—am I going to listen?"

Greta loved chocolate. Not cheap chocolate. Not mud. She loved expensive chocolate, chocolate made with pleasure. Chocolate was childhood. Childhood was life.

And what did these people here, in this city, know of pleasure? They took no pleasure in anything, they moved about from sunset to sunset to dawn to sunset, and their weeks became years until their years were done.

Hers were just beginning.

Chapter Thirty-five

Summer, outside the House on Four Mile Creek

The man asked, "Is it salvageable, do you think?" His own guess was no. The paint had long since flaked off the clapboards, the grouting had crumbled from much of the stone foundation, the chimneys were little more than stumps.

The real-estate agent was a woman who was new to the area, but she wasn't new to real estate, or to architecture and construction, and she said, "I think it is. It's a beautiful house underneath that dark patina of age."

The man looked at her and smiled. "You're something of a poet, aren't you?"

She blushed. She didn't know what to say. She had seen her phrase merely as a descriptive enticement, although it was true enough as well—the house was certainly sal-

187

vageable. She explained, "All the windows are intact, as remarkable as that may seem. Some of them are cracked, certainly, but they can be repaired. And since the windows are intact, and the roof itself is not too far gone, then the house hasn't been victimized by the elements in the way that it might otherwise have been."

"Even though it's been empty for how long? Thirty-five years?"

"Thirty-five years? Yes. About that long."

They were standing just outside the house's gray, stylized picket fence—much of it had fallen; only a few tilting sections remained—and the man said, "This is very pretty. It looks hand-built."

The real-estate agent nodded. "It is."

"What a pity that it can't be salvaged as well." Short pause. "Could we look inside?"

"Of course."

PARTIAL TRANSCRIPT OF THE INITIAL INTERROGATION OF ROBERT W. GARNISH, AS CONDUCTED BY DETECTIVE PAUL MCBRIDE, OF THE 20TH PRECINCT:

P.M.: This won't wash, and you know it, Robert. This is crap from the get-go.

R.G.: My name's not Robert. It's Bob.

P.M.: Okay, Bob. Your call.

R.G.: Shit, too.

P.M.: Yes, you're right, Bob. It's not your call. It's our call. And I'd say our call is for twenty-five to life. Shit, Bob, if it were up to me I'd feed you to the fucking bears at the fucking Central Park Zoo. That would be a fitting punishment. That would be . . . shit, that would be fucking irony, Bob. But it's not up to me, and you can thank your lucky stars for that.

R.G.: *I don't have any.*

P.M.: *Any what, Bob?*

R.G.: *Lucky stars.*

P.M.: *Damn right, Bob. All the fucking stars in the sky and not a lucky one for you. You've had a fucking tough few months, haven't you, Bob? No job, no place to live, nothing to fucking eat!*

R.G.: *Yeah.*

P.M.: *Sure, you have. We've all had a tough time. Life's tough. Living's tough. Finding enough to fucking eat is tough, isn't it?*

R.G.: *I didn't do that to her. I told you who did it, and it wasn't me.*

P.M.: *Yes, you did, Bob. And the amazing thing is this: The amazing thing is—you actually expect us to fucking believe that fantasy. Naked woman, my ass!*

R.G.: *It happened.*

P.M.: *No, it didn't. We both know what happened. We both know what happened. So tell me, Bob—how was it? Was it finger-licking good stuff? Did it go down good? Was it nourishing, Robert? Did it contain your daily allowance of vitamins and fucking minerals?*

R.G.: *Shit on you!*

P.M.: *Tell me something, Bob. How do you feel about chocolate?*

Two Miles from the House on Four Mile Creek

What had he expected? Had he expected to find her here? Had he expected to see her sitting by this stream and spooning mud into her doll's mouth? That was the past. That was thirty years ago or more. She had been a child, then, and so had he.

He turned his head. He was in a valley, and the tall golden grasses were swaying in a soft breeze. The white noise they created was comforting, and called up memories he had long suppressed. He thought that, from this vantage point, he could see the house. But he could not. It was too far away, over the hillock. He would have to do a lot of walking and climbing if he wanted to see it.

He looked at the little stream again. If there were ghosts, would she be sitting there, doing what she had been doing so long ago? Perhaps. If so, he did not have the power to see her.

Why had he come back here? he wondered. The answer was obvious. He had come back because this was where he had begun his life. There was something sacred in that. Childhood itself was sacred. Adulthood wasn't. Adulthood was profane, violent and perverse. But he was trapped in it. There was no way around it. He was trapped in it, and he had to make the most of it.

He climbed the hill that was on the opposite side of the stream, and went back to his rented car. He sat in the car for a long while and asked himself if, after driving all this way, he was really going to simply turn around and go back to his city without returning to the house he had grown up in. Yes, he realized. That was what he was going to do. The house itself meant nothing. The house was simply a dark blotch on the tall, golden grasses. It was wood, shingles, cement, stone, and memories that were not as delicious as they had once been.

And he had work to do.

He started the car and drove off.

* * *

They were on the second story of the house on Four Mile Creek and the man lifted his foot and brought it down hard on the wood floor. "Solid enough," he said.

"It is," agreed the real estate agent.

They were near a window. It looked out—through the sad remains of a lace curtain—on hills and fields lush with golden grasses that were swaying gracefully in a playful breeze. The man stepped over to the window, parted the lace curtain, looked out at the golden grasses. "This is beautiful," he said. "Very beautiful."

"Best place on earth," said the real-estate agent. "A great place to raise kids."

"I would say, though," noted the man, "that it's hell in winter."

"Before the bond issue was put through," explained the real-estate agent, "I would not have recommended that anyone live here in the winter. But, as you know, there is a road being built to take the place of the one we drove on to get here."

"Uh-huh," said the man. He seemed suddenly distracted. He glanced back at her, said, "I see some dust rising at the horizon. What do you think it is?"

She came over to the window, looked out. "It's that dirt road. When it's dry like it's been, cars can kick up a hell of a lot of dust on it."

"Yeah," he said. "I see." He paused, continued. "And what do you think that is?" He pointed to indicate an area a hundred yards from the house.

She looked, said, "An animal."

"What animal?"

"Take your pick."

"Yes," he said. "I see now. It's a raccoon." He paused, continued. "I thought they were nocturnal."

191

"Yes, well, they usually are," said the real-estate agent with an odd tone of apology.

"Then what's that one doing out in daylight?"

The real-estate agent hesitated, then said, "I should caution you about some of the wildlife."

Book Two
Williamson the Loon
or
The Species Returns

Chapter One

"Oh, there is so much to see in the country—little tiny insects, and great insects (like burying beetles, which are as large as postage stamps—even larger, some as large as the caps on Mocha Frappucino bottles), and you can see animals, too, like coyotes (which are abundant in some parts of the state), and bears (which you can see at Letchworth State Park, though mostly you hear them when you're trying to sleep in your tent or your cabin, and it scares the crap out of you; and you can see them, too, in the Adirondacks, though these are just black bears, not brown bears, which are very dangerous), and small wildcats, and wolverines, and beaver, and various kinds of ducks and geese and swans. The red-tailed hawk is quite prevalent in all of the state, and it's a noble and beautiful bird, especially when the sun catches its tail feathers and turns them a bright, screaming red (hence the name).

"In the countryside, death happens as easily as rain. If you look closely enough, you see it happening. You see one large bird attacking a smaller bird (and sometimes it's the other way around), or you see that your cat has brought a headless mole into your yard, where it eats the rest of the poor creature, or you see roadkill, which is everywhere (on the roads).

"The countryside is very different from the city. There's grass and trees in the city, it's true, but mostly there's just asphalt and tall buildings, cars, sewers, and people looking for work, or people working. The deaths that happen in the city are usually the result of one person killing another, not the result of some animal killing a person, or some animal killing another animal.

"I saw a person kill someone else when I was visiting the city. I saw a large person beat up a small adult person who seemed to be minding his own business. After a while, police came and took the large person away, and a medical examiner's van came and took the dead person away. It was a sad sight to see, even sadder than rain (which isn't really sad), or fire that burns the countryside, though probably not that sad.

"I think you must understand that death is not a part of life, and if it were a part of life then it would be strange, because death is death, which is 'no life,' and life is life, which is 'life.' I don't understand it when I hear people say that death is a part of life. It's like saying that an empty Mocha Frappucino bottle is like a full Mocha Frappucino bottle. They aren't alike. One is an empty bottle, and one is a full bottle.

"And that doesn't mean that I don't know what people are talking about when they say that death is a part of life. They think they're being pretty smart saying it. They think, well, there you are, alive, but you won't always be alive, because death will catch up with you eventually, then you'll be dead. But that's stupid, because death doesn't catch up with anyone, *people* catch up with *death*. They run toward it all their lives, know what I mean? They smoke cigarettes and eat too much and have sex with people who have diseases, or they do stupid, hazardous things like ride three-wheeled bikes in the countryside, or hop on freight trains or bungee jump. I think people are always chasing after death as if it's some kind of lover, and if only they could touch it for a moment or two, it would be the best sex they ever had. People are stupid. People make things up as they go along. People can't be trusted. And most of all, people are born of women with red lips and breasts brimming with milk. They aren't born of a mother with hollyhocks in her forehead and rivers running through her belly.

"I'm telling you this, though—I'm telling you that there are things everywhere in this world that will kill you quick as a wink, no matter who your mother is, and it will be so seductive, like the lover, so teasing and fantastic and seductive, that people will fall all over themselves just to have it, like it's a great big bottle of Mocha Frappucino.

"Well, you know, that's this guy you're talking about. This Fred. That his name? Fred? Yeah? Good. Fred. Stupid name. So many people named Fred. It sounds like a kid's name. Hey, Fred, get your ass in here and eat your goddamned macaroni and cheese and drink your Kool Aid. Fred, ha! Anyone named Fred deserves what this Fred got. Well, not having their insides eaten. Not that. I mean, think about it. Just think about it a little. You're not really dead when your insides start getting eaten. You're still alive. And you're watching your insides get eaten. Maybe your intestines first (which you can live without for a couple of minutes), your spleen (same thing), or your stomach. Of course, it depends a lot on how fast your insides are getting eaten, I guess. Quick is good. Not so quick is not so good. I guess Fred's wasn't so damned quick, is that what you're telling me?

"But if you think I ate Fred, then you got to think again, because I'm a vegetarian. I don't eat people. I eat vegetables. Okra, especially. And greens. Celery is good. I don't much care for tomatoes, though. But they're a fruit. Do you know that? They're a fruit. Like Fred. I guess Fred was a fruit. Not that I have anything against fruits. If you want to drill someone who's got the same plumbing as you, that's your business.

"But it doesn't mean I killed him and ate him because, like I said, I eat okra, and celery, and carrots. Not the cooked kind. I hate that. Mushy crap. Or cooked cabbage either. Mushy crap.

"Do you know that Mocha Frappucino is a Starbucks product? Other manufacturers manufacture it. Some of those manufacturers are in New York State, my home state. One of those manufacturers is Upstate Farms, and they make a Frappucino that they call Cappucino, I think because Starbucks has a trademark registered on Frappucino, which means, I think, that if you use the name in some press release regarding the killing and eating of Fred, then you have to get permission from Starbucks. You don't want to get sued.

"And speaking of which, I think I'm talking to my lawyer about suing someone here. You know, for false arrest, or harassment, maybe, or internal prejudice—wait. What is that? Internal prejudice? It just came to me out of the blue. It's nothing, right? It's something I made up, right? Okay. Sorry. I'll stick to those other things. Harassment and false arrest.

"Because, I'll tell you, someone else killed fruity Fred,

and I can guarantee it. And someone else did those Chocolate Murders, too. I heard about them. I read about them. How can you live anywhere and not hear about them or read about them? You'd have to be living underground, I think. You'd have to be living in the great bacterial underbelly that breathes and moves and reproduces just a thousand feet below our feet (hmmm, rhyme?). You'd have to be expelled from the great bacterial underbelly that lives and breathes beneath our feet not to have heard about the Chocolate Murders. How calculated. How human. How perverse. Better to eat poor fruity Fred because you're hungry and there aren't any vegetables around—no okra, no broccoli, no yummy asparagus."

Erthmun flipped the interrogation sheet over, then back again, and said, "That's his whole statement?"

Peabody said, "Uh-huh. Then he clammed up tighter than beeswax in Detroit."

Erthmun gave Peabody a quick questioning look, wanted to say, " '*Beeswax in Detroit*'?" but didn't, because Peabody—who'd been with the force for twenty-five years—was known for talking strangely. Instead, Erthmun said, "And the confession?"

Peabody said, "Isn't worth two hams in a cracker box. I guess the guy's lawyer walked in when someone was putting a little pressure on him."

Erthmun sighed. "Well, shit, he did it."

Peabody, who was tall and bald, shrugged. "Yeah, of course he did it. That's as clear as tomorrow's orange juice. But, Christ, the guy *still* isn't talking. He hasn't said a goddamned word since that interrogation . . ." Peabody glanced at the date on the interrogation sheet. "Ten days ago."

Chapter Two

Williamson's head felt like a jar of snails, and he desperately wanted some Mocha Frappucino®. This was cruelty. Milk and bologna sandwiches on fucking white bread, and he a vegetarian. Didn't they know what all that goddamned protein could do to a body? Now if anyone knew about protein, it was him. He should have told them that. A rat couldn't live on bologna and white bread!

Pictures of Mama. Good old fat Mama singing gospel songs on the porch in the fall and strumming her banjo, all three of her teeth as white as a fish's belly, voice as clear as a mountain stream, and all that lisping and mangled chords and farting. Marvelous as dewdrops, spring leaves, frogs' tongues.

Williamson banged on the bars of his cell with his shoe. It made a dull noise that nobody beyond the closed door outside the cell would be able to hear to the point of annoyance, but the mere act of hitting the bars was gratifying. "Hey, coppers," he called, "you get that bitch in here and I'll teach her to go spilling her guts!" There was no bitch who had spilled her guts, but it sure sounded good. "Damn bitch!" he called. "Damn whore! Ludmilla! Ha!" He banged on the cell bars with his shoe. "Ludmilla is a stupid name. It's no one's name! Ludmilla! Ludmilla!"

Head felt like a jar of snails. Williamson liked that. Lots of snails in a jar, moving around real slow, leaving slimy snail trails. That's what his head sure felt like. And there were marbles in there, too. And jelly beans. Little grains of wheat. Raindrops. Pieces of dreams. All in that jar. Big jar. Bug jar. Bugaboo. Bugaboo joy juice. Bug juice. *We need more bug juice, Mama. Look at that windshield! Full of dead tsetse flies. Ugly! Stop there, get the bug juice!*

Williamson frowned. Awful to have a head full of snails, really. Like having a head full of mushy crap. *Mama, Mama, wherefore art thou, Mama?* And who knew? There was this Mama and that Mama, and that other Mama, a thousand Mamas, all different, all doing different things—swimming, knitting, cooking, hiking, laughing, crying, Mamas everywhere in his head, and Daddies, too. Daddies with rifles, briefcases, ladders, pickup trucks, limousines, Corvettes, and a thousand brothers and a thousand sisters—big ones, little ones, ugly ones, smart ones . . .

Bang the bars with the shoe. *Bang, slap, bang slap!* "Okay, coppers, you get that bitch in here or it's curtains for the kid!" *Bang, slap, bang, slap, bang, slap!*

He could keep it up all the damned long afternoon. Let them try to come in and stop him. He'd tear them ass from toenail, rip them up like they were soggy, chow down on them like they were escargot, then make clean his escape, into the dawning night, into the arms of his Gwynethe, Gwynethe waiting, Gwynethe the lithe, the lithesome, the libidinous!

He dropped the shoe. *Kerplunk!* He looked at the shoe. So who wore shoes but the shoeless? Why deprive the sole of the good earth? The green and dewy grass. The dunes!

Then there was Fred the fruit. Fred fruit. Apple Fred, Tomato Fred. Fruity Fred. Poor Fred without guts, hollowed out like a bowl of oatmeal, left to rot and stink up the place. Poor dead Fred. Eaten by the protein poor.

Bang, slap, bang, slap!

"What in the hell is he doing in there?" the visiting guard asked the resident guard.

"He's banging his cell bars with his shoe. He does it all the time. Morning, noon, and night. All the time. He's crazy as a goddamned bedbeg, a goddamned loon. Jesus, he *ate* someone."

The visiting guard looked wide-eyed at the resident guard. "You're kidding!"

The resident guard shook his head. "No. It's true."

"Ate who?"

"A guy named Fred. A big guy named Fred. Ate his guts."

"All of them?"

The resident guard nodded grimly. "Uh huh. Left nothing. Not even an entrail."

"What's an entrail?"

"Guts."

"Oh."

"Well, you know, it's the whole thing. All the intestines. They're entrails. That's what they're called." He gave the visiting guard a suspicious look. "You didn't know that?"

"Well," said the guard, "I did, sure. I knew that. But I just didn't know the technical term."

The resident guard gave the visiting guard another suspicious look. "Huh?"

The visiting guard said, with a glance toward Williamson's cell, "Really ate him, huh?"

"Yeah. Just his entrails. But the guy was big, so I guess that was enough."

Chapter Three

For a moment, Erthmun couldn't remember his name. For a moment he had to think about it. For a moment, he latched onto Jack Eberling, then Jack Entwistle, then Jack Earwig, which gave him a shiver. Then he remembered. Jack *Erthmun*. This temporary loss of memory had been happening quite a lot as he woke. His sleep had been very deep lately, deeper than dreaming, so he guessed that—somehow—his brain was merely shutting off, and that when he woke, his brain took a while to click back on. It was a good explanation, he thought. And it had happened more times than he could remember during his recently ended six-month hiatus from the force, six months he had needed away from chocolate murders, dead vagrants, and homicidal bag ladies more than an old dog needed a feather bed. Besides, come to find out that no one was within two hundred miles of solving the Chocolate Murders ("It's not just a dead end, Jack," Captain Hogarth had told him, "it's a slippery slope into a bottomless pit. The killings stopped, and suddenly we had nothing. Only some names and some suspects who just didn't pan out. Or they didn't pan out into gold."), well, no one much cared about dead vagrants, and although homicidal bag ladies were fascinating, they were few and far between.

Erthmun was sitting at his little pale green dining room table and he was drinking coffee, eating a poppy seed and sour cream muffin, and looking at photos of the fat, middle-aged man named Fred who had been eaten by the loon named Williamson.

Erthmun liked poppy seed muffins, even though his co-workers had warned him that if there were a surprise drug test, he'd flunk, because the poppy seeds would make him come up positive for cocaine. He thought this was stupid, though; "I'll just tell the guy doing the test that I've been eating poppy seed muffins," he said. "He'll understand."

His coworkers laughed. One of them said, "The guys who do these tests don't understand nothing but, *Hey, we got a positive for coke*," to which Erthmun merely shrugged. He wasn't going to give up his poppy-seed muffins just because there were stupid people in the world.

Fred, the guy who'd been eaten, was a handsome man, Erthmun thought. He was noble-looking, like a Viking. But if you looked at the huge, empty red bowl that was Fred's stomach, it was a different story. A goddamned bloody story. A horror story.

Erthmun picked up one of Fred's autopsy photos and studied it very closely. He'd wanted to be at the actual autopsy, but had been too late getting back from the Adirondacks. So he had to settle for 8X10 glossies. Good glossies, prepared from very-high-definition digital photographs, and they showed every nuance, every white and red curve of Fred's emptied belly. They even showed the bite marks on Fred's ribs, and on his spine. Very good photography. But Erthmun missed the sounds and the smells of autopsy. The heady aroma of flesh on the verge of decomposition, the chatter of bone saws and the snap of autopsy scissors. It was quite a sensual celebration of the real meaning of death—the poking, the probing, the prodding, the ghastly invasion of privacy. It always put Erthmun in another place, in a universe where death and life intermingled as easily as coffee and cream, rainwater and earth, love and poetry. And hey, hell, he thought, death and life had always combined to produce the ultimate poetry.

He took a great chomp of the poppy-seed-and-sour-cream muffin. It was the last of three he'd bought the night before at Vittorio's Deli, on Second Avenue. He'd eaten one before bed, with a cup of hot chocolate, and it had been soothing for sleep, but now he wished he hadn't, because two muffins simply didn't comprise an acceptable breakfast, and he felt empty, as empty as Fred, he thought, then sighed, grinned, and chuckled.

Perhaps he had eggs.

"Poppy seed?" he heard, and ignored it.

He got up from the pastel green table and lumbered over to the refrigerator, way across the kitchen, pulled the door open, and peered in. Nothing much. A can of cannelini beans. A slice of bread. Half a glass of what looked like water. Some aluminum foil covering nothing. Odd stuff to keep in a refrigerator, he thought.

But no eggs.

He closed the refrigerator door, lumbered back to his table, and felt suddenly cold. Maybe it was time he put underwear on, at least. After all, who was he trying to impress—the old women across the way, who hung all their graying undies on a clothesline that sagged between their building and his?

But being naked was okay, he thought. There were probably millions of naked people in the world at that moment, and very few of them actually ashamed of it.

He took the last bite of his muffin, chewed it slowly, swallowed, and picked up several of Fred's autopsy photos again. He sighed. He wasn't interested, suddenly. Fred didn't matter. Fred was stale, his life over, his story finished, his photographs taken, and his entrails ingested by Williamson the Loon. Nothing more needed to be said or done, except to face Williamson and extract a confession in the usual way.

Patricia thought that, ultimately, everyone was weird. They lived inside the sweaters and suits and gray pants of civilization, brushed their teeth, washed their hands, became enthralled with football or hockey or movie stars or swimming pools, attended church (some of them), where they genuflected or crossed themselves or ate wafers and decided that it was homage enough to the shadowy creator of the universe. But when the universe itself congealed and swirled around them like dirty laundry, they became weird, they became the people they really were beneath the sweaters and suits.

It had happened to Erthmun. That was obvious. Why else would he be sitting naked at his table eating his favorite muffin with his front door wide open?

She wanted to say the correct thing. She didn't care that he was naked. It was no big deal. And she knew that he didn't care either. But surprising him this way, while he was clearly embroiled in a process that brought him pleasure (looking at autopsy photographs, eating muffins, drinking coffee) required the right words.

She thought of clearing her throat. No good. Obvious. Cliché. He'd hate it.

Okay, then, blurt out something. Let it erupt from that sane, safe, and deliberate place in the brain that knew best about such things.

"Poppy-seed?" she asked.

He said nothing. He put the remainder of the muffin on his plate, set the autopsy photographs down, stood, lumbered to his refrigerator, way across the kitchen, opened the refrigerator door, peered in a moment, shut the door, and went back to the table, where he put the last bit of the muffin into his mouth and chewed slowly.

She repeated herself; "Poppy-seed?" paused, then added, "Jack? Poppy-seed?"

He turned his face toward her, looked through her, looked back at the autopsy photographs, looked back again at Patricia, put the autopsy photographs down, said, "Yes, poppy-seed." He looked at the autopsy photographs again, then again at Patricia. "I'm naked," he said, as if she hadn't noticed.

She grinned. "Well, yes, you are. Do you want me to go away?"

He shook his head. "I don't suppose so. Unless you're embarrassed. But you'd tell me that, I think. If you were embarrassed."

"Yes, I think I would. Or I'd close the door."

"Perhaps that would be a good thing."

"To close the door?"

"You can come in and close the door or you can stay out in the hallway and close the door."

"Are you going to put clothes on?"

He shrugged. "Yes, I imagine that I am."

"I mean soon?"

He shrugged again. "Would you prefer it?"

"It might make having a business discussion more . . . businesslike, Jack."

"Business discussion?"

She reached out, put her hand on the doorknob, said, "Let me know when you're dressed, okay?" and closed the door, leaving herself in the hallway.

Dark enough in this place, thought the creature who had named herself Tabitha. Darkness was as important as oxygen. She felt comforted in it, secure, able to breathe and see. She saw *the now* when it was dark. The now of her heart beating—*clip, trip . . . clip, trip*—and the now of her blood coursing through her body. She could not always hear the movement of her blood, but when it was dark and very quiet, as in this place, she heard it. It made the same rushing noise that a river makes, and she felt power in that sound. The power of water, and air. The power of stars.

She was, of course, as powerful as the sun. She was made of stardust, earthshine and clouds, and—her real self—of soil and its great bacterial underbelly, which existed beneath granite and sandstone, which existed beneath the igneous layer, and the substrata, and which was the greatest mass of life on the planet—greater even than all the life in the oceans, all the life that moved on the land, all the life that flew through the air.

She was not hiding in this place; she was merely seeking the darkness, because there was no need for vision when she had no need to see. Her only need here was to draw closer again to Mother and Father, now that she was sated.

Now that nourishment had been inserted into the

mouths of the always dead who lived and corrupted the earth and died and lived and corrupted the earth. The nourishment of their own design and need. The chocolate.

Erthmun's mother couldn't believe the story that she had never told. The story of her son and her other children and her husband—God rest his soul (wherever God was keeping it). She couldn't believe she had never told that story, and couldn't believe, either, that it had happened, although she knew only too well that it had happened. Erthmun himself had been produced because of it, and Erthmun was undeniable.

She didn't like looking at herself in mirrors and hating what she saw—a woman on the verge of disintegration. She hated her poetry, too—it was so self-indulgent now, so full of the angst of the aged and the depressed trying hard to avoid cynicism.

But it was wonderful knowing so much more about the universe than anyone else. It gave her a feeling that she harbored a secret she would never share because only she could understand it, because only she could understand her son and the others like him, who were so *unlike* him. It was like harboring the secret of creation itself, and it made her feel all knowing and all-powerful (because she *was* all knowing), even in the midst of disintegration.

Chapter Four

When Detective Vetris Gambol awoke, he found, and not for the first time, that his cat was sitting on his chest, kneading and purring with great pleasure. The cat's name was Villain and he was very large and usually quite unfriendly and standoffish, except when Vetris Gambol slept. At other times, it was all Vetris could do to get even a glimpse of him. Vetris fed him by putting a small plate of canned cat food on the kitchen floor and leaving the room. If Vetris tried to look in on Villain surreptitiously, Villain almost always seemed to know and ran off.

Vetris had never been able to determine if the cat hated him, was afraid of him, or was simply, and painfully, shy. He thought it was very strange that the cat slept on his chest while he—Vetris—slept, although, at all other times, Vetris couldn't even get near him. Was it, Vetris wondered, because Villain sensed something warm and cozy about him—beneath his gruff exterior—but could only gain access to this warm coziness while he was asleep? Or was it because Vetris was simply immobilized during sleep, and therefore not a threat? Or was it something even deeper, something almost unknowable? Something that existed deep within the noble and nasty and predatory mind of the cat. (Perhaps, Vetris thought with some alarm, Villain was merely waiting for the moment, while Vetris slept, that Vetris's shallow breathing stopped at last and Villain could easily make several tasty meals of him.)

Vetris did not ask himself why he didn't give the animal away. He knew that he loved Villain, loved his predatory nature, his stealthiness, even his strangeness. And Villain was, as well, possessed of the kind of nobility that only a large cat possesses—a nobility that is completely inborn, completely without affectation, completely real. He even seemed to possess this nobility as he slunk off—many times a day—to hide from the man who pretended to be his owner.

Vetris had also realized for some time that he was just a little fearful of Villain. A large cat could be dangerous in the right circumstances, and a cat that spent much of its time slinking away from the human being who fed it was a cat with a problem. What if, while Villain camped out on his chest one night, he—Villain—decided he'd had enough of slinking away, perhaps in cowardice, and was going to go after Vetris's jugular, or his eyes, or—Good Lord!—his genitals.

But Vetris knew that, deep down, he enjoyed such vague possibilities. It made up for an essentially boring life.

Vetris's bedside phone rang. He groaned and snatched it up, said, "Hello."

"Hi, Vetris, yeah," he heard, "this is Jerry, at the office."

Vetris sighed. Villain slunk away. Vetris said, "I know your voice, Jerry. You don't have to tell me who you are."

There was silence on the other end of the line.

"Jerry, did you hear what I said?"

"I did, yeah. I'm sorry." Silence.

Vetris sighed again, threw his comforter off, and swung his feet around so he was sitting up on the edge of the bed. "There's no need to be sorry, Jerry. Just tell me why you called."

Silence. Vetris heard what sounded vaguely like air passing through the line. "Jerry, are you nodding your head?"

"Yeah, I am. How'd you know?"

"Just tell me why you called."

"Yeah, I called because you got to get down here, okay? I mean, like now."

"Can you tell me why?"

"I can, yeah, I can tell you why." Silence.

"Before I get there, I mean."

"Oh. Sure. I can. It's because there are people missing. In the park."

Vetris said, "People go missing in that park every month. Why is it my business?"

"Yeah, because they left lots of blood behind, Vetris. It's all over the park, practically. God, it's everywhere. I seen it. It's like someone ran through there with a couple dozen gallons of red paint. Know what I mean?"

"Jesus!" breathed Vetris.

"Sorry?" said Jerry.

Vetris hung up and very reluctantly got dressed.

* * *

Erthmun opened his front door and said to Patricia, who had been waiting for him to get dressed, "See, I'm fully clothed now."

She nodded, said, with a little smile, "Yes, I see," moved past him, into his apartment, and stood with her back to him in the middle of the room, so she was outlined in sunlight streaming through the windows. "We have a problem, Jack," she said, and turned around to face him. "Actually, several problems. All of them the same, and all of them different."

He smiled. "Puzzles? It is not something I expect from you, Patricia."

She shook her head. "No puzzles, just enigmas."

He looked confused. "And they would be?"

"Enigmas?"

"Yes."

"I guess you could say they're conundrums."

"Which are?"

"Mysteries, of a sort. A conundrum is a kind of mystery."

"So enigmas are conundrums that are mysteries?"

Patricia grinned. "Yes, I suppose."

"They are puzzles, then, you would say?"

She shrugged. He enjoyed her shrug. It was as sensual a shrug as he had seen. "Yes," she said. "You're right."

"And these puzzles are what?"

She glanced around at the table at which Erthmun had been sitting. "Can you make me some coffee?"

He nodded. "Yes, I can," he said, and moved past her, to the cupboards. "Which of the kinds do you want?" he asked.

"Regular."

He nodded, opened a cupboard, pulled out a can that

was labeled decaf, said, "Then the conundrums are what?"

"Missing people," she said, and nodded at the can of decaf. "I'd prefer regular, if you've got it, Jack."

"Regular, then, it is," he said, and dragged the percolator out from under a cupboard.

"That's a green can, Jack," she said. "It's decaf."

"No," he said. "It's the regular coffee. I put it in this can. I like it. I like the color of it. I took the regular coffee out of the brown can it came in and I put it in this can. I like green. It's a nice green, don't you think?"

"You're a very odd man," Patricia said.

He poured water into the percolator. "Ah, I think that I am," he said. "And these missing people? How are they a puzzle?"

She sat in the same chair that Erthmun had been sitting in when she came to his open door. "They're a puzzle, first, because there are so damned many of them, and, secondly, because they seem to have simply vanished out of their nicely furnished apartments and houses, and some even from their places of work. Hell, there's a desk sergeant in the 5th Precinct who went to the bathroom and simply never returned."

"And he is?"

She took a small notebook from the pocket of her sport coat. "His name is O'Reilly."

"And the others?"

"You want all the others, Jack? Here and now?"

He shook his head, turned the percolator on, waited before speaking until it started perking, then said, "That's a very nice sound. I like it. Sometimes I put water on to percolate just to hear it." He put his hand on the side of the percolator, took it away quickly, muttered, "Hot," then said to Patricia, "No, I want you to tell me about these other people. How many are there? Where were they last seen? I need you to . . . capsulize and tell me about this mystery."

So she did.

Chapter Five

Williamson had a longing. He'd had many longings in his life. Some of them were closer to obsessions than mere longings. But this was simply a longing, he thought. Simply a need. Simply a simple need. Simply the simple need of a simple man who wanted to live simply on the green earth, among the green trees, to be as one with the brown soil and the gray rocks and the other creatures that shared his need. The hedgehog. The cormorant. The Canada goose. The black snake, the burying beetle, the barking tree frog, oh, yes, and all the flora and fauna of the earth.

But such a simple need could not be met here, where breakfast was composed of bologna on white and half a pint of milk, where the air was as stale as the breath of a dead man, and the closest approximation to gray rock was the iron cell that held him, trapped him, made him immobile, and discomforted, made him as one only with the sadness and panic and agony of the others trapped with him—like one of a thousand flies caught in a massive web.

It was an insult to life, this place. And for what? Because he was a vegetarian! Because he ate the flesh of others only when his longing prescribed, only when his longing became greater than his ability to ignore it, only when his longing told him more about himself than he had ever wanted to know.

Patricia read from a list of names and occupations:

"Tabitha Reed, stockbroker; Jonathan H. Lewenthal, jewelry store owner; Manny Incitus, real-estate agent; Vicky Morgan, model; Renee O'Byrne, playwright . . ."

Erthmun held his hand up and she stopped reading. He said, "You're giving me a pain in the head."

She grinned, sipped her coffee, longed to tell him that it was probably the worst coffee that had ever passed her lips, said instead, "Oh? Why?"

He said, "These names mean very little. You say they're gone, poof, vanished. No one knows where. But who were these people? That's the important thing."

Patricia said, "Well, they were who they were, Jack. They were playwrights, models, real-estate agents. That's who they were."

He shook his head, sipped his own coffee, said, "No one makes coffee like this, do they?"

She grinned.

He went on. "No, no. That's what these people *did*. They modeled and they sold properties and they managed people's portfolios. But that is not who they *were*. Do you *know* who they were, Patricia?"

"I think you're being argumentative, Jack."

"No, I don't do that. You do that. I've heard you. It's

a thing you do. It's a thing that many do. I don't. I say what I believe. This is what I believe. I believe that these people were not what they *did,* they *were* who they *were.* We all are, I believe. I know that I am."

She sighed. "Jack, do you want to know the circumstances of these people's disappearances?"

He shook his head. "You said that there were no circumstances, Patricia. You said that they simply weren't there after being there in the previous moment."

"Well, no, I didn't say *that,* precisely."

"But it was your meaning? It was what you intended?"

"Not exactly. They didn't simply vanish into thin air. They're gone, true, and no one knows where the hell they are, so in that sense, I guess they did vanish. But it's not as if they were standing there and then they . . . *vanished*!"

"Oh, of course, Patricia. I may sit around naked eating poppy seed muffins with my door open, but you must know by now that I'm not stupid. I intuit that you're telling me these people didn't leave any notes saying where they were going, and that they didn't tell anyone, either, where they were going. That's what I intuit."

"Intuit?" she said. "I've never heard you use that word before, Jack. But you're right. You intuit correctly. No notes, no final words to friends. Nothing. They're simply gone."

He shrugged. "Well, then, we'll have to find out where they went, I think."

Vetris Gambol did not like the sight or smell of blood, but he liked being a detective, which is why he had hooked up with the South Oleander Police Department. It consisted of six deputies, two detectives, and a police chief named Myrna Guffy, who was pale, redheaded, and

T. M. Wright

as smart as an Armani suit. But she wasn't smart today. She was panic-stricken, because this was the first multiple homicide she'd encountered during her ten years at the South Oleander police force. It was Vetris's first multiple homicide, too, and the bloodiest homicide he'd encountered—judging from the photographs that Myrna was showing him.

He was standing in front of her desk. She was standing, too, and putting the photographs on the desk in front of him. The photographs had been taken several hours earlier, just before sunrise.

"How do we know we're talking about a multiple homicide," he asked, "if we haven't yet found bodies?"

Myrna snorted a little, as if in derision. "Oh, c'mon, no one person carries this much blood around inside him, and no two or even three people can lose this much blood and still be walking around singing hallelujah."

Vetris mumbled, "They were singing hallelujah?"

"Yes," Myrna said, "and playing bagpipes. Are you coming out there with me?"

"Why wouldn't I?"

She raised an eyebrow. "Do I need to answer that?"

He shook his head.

"Then let's get going." She picked up the photographs, straightened them, put them back in their folder, and came around the desk. "How's that evil cat of yours?" she asked as she and Vetris started for the door.

"Still evil," Vetris said.

"God," said Myrna, "I'd shoot the damned thing."

When Erthmun and Patricia walked into squad room at the 20th Precinct, Peabody looked up from his work and said, "Your mother called."

Patricia asked, "My mother called?"

220

"No," Peabody said, then nodded at Erthmun, "*His* mother called. She said it was urgent."

Erthmun asked, "Did she say what it was about?"

Peabody shook his head. "Not so's anyone but a jack-rabbit would notice."

"Huh?" Patricia said.

"Never mind," Erthmun said. "It's how he talks."

Peabody said, clearly annoyed, "How do I talk?"

"Like a man who has no Gatorade," Erthmun said, and went to his desk, behind Peabody's.

"Huh?" said Peabody, and turned around to look at Erthmun, who was dialing his mother's number.

"Huh?" Patricia said, to no one in particular.

"Hello," Erthmun said into the phone, "is my mother there, please?" After a moment, he said, "This is her son." After another moment, he said, "Why?"

Patricia said, "Jack, is there a problem?"

Erthmun said into the phone, "Damnit, just tell me what the problem is." There was a silence, then Erthmun said, "When?"

Patricia said, "Jack, what's going on?"

He said into the phone, "Yes. As soon as I can," hung up, looked blankly at Patricia, then at Peabody, then at Patricia again. He sighed—it was a big sigh that made his whole body shudder—looked down at his desk, looked at Patricia again, back at his desk, then out one of the tall, narrow precinct windows—it faced the solid brick wall of an office supply warehouse. "She put her head into her oven and turned the gas on and killed herself," he said, and looked at Patricia. She saw that his eyes were moist. He added, "She did it this morning. After having her tea. And scones."

Peabody said, "Scones?"

Patricia said, "My God. Jack, I'm so sorry."

He stood. "I'm going there," he said.

221

Chapter Six

Myrna Guffy, Chief of Police at the tiny South Oleander, New York, Police Department, thought for a moment that some of what she was seeing had, indeed, to be red paint, because there couldn't possibly be so much blood in even a dozen people. Then it came to her that barns were red because it had once been the practice to paint barns with the blood of cows and bulls that had been slaughtered, which was cheaper than paint. A quaint, if horrific custom, a simple, financial consideration that was, on balance, completely reasonable. Make use of the entire animal, not simply its flesh. Waste not, want not. A penny saved is a penny earned. And who knows, maybe blood paint was more durable than paint paint. Maybe it bonded with the wood in a way that Sherwin Williams simply couldn't.

"Are you all right?" she heard. It was Vetris.

She glanced quickly at him. "Yeah. I'm fine. This"—she nodded—"is just very . . . difficult."

"I think Villain would love it."

She gave him a curious look. She hadn't expected such a flip remark from him, under these circumstances. Blood made him queasy. But maybe this much blood was simply overwhelming. At some point, blood stopped being blood, stopped being something trickling and suggestive and became something much more than blood, or much less. She remembered a scene from *The Shining*—a thousand gallons of blood flowing from the closed doors of an elevator. Instead of being gory or upsetting, it had been, for her at least, simply like watching a river that was an odd color.

Vetris added, with a wave of his hand, "It's like it's not blood at all because there's so goddamned much of it. It's like it's . . . I don't know, paint."

There were several state police investigators nearby, collecting samples of the blood, taping off the area, and they looked very grim. Vetris thought they should look grim; this was damned grim work. Somewhere in this park, there were . . . remains, and the awful process of collecting those remains would be doubly grim. He didn't know if he wanted to be a part of it, though he knew that he would have to be a part of it, that *being* a part of it would be wonderful for his career. But still, it was work that a creature like Villain, human or otherwise, would adore; he—Vetris—was simply not up for it.

Myrna Guffy said, "Yeah, but it isn't paint. Jesus, it doesn't *smell* like paint."

"I don't smell anything," Vetris said.

She shrugged. "You never do."

*   *   *

223

Peabody declared, "You know, it's as baffling as a shoe store in Milwaukee: a cop gets up from his desk and goes to take a piss, and never comes back. I mean, people actually *see* him go into the goddamned bathroom, but no one sees him come out."

Detective Tony Julia said, "It's as strange as a three-headed snake."

"No such things as three-headed snakes," said Peabody.

Detective Julia frowned.

Peabody said, "And these other people. This stockbroker, and this model and the others. I know that people go missing every day in this goddamned city. It's like clockwork. But not people like this. People who *know* people—people who *are* people!"

"That would be everyone, I think," Patricia said. She was standing next to Detective Julia, who was standing in front of Peabody's desk, because, for reasons Peabody couldn't understand, he'd been delivered the file on the recent disappearances. It was a thick file, and Peabody had been poring over it for fifteen minutes, trying to get all the high points.

Peabody shook his head. "Nah, some people aren't anybody, and they don't know anybody either. But I take your point, Patricia."

"Uh-huh," Patricia said.

"Has anyone heard from Erthmun?" Detective Julia asked.

Patricia shook her head grimly.

"Who would anyone kill themself like that?" Peabody asked. "I mean, putting your head in an oven. It's as weird as crazy glue at a flea circus."

Patricia sighed.

Detective Julia said, "Sylvia Plath did it."

"Who?" asked Peabody.

"She was a poet," Patricia explained, and Julia—new to the precinct—gave her a surprised look. "She wrote a lot of . . . I don't know . . . confessional poetry. People ate it up. She killed herself by putting her head in an oven."

"You'd think the heat would make her . . . jump back," Peabody said.

Patricia sighed again. "No. No. She didn't light the oven. She died of asphyxiation."

"No shit?" Peabody said.

Detective Julia said, "She was married to Ted Hughes."

"Big deal," said Peabody. "One billionaire's the same as another."

"Huh?" Patricia said.

Peabody said, "So no one's heard from Erthmun. Poor slob, to have his mother off herself like that. I can imagine how it must make him feel."

"No," said Patricia, "I don't think you can."

In another part of the city, a creature was waking that never really slept. Only its needs, its hungers, and its appetites slept, though just briefly. But this was sufficient, because the creature's needs and appetites comprised nearly its whole being, like an infant whose whole self is dedicated to growing. But this creature was no infant, though it was new to the earth. This creature was tall and strong, and as graceful as a cat; its long dark hair was a thing of consuming beauty, and it spoke with eloquence in a voice that was music.

It knew what the earth demanded of it, and it was not reluctant. Or regretful.

Erthmun thought, *Who in the hell can know about such things?* The thought upset him because it seemed so callous. After all, there was his mother in front of him, dressed in a long blue terry cloth robe with small white frogs imprinted on it, on her knees, leaning into her oven, and she was dead. He could see only the back of her head—straight shoulder-length gray hair recently permed, he guessed—the clean, white soles of her bare feet, her bare hands sticking out of the terry cloth robe. One hand was palm-down, on the inside of the oven door, so her elbow was bent; the other hand hung over the edge of the door, so her fingertips grazed the black and white tile linoleum. Erthmun could smell the awful odor of the gas, though the oven had been turned off nearly ninety minutes earlier.

"Coming through," he heard, and when he turned his head, he saw a couple of men from the Medical Examiner's Office carrying a stretcher in. "Step aside," the lead man said to Erthmun, who nodded and stepped aside.

He felt someone tapping his shoulder. "Jack?"

He looked, saw the round and pleasant face of Lieutenant John Blair, from the 11th Precinct, with whom he'd worked on a couple of cases.

Blair said, "I'm awfully sorry, Jack. Really. This is terrible."

Erthmun nodded a little.

"Jack," Blair said, "you know that your mother left a note, right?"

"No," Erthmun said, "I didn't know that. I just got here."

Blair nodded. "On the table." He gestured toward it. Erthmun went over to the table and bent a little to read the note, while keeping his hands at his sides.

"The element of truth in all this is the rape, of course," he read aloud. His mother's handwriting was elegant. "The rape is not a kernel of truth. The rape is a hard and grim truth, with which I have tried to live peacefully within myself for a very long time. But the hard truth of the rape has jumped on me like an animal, and I cannot rid myself of it.

"Because I wonder, of course, what the rape has produced, and I know only a little of what it has produced—perhaps as one can know only a little, a very little, of what the infant at one's breast will become, what its potential is, what strange, horrific, ghastly, or beautiful creature actually dwells inside it.

"Oh, I love all my children, none any more than another, but some of our children become mysteries to us, to everyone, and we make excuses for them. We say, 'He's his own man,' or, 'He's in therapy; everyone should be in therapy, don't you think?' even when it isn't true. Or we simply believe that one or another of our children is on a different path than the rest of humanity, although the sky they peer into is just as blue as ours, and the flowers they pause to enjoy are the same flowers we all enjoy—these children are simply on a path of their own.

"But such excuses eventually pile up and become mountainous and we can no longer cope with the simple fact and process of being alive. It becomes a great and unbearable burden.

"And at some point we realize not only that we are doomed, but that our children are doomed as well. That some of them, one of them, not all of them, is as strange in his skin as a frog with wings. But the frog would never dwell on the fact of his wings. The wings would simply be a burden because the frog could never fly—it's too heavy. But the frog wouldn't fret about the burden; the frog would simply carry it. We humans, and those so much like us—those to whom we may have given birth—are not made that way. We sometimes spend a lifetime in regret at this or that. We do not shoulder lifelong burdens well. We become cranky. Strange. Or suicidal. There, the word.

"Who can bear to outlive her children?

"I'm sorry."

Erthmun glanced solemnly at Lieutenant Blair, then silently read the note again, straightened, glanced at the oven—his mother's body had been removed while he had read her note—then at Blair again.

After several seconds, Blair told him, "It says a lot, and it says very little."

Erthmun said, "I think it says everything that she wanted to say."

Chapter Seven

Williamson the loon, as Erthmun liked to think of him, believed everything about himself that he remembered. And he remembered much—a father who took him fishing at a place called Beaver Pond, who taught him to ride a two-wheeled bicycle, how to piss against the side of a car stopped on the expressway, how to swear, size up a woman, make people afraid. And he remembered a mother who was as beautiful as blood, as beautiful as floods and tornadoes, who taught him to cherish his needs as if his very life depended on them, which it did, and how to grow and carry on a conversation and eat a school lunch.

Many of these memories were real, and gave him comfort in the noisy hours between the frenzied satisfaction of his needs and the time for blissful sleep, the hours when people talked to him about this and that, over and over and over, like squirrels chattering, when he needed to smile and react—the hours when the woman he lived with pestered him about children or groceries or car payments, and he had to smile and react and pretend that it wasn't really his need, in those moments, to tear her brain from her skull.

So, in this place where he'd been put, he dwelt on his memories, leaned into them, made them a part of the gray bars, the hard, pencil-thin mattress, the cement floor and foul air; he saw his mother there, as naked and appealing as trees, and his father, too, standing naked with her, hard and ready, like a summer rain. They were two naked creatures of a day that dawned and dawned again; two who sprang from sassafras root, limestone, the bacterial deluge of the earth's living under-layer.

He found arousal in all this, but it was no great thing because he found arousal often, even in the mundane, especially in the mundane, in snow that lingered at the edges of sidewalks, in a woman's arm moist with sweat, in naked feet, in cats battered bloody after a fight.

He did not hear the guard. "Okay, Williamson, you're gone." He heard only his father—standing naked with his mother under a towering oak at the edge of a woodland he recognized too well—telling him with a fist raised, as if in anger, "Go on out there, boy, and do what you have to do." Which was advice that he gave himself often, and followed religiously.

"Williamson, you listening to me? I said you're outa here."

"Son, you can go," Williamson's father told him.

"Go where?" Williamson said. "I don't want to go." He missed his mother and father very much, hadn't seen them in decades, wondered often if he had ever seen them.

230

"Well, that's too damned bad, isn't it?" the guard said. "Because you ain't got no say in the matter."

"I'll tell you what she was doing the last time I saw her," said a man named Berko. "She was fixing her hair. She was sitting at her table there, looking in her mirror, and fixing her hair. She fixed her hair a lot, even if it didn't need fixing. She loved to fix her hair."

Patricia said, "Do you mean she was combing it?"

Berko gave her a quick, disbelieving look. "Did I say she was combing it? No. I said she was *fixing* it. She was messing with it the way women mess with their hair— you know, poufing it and straightening it and scowling at it like it was a bad movie. I'll bet you mess with your hair, right? Well, that's what she was doing. She was messing with hair. She was fixing her hair. She thought it was beautiful. It was, I guess. But she fixed it, anyway."

Patricia said, "It's not important what she was doing with her hair, Mr. Berko. Did you say anything to her then, or did she say anything to you?"

"Yeah, she said, 'Don't bother me, Tommy. I'm fixing my hair.' So I closed the door."

"And that's all she said? You said nothing to her? You just closed the door and that was that?"

Berko sighed a long-suffering kind of sigh. "Listen, if Tabitha told you she didn't want to talk, you didn't talk. That's the kind of woman she was."

"And when you looked in on her later . . ."

"I didn't look in on her. No one just 'looks in' on Tabitha, unless they want to get their head handed to them. I knocked a couple of times, waited a minute, knocked again, then I called to her, and when she didn't answer, I opened the door. She wasn't here."

"And you'd been waiting out there"—Patricia nodded

to indicate the living room—"the entire time and didn't see her leave this room?"

Berko nodded. "That's right. I didn't go and take a piss, or make a sandwich, or watch TV. I just waited for her to come out. And when she didn't come out—I guess it was an hour—I knocked on the door."

Patricia glanced about. The bedroom was large and sported a dark cherry four-poster bed, two huge armoires, a glass dressing table, and a walk-in closet. There were also two long, narrow windows that looked out on 42nd Street, thirty stories below. She said to Berko, "It's a very strange story."

He shrugged. "Shit," he said, "Tabitha is a fucking strange woman."

"It's what I'm telling you," said the head of the search team in South Oleander. "We haven't found anything. Just lots and lots of blood. But no bodies. No parts of bodies either. Nothing."

Vetris Gambol didn't know what to say, and when he glanced at Myrna Guffy, he could see that she didn't know what to say either.

After a few uncomfortable moments of silence, Myrna said, "Well, Jesus, then you haven't looked far enough, have you?"

The head of the search team—a balding, rotund man who wore brown horned rim glasses and spoke with the hint of a wheeze—said, "You know, first we looked until we reached the perimeter of all that blood. Then we looked further. A couple of miles further. Then we did it all over again. Now we're going to do it a third time. But I can tell you that I'm just about positive we *still* won't find anything because I'm just about positive that there's nothing to find."

Myrna scowled. "Well, I can tell you this—all that blood means bodies. A dozen bodies. Two dozen. I don't know. But bodies. Or pieces of bodies. And they weren't eaten by forest rats!"

"Maybe it was a prank," Vetris Gambol offered.

Both the head of the search team and Myrna Guffy looked wide-eyed at him, as if he'd sprouted a third arm.

"Because," he explained, "you're right. All this damned blood *has* to mean bodies. Or small pieces of bodies. Maybe just fingers, or tips of fingers, or—I don't know—an eye or two, a cuticle . . ." He shook his head. "Forget that. Sorry. It was stupid." He sighed. "I'm merely suggesting that since we're looking at what seems to be an impossibility that we need to rethink what's possible and what isn't." He paused to give Myrna and the head of the search team time to jump in; they said nothing. He went on. "And since it's literally impossible, considering all this goddamned blood, that we *wouldn't* find bodies or parts of bodies, then, ipso facto, there are no bodies or parts of bodies to be found. Just blood. Because someone dumped it all around as a prank."

Myrna said, "And where would they have gotten so much blood, Vetris?"

"Don't you see?" he said. "Don't you see? That's just secondary. If we determine that all of this blood has been dumped here as a fucking prank, then we—"

A uniformed state trooper came quickly up to them; "We found something," he said. "We found some pieces of bone."

Jack Erthmun's sadness over his mother's suicide was like a lingering dream of claustrophobia, as if he were within his mother at the moment that she had decided to end her life, and at the moment before her life ended. Within her, too, minutes earlier, when she had thrown the green robe festooned with white frogs around herself, and within her when she stared at the oven and wondered if her plan really would work, if she would allow it to work, if sleep induced by the gas would overcome her before she could change the plan, and hoped it would, knew that such a sleep had, after all, to be quiet and thankfully peaceful, and blessedly eternal. Erthmun knew that had always been the way she thought. As if life and death constituted nothing more than a dream wrapped up in poetry, wrapped up in confusion, wrapped up in heart-break.

Good for her, Erthmun thought. She had lived and died as a poet, which she had wanted. But no one would ever know or care or remember. Except him. And for Christ's sake, what in the hell did *he* know about poetry? He knew as much about poetry as he knew about himself. His mother had gotten that right, for God's's sake. He was the odd man out (among himself and four sisters); he was the stranger, the one she had written about in her suicide note, the one she thought she'd outlive, and, since she couldn't bear that thought, she had decided to go first.

Christ! Christ! He wished he could chalk it all up to simple craziness. But his mother wasn't crazy. She was loving. She loved him.

And the irony of it all, he thought, was that he expected to live another seventy-five years, at least. So what in the hell had she been talking about?

When Vetris Gambol woke to the ringing of the telephone, he found that Villain was on his chest, furiously kneading the base of his—Vetris's—neck, purring with great and disturbing enthusiasm, and feverishly licking Vetris's chin, as if it were meat. And when Vetris reached for the telephone, Villain leaped to the floor and slunk off.

"Yes?" Vetris croaked into the phone.

"Vetris?" It was Myrna Guffy. "We got the report on those pieces of bone."

"Uh huh."

"They're human."

"Is that surprising?"

"No. But what is surprising is that they've been partially digested."

"Jesus," Vetris said. "Digested?"

"Partially digested," Myrna corrected him. "I don't think any creature completely digests bone."

"Meaning?"

"They pass it. Most of it. Except the marrow."

Vetris sighed. "Good Lord." He paused. "What time is it?"

"Very early," Myrna answered.

Chapter Eight

She thought, *A happy death is happy disintegration*; oddly, the thought warmed her, made her feel at a comfortable distance from the ebb and flow of human events that she'd been a part of for as long as she could remember.

It was as if, on this balmy early evening, with the clatter of traffic around her and the taciturn pedestrians avoiding her gaze—for she had always had the habit of catching the eye of people—she had received a letter from a mother and father she had never known, but, through the letter alone, was finding them for the first time, loving them, and needing to be with them. Even if that reunion required a happy death and disintegration. After all, she was not *one*, she was part of the great pool of life, and returning to it would insure that that life would continue—perhaps in another form, with another personality, perhaps as another being, but another being who was also aware of herself and her existence—as *she* was now—and aware, as well, of the great pool of life from which she had sprung.

Her name was Elizabeth. She had always liked being called Liz. She remembered brothers and sisters—Constance, Samuel, Valorie—but knew without being able to verbalize it that they were no more real than the mother and father she also remembered.

And she remembered the place of her creation, too—deep below the surface of the earth. Remembered the first moments that she had breathed air and felt hunger. And she realized, with something like joy, that she would experience those moments again, in the form of a creature who was not her, and who had never been her.

Although the knowledge mystified him, Vetris knew that he enjoyed being afraid of Villain. It was like living with a demon that purred and licked and kneaded and bore the exquisite face and form of a cat. A demon that could grace a calendar, be grinned at and fawned over by small children, although he—Vetris—knew the identity and predilections of this creature. The killer with golden eyes.

Vetris set out a plate of tuna for the cat. He always set the plate in the same place—between the refrigerator and the cupboards. And when he left the room and returned ten minutes later, he always found the plate empty. This morning, he had not been able to wait.

Warm morning, just past 5:00, the faint, soft pink glow of sunrise against a cloudless sky. Vetris had his car window rolled down, and the air moving past the side of his face was moist. He guessed that there'd be rain later in the day. He was driving below the speed limit of fifty-five, and assumed this was because he was in no hurry to begin this particular morning.

Far ahead, he saw someone walking at the side of the road, caught in his high beams. He guessed at once, from the way the person moved, that it was a woman, and as he drew closer, he saw that he was right. He saw also that she was naked.

"Jesus," he whispered, and slowed the car. She was dark-haired. She moved beautifully.

When he was alongside her, he slowed to her walking speed, rolled down the passenger window, and said, "Miss, are you all right?" He could see her just dimly, now that she was out of the glare of the headlamps. She did not answer him, and he repeated, "Are you all right?"

She looked briefly at him, then looked away. He saw her face unclearly through the mask of darkness.

"Miss," he said, "I'm sorry, but what you're doing is illegal." And indeed he was sorry, he thought.

She looked at him again. "Enjoy it while you can," she said, looked away, and continued walking. Her voice was high-pitched, the voice of a woman, but her tone had been brusque and toneless.

"Good Lord," he muttered. "Miss?" he said again, and she turned to look at him.

"You're bothering me," she said, her tone again brusque and toneless. "Don't bother me. You don't know what you're bothering."

Of course I do! he thought. *I'm bothering a woman who's walking down the road naked.*

He pulled fifty feet ahead of her, stopped the car, got out. He saw that her body bore a reddish tint from the car's taillights. He stood silently and watched her approach. She was tall, almost as tall as he, and—he thought in so many words—as graceful as a cat; she wore her straight dark hair to just past her shoulders.

She called to him, in that same brusque voice, "You don't know what you're bothering! This is my own business." He strained to see her face, saw it unclearly.

"Miss," he called back, "I think you're in trouble somehow. I only want to help you."

"I don't need you to help me!" she called back.

She was within a dozen feet of him now, and he could see her face as a reddish mask—large eyes, small nose, full lips, high cheekbones. A mannequin with soft skin, and eyes that reflected the dim early morning light in a harsh and brittle way. Beauty that was too perfect.

He stepped back, uncertain why, as she passed him. He thought briefly that it was fear. And he smelled her as she passed—the tangy odor of moist earth freshly turned, the cloying odor of growth and decay. His hand went for his .38 in his shoulder holster; he touched the grip of the weapon, let it go. Clearly she was unarmed, he thought.

Chapter Nine

Williamson the Loon had done more than a few murders, though he did not think of them as murders. The concept of *murder*—with its accompanying aura of judgment and moral decay—was not part of the way he saw the whole matter of being alive. You smiled when it was necessary, you fucked when you needed to fuck, you bought shoes when your old shoes wore out, and you killed when the occasion demanded.

Well, his own father had taught him that, and his father had never misled him. His father was a naked, grinning saint, a dirty naked saint with an erection the size of Betelgeuse and enough sperm to populate the galaxy in Andromeda.

Williamson had learned quite a lot about astronomy because he was—he'd explain if asked—a creature of the earth. He was a spaceman riding starship Earth to realms that were all but invisible, now, but which would become all too visible within the span of his years, which would be innumerable.

He was in a pawnshop. He was looking at watches because he enjoyed the keeping of time, enjoyed the futility of it, in the face of eternity, enjoyed the attempt at measuring a thing which could not be measured because its parameters were limitless, so it effectively had no parameters (*Here are three seconds in eternity*—so foolish trying to parcel out bits of a thing that had no beginning and no end).

The owner of the pawnshop was a short, fat man named Lewis, and he was growing tired of Williamson's questions. Williamson had been in the shop for almost an hour asking questions—"This timepiece, it looks old. How old is it?" "Is that real gold? If it's not real gold, I'm not interested." "Do you have any idea why clockwise is *clockwise?*"

Lewis said now, "Listen, I've got work to do, so why don't you make up your mind."

Williamson liked this no-shit approach. He smiled at Lewis, which made Lewis a little weak in the knees, because Williamson's smiles were part humor, part malevolence, and mostly bizarre. "Oh," Williamson said, "you have been a pawnbroker for many years, I see, to have cultivated such a direct approach to annoyance. Even if I buy a watch from you—and it's a good possibility that I will—then you will earn too little from the purchase to make your time with me profitable."

Lewis gave a small, nervous shrug. "Yeah," he said. "Sure."

Williamson said, "But there's no one else in the store." He glanced about quickly, then once again at Lewis. "Only the two of us. Two men caught up in an act of commerce, which, I might remind you, is your business. Commerce."

Lewis said curtly, "Please choose a watch."

Williamson smiled again and leaned over the glass counter that separated him from Lewis. "I want many watches. I want all your watches, but I will take only one. And that process, deciding on which watch to take, requires time. Ironic, isn't it? Taking time to select a timepiece." He waited for a response from Lewis and when none came, Williamson went on, at close to a shout, "I said, don't you think that's ironic? Taking time to choose a timepiece. Isn't it ironic?"

Lewis glanced at an area below the counter.

Williamson said, "I'm not going to rob you."

Lewis shrugged again. He'd begun to sweat.

Williamson said, "Yes, yes, I know about your gun. Pawnbrokers have guns. But leave it where it is because I'm here only to buy a timepiece and to engage you in philosophical discussion of the purchase of timepieces. No gun is required for that."

Lewis shook his head quickly.

Williamson said, "I may eat you. I may buy a timepiece from you and then eat you. But I will not rob you."

Lewis said nothing. His eyes were wide.

Williamson leaned back. "There you go, taking my words literally when, in all likelihood, you should take them figuratively. Don't think of *eat* in the classic sense of mastication, ingestion, and digestion. Think of *eat,* instead, as a philosophical term, a term of psychosis, or, for that matter, drama alone. If I were to say to you that I am going to *eat your eyeballs,* then you cannot really assume that that is precisely what I intend to do. Assume nothing and you enter a world of great possibilities, sir."

Lewis once again glanced at the area below the counter.

Williamson said, "Oh, stop glancing at that gun, Mr. Pawnbroker, and pick out a watch that will suit my needs, much as a tiger's stripes suit its needs."

Lewis managed, "Please leave my store."

Williamson cocked his head. Smiled. "Surely," he said, and left the store, though not before quickly dispatching Lewis with a deft, sharp, and crushing blow to Lewis's windpipe, then eating Lewis's eyeballs, his genitals, his entrails, and the soft tissue of both his hands, and, then, finding a beautiful solid gold pocket watch, circa 1926, with the name "Roland" etched in script on the case.

How interesting, Williamson thought, that the idea, or fact, or knowledge, or premonition—whatever the people in the culture in which he lived might choose to call it— of the end of existence would allow him to know, so clearly, the possibilities and realities of his existence as it now . . . existed. He'd never had any idea of those possibilities, *his* possibilities. The simple magic of being! He'd always spent too much of his energy on . . . existing, and had left most of the magic trapped inside himself. Now he could use it. All of it!

Vetris Gambol knew what he had to do. He had to confront the naked woman—who now was fifty feet from him and walking briskly—put a coat on her (his own coat, perhaps, though—he realized—he had no coat here, although there was a soiled yellow blanket in the trunk of his car), and take her to the police station for observation. *For observation?* He grinned.

"I'm sorry, miss," he called, "but you will have to come with me."

She made no reply, and the near-darkness at the perimeter of the headlights was quickly swallowing her up.

"Shit," Vetris muttered, got back into his car, and drove after her.

He pulled alongside her again as she walked, kept the car at her walking speed, said through the open passenger window, "Miss, I'm going to have to ask you to get into the car. I'm a detective with the local police department. My name is Vetris Gambol. . . ."

She broke into a run.

Vetris cursed again, hit the accelerator, caught up with her, kept the car at her running speed—which, he thought, was very fast, almost unnaturally fast—and yelled, "You'll have to get into the car, miss. I'm ordering you to get into the car!"

She quickened her pace.

He nudged the accelerator, caught up with her. "God-damnit!" But then, impossibly, she was ahead of him. He nudged the accelerator again, caught up with her, pulled ahead of her, veered sharply to the right, hit the brake pedal hard. He heard a dull thumping noise from the passenger's side of the car. "Oh, shit!" he breathed, because he knew instantly what had caused the thumping noise. He cursed again, took a breath, opened his door, got out of the car.

The sun had just begun to rise. It was behind him.

His car was a white Dodge Intrepid. People had told him that white contained a pigment that actually encouraged rust, and even though the car was only two years old, he had indeed seen the beginnings of rust under one of the wheel wells. He liked his car. He liked its shape and its power; he liked its interior—gray cloth—and its sound system, too. It was a good car, except for the beginnings of rust under one of the wheel wells.

He thought now, as he stood by the driver's door, that the rising sun was painting the car's hood and roof a soft rust-red. It ran in long irregular striations from the opposite side of the car toward him, and it took him only a moment to realize that the sun, which was behind him, could not cause such a pattern.

"Jesus," he whispered. "Jesus, God," he whispered. And realized that he was seeing the blood of the naked woman. It covered the car. It glistened in the early morning light. In spots it was rust-colored, nearly brown, in spots it was bright red, and in spots it was black. It flowed in rivulets over the curve of the hood toward him.

He moved around the front of the car, and his hand went to the .38 in his shoulder holster. He moved cautiously and when he was near the car's right-side headlight, he leaned over to look at the side of the car. He saw only the rough impression of a body in the Intrepid's fender. Only blood. He looked further down the road, saw only the road, came around to the side of the car, saw only the side of the car, the smooth shoulder of the road. "Where the hell is she?" he whispered. "Jesus, where in the hell is she?"

Chapter Ten

Patricia said, "Jack, I'm so sorry. I'm so very sorry."

Erthmun said, "Patricia, I think that there's a lot of death everywhere. All over. In every county and state and nation. People talk about the river of life. They talk in poetry about the river of life. Or they talk in philosophy about the river of life. When there is a river of *death,* too, flowing alongside it. Or maybe not. Maybe the river of death and the river of life are the same river."

They were seated opposite one another at Erthmun's small dining table; Patricia had made coffee for both of them, which Erthmun had sipped and about which he had congratulated her—"Much better than any made here previously," he said, and gave her the ghost of a smile.

Patricia said now, "You were very close to her, weren't you, Jack?"

He shook his head. "I may have been. I'm not sure."

She cocked her head. "That's an odd answer. How can you be unsure of something like that?"

He sipped his coffee, smiled a little, as if in response to the taste of the coffee, set the cup down gently. "Well," he said with a strangely earnest matter-of-factness, "I believe that I'm unsure of my real feelings about practically all relationships, familial or otherwise."

"Familial?"

"Of the family," he answered.

"Yes," she said, "I know what it means. I simply didn't expect—"

The phone rang. Erthmun snapped his gaze to it, grimaced, got up and answered it. Patricia heard him say after a minute, "Okay. Yes." And he hung up.

"A problem?" Patricia asked, because she saw a troubled look on Erthmun's face.

"Who's to know?" he said. "Problems may simply be opportunities."

She smiled quickly.

He went on, "There's a place called South Oleander, New York, where we have been asked to go."

"Why?"

"Because a woman ran into a car there and left behind only her ring."

"How does that concern us?" Patricia asked. "And what do you mean by 'left behind only her ring'?"

Erthmun shrugged. "Well, yes, you have posed two questions, I think, and I can really answer only one. It appears that this woman was named Tabitha Reed and she was one of the people who went missing here not too long ago."

Vetris Gambol didn't like being grilled by state police investigators. He'd told them a dozen times or more exactly what had happened, and they still seemed to believe that he was hiding something.

One of the investigators was a very tall and athletically built man who wore an expensive blue suit and a paisley tie. His name was Tony Grigoli. The other investigator was a man named Tim Christmas; he was dressed in a threadbare hound's-tooth sports coat and blue jeans that should have been thrown out a year earlier. It was clear that he hadn't shaved that morning, and his breath smelled of eggs and garlic.

Vetris was seated in the interrogation room at the South Oleander Police Department. He knew that Myrna Guffy was standing just outside the door because she peered in through the small window every now and then. Christmas and Grigoli were seated across from Vetris.

Christmas said, "You know, Detective, it's not like we think you killed this girl. We don't think that." He glanced at his partner. "Right, Tony?"

Grigoli nodded a little.

Christmas went on. "But we do think you're not telling us everything we need to know."

Grigoli added, "Like where you put her body, for instance."

This was something that Vetris had heard too many times in the past several hours, and he was near the boiling point. He sighed heavily and said, "There was no *body*. There was only blood. Lots and lots of blood. That's it. And a ring."

Christmas nodded. "Yeah, her wedding ring. Had her name etched in it. Tabitha."

Vetris said, "Listen, if you don't mind, I've got to get home and feed my cat. If I don't feed him—"

"Fuck your cat!" Grigoli cut in.

Christmas looked sternly at Grigoli. "Tony, cut it out.

The man's a cat person. So am I. You know that."

"Yeah, well, fuck you, too. This guy's dishing out shit like it was devil's food cake, and he tells us he's got to feed his *cat*?"

"If I don't feed him," Vetris began to explain, "then he gets—"

"Goddammit," Grigoli cut in, "I don't give two shits in a handbag *what* your goddamn cat does if you don't feed him. I don't care if he eats *you*, for the love of Jesus."

"Yeah," Christmas agreed, "why don't you get off the cat business, okay, and simply tell us what we both know you're not telling us."

Vetris sighed again. "Listen, I'm sure you guys are very, very good at what you do. But keep in mind the situation we've got at the park. Keep in mind that it's *identical* to the situation you're looking into here, except on a much, much larger scale."

Grigoli leaned over the table so his face was uncomfortably close to Vetris'. "Except, in this case, Detective, *you* were there, weren't you? You *created* the situation."

"Oh for the love of Pete," Vetris whispered.

It was a three-hour drive to South Oleander from New York City and, since Erthmun had agreed, reluctantly, to drive—because Patricia was having trouble with her new contact lenses—he drove while Patricia fiddled almost constantly with the radio, and complained almost constantly that there was nothing to listen to.

"Patricia," Erthmun said—they were twenty-five miles northwest of the city, in a bucolic area.

"It would be very nice if you stuck with one radio station. Or turned the radio off. We could talk."

She turned the radio off, looked expectantly at him. "So?"

"You want me to talk?" he said.

"It was your idea. And it was a good idea, too. We *should* talk. About this case, about this woman named Tiffany . . ."

The slim file on Tiffany Reed was on the backseat. Erthmun inclined his head toward it and said, "Okay, get the file, read it to me, and we'll talk about it."

Patricia shook her head. "It makes me nauseous to read in a moving car. It always has. I'm prone to car sickness."

"Well, you can drive, and I'll read," Erthmun said.

"No, we've both read the file. There's not much of interest in it."

"You don't think so? What about her connection to—"

"The Chocolate Murders?" she cut in. "There is no connection, Jack. She was the victim of coincidence. She was in a place where a murder happened at about the time the murder happened, but that doesn't really mean anything, because my guess is that there were hundreds of people in the general area of that particular murder. When it happened."

He glanced quickly at her. "Is it because you don't believe a woman could have committed those murders, Patricia? Is it because you don't think a member of your own sex could do things so horrific?"

She pursed her lips. "Good Lord, Jack—how can you ask such a question? Women are as capable of just as much sick crap as men are. We've both witnessed it. And I don't believe, as you're suggesting, that my"—she held up her fingers to form quotes—" 'sisters' are inherently any less violent than you or any of the other three billion men in the world are simply because they don't have a penis and balls and aren't choking with testosterone."

He said nothing for a long moment, then said, "Okay,

go ahead and listen to the radio. It's better than your speeches."

She pursed her lips again, but decided to ignore his comment. "No. I'd like to talk with you about your mother."

He glanced questioningly at her.

She said, "I'm sorry, Jack, but the dynamic that apparently existed between the two of you is fascinating."

He looked at the road again. "Dynamic," he said, as if to himself.

They were entering a small town. A large white sign shaped roughly like a shield read, in bold black letters, "Welcome to Mallsberg, Home of the Mallsberg Maulers."

Patricia read the sign aloud and grimaced. "So much aggression. It's almost epidemic."

"They were playing with the name of the town," Erthmun said. " 'Mallsberg.' 'Maulers.' It means very little, I think. They were excited about the alliteration."

"I realize that, Jack."

"My mother," Erthmun said, "was a poet. She got excited about alliteration, too. It's a poetic style. Alliteration. Like, 'Many marvelous men make merry.' "

"I know about alliteration, Jack."

"As do I," Erthmun said. "And my mother, too. A poet."

Patricia nodded to indicate the speedometer. "You're speeding. This town probably has a speed trap. Any town with a sports team named the Maulers would have a speed trap, don't you think?"

"Let me quote you a poem of my mother's," Erthmun said; he didn't let off on the accelerator.

"Yes," Patricia said, "I'd like that."

Erthmun said, "Such as her poem 'Unable, Unlike Anyone.'"

"Sorry?" Patricia said. And added, "Please slow down, Jack."

Erthmun said, " 'Unable, Unlike Anyone.' It's the alliterative title of one of her poems. Three 'un' sounds. And the poem goes:

> *I, unable, unlike*
> *anyone,*
> *release, not recapture*
> *a past that is*
> *too present,*
> *living the lie*
> *of hegemony.*"

He smiled broadly. "Do you like it, Patricia?"

"It's a lovely poem," she said.

"And very meaningful," Erthmun said.

"Yes," Patricia said, "I'm sure that it is."

"It means that she saw herself as outside the natural order of things."

Patricia nodded. "Yes, that's clear to me."

A siren wailed behind them.

"Enough about the cat!" Grigoli screamed.

And Vetris shot back, "Listen, you don't *know* this cat. He's not like any other cat. He's . . . unique! He's got a mind of his own, and if he doesn't get fed . . ."

"I don't give two snails in a peach pit *what* your cat does if he doesn't get fed. I simply want you to—"

"Shit," Christmas cut in, "go home, Detective Gambol, and feed him, for Christ's sake."

Vetris stood at once, said, "If you have any other questions, you know where I am."

"No, we don't, but we'll find out," Christmas said.

"You can count on it," Grigoli said.

Vetris left the room, told Myrna Guffy he'd be back soon. "I'll see if I can get them to lay off, okay?" she said.

Vetris shook his head. "They're just doing their damned job. I'd be the same way." Then he drove home.

Villain was waiting for him, and he was pissed.

Williamson the Loon felt sated. It was such a happy feeling—sated and warm and at peace within himself, with the universe and with the earth. The sky was never so blue as when he was sated, and the grass never quite so vibrantly green, and the great ocean never greater. The wind itself caressed him as a lover might, as the outstretched branches of a magnificent oak might, or the living tendrils of a catfish.

And all that inner beauty, peace, and strength came to him merely through the necessary and passionate act of eating Lewis the pawnbroker, and in finding a watch that pleased him. Life was surely no grander than at such times as this.

Williamson was walking. He walked vigorously. His arms swung in a wide arc, his long legs produced very long strides, and his torso remained ramrod straight. People asked him from time to time if he was "power walking," and he answered that of course he was, that walking itself was power, that every step produced a gram of muscle, and every mile a new caress of mother earth. People usually smiled politely at this and went on their way.

He was near a restaurant ten miles from Manhattan. The restaurant was called "Sim's Eats," and because the name appealed to him—terse, no shit—he went in and sat at the counter.

The counter was full, and he found himself between a beefy man in khaki and a beefy woman in a blue dress. These beefy people looked askance at him, as if he were taking someone's seat, so he asked, "Was someone sitting here?"

The beefy woman in the blue dress shrugged, said, "Who knows?" though it was clear from her tone and expression that *she* knew, and the beefy man, whom Williamson turned to after the woman had spoken, said, "It's all right, I guess. That was Balloo's seat, but he's dead."

Williamson loved this. He said, "You save a seat at the counter in a restaurant for a dead man named Balloo?" He gave them a grin that was big and full of happiness: he was tickled.

The beefy woman said, "If you're making fun of us, or Balloo, then I think you can move off."

"Yeah," said the man, "you can move off."

Williamson shook his head enthusiastically. "I'm sorry, no, I really don't want to move off. I want to hear about your friend, Balloo. I'm quite interested."

"Huh?" said the man, as if Williamson had spoken to him in another language.

"Tell me about Balloo," Williamson said. "And why he had that name. It's a funny name. It's the name of an elephant."

"What elephant?" said the beefy woman.

"Well," Williamson answered, "the elephant in *Dumbo*, I think. In the movie *Dumbo*. Certainly you've seen it."

The waitress came up and asked what Williamson

wanted. He answered, "Do you have any Mocha Frappucino?"

"What's that?" the waitress asked.

"It's a Starbucks product," Williamson answered. "It's milk, coffee, and chocolate in a creamy blend."

"You're shittin' me!" said the waitress.

"He ain't," said the beefy woman. "I drink it. Mocha Frappucino. I love it. Try it sometime, Gwen."

"Hey," said Gwen, "I'm up all night with the goddamned kids! I don't need no more caffeine or nothin' keepin' *me* awake."

"It's made with low-fat milk and decaffeinated coffee," Williamson said. "So its caloric content is quite low."

"Caloric content?" said the beefy man.

"The number of calories," said the beefy woman.

"Whatever," said Gwen, "we ain't got it. We got coffee, high test and decaf, and we got breakfast, if you want."

"I don't want breakfast," Williamson said. "I want Mocha Frappucino. And I want my new friends here to tell me about Balloo." He frowned at the beefy man, first, then at the beefy woman. Then he looked earnestly at Gwen. "But my interest in Balloo has faded, I'm afraid, because you have no Mocha Frappucino."

Gwen gave him a suspicious look. "Mister," she said, "I think you ain't playing cards with all your ducks lined up in a row."

He gave her a wan smile. "Ah, a mixed metaphor. How delightful."

"Jesus," breathed the beefy man.

The beefy woman said, "I can tell you where there's some Mocha Frappucino, mister. Right across the road there"—she turned on her stool and pointed out the restaurant's big windows—"at the SaveRite. But they get almost two bucks for it, when you can get it anywhere else for like a buck-fifty—"

Williamson reached out as quickly as a cobra, a cat, a mongoose, and tore her beefy throat out before she could finish her sentence.

Chapter Eleven

Erthmun felt foolish explaining to the local cop that he—Erthmun—was a Manhattan Homicide detective, and could the local cop please give him a break and forget the damned speeding ticket.

Patricia had already offered her two cents worth: "Listen, Barney, we're on an investigation. We're with NYPD, do you understand that?"

But the cop was not to be swayed. "Mr. Erthmun," he said in a parental tone that was ludicrous from one so young, "we get people from the city coming through here all the time. And you know what? They always speed, like we don't have any laws, or like there aren't any kids playing, or like we don't care. And I made up my mind a long time ago that it doesn't matter *who's* doing the speeding—it doesn't matter if it's the mayor himself—he gets a speeding ticket. I'm sorry, but that's the law."

T. M. Wright

And he gave Erthmun a speeding ticket, said, "Have a nice day, now, watch your speed," and walked back to his car.

Erthmun stuffed the ticket into his shirt pocket, pulled away from the curb, and said, "Who's Barney?"

"No one," Patricia answered. "A TV character. What's the matter—you didn't watch TV when you were growing up?"

"We didn't have a TV," Erthmun said. "My father wouldn't let us have one. He said that TV was a reprehensible spawn of the devil." Erthmun smiled a little. "That's what he said. Those words exactly."

"Oh," Patricia said. "One of those."

"Those?"

"Yeah. A Jesus freak." She sighed. "I'm sorry. That was pretty damned stupid of me. My sister . . ."

"No, he wasn't a Jesus freak, Patricia," Erthmun cut in. "I don't know. I don't remember him reading the Bible or going to church. But I remember him saying that TV was a reprehensible spawn of the devil. I guess he knew about devils. I think he knew about devils. He said he saw them everywhere. He said he saw them running around the house. He said he even saw them *in* the house."

Patricia glanced nervously at Erthmun, out the window, then at Erthmun again. "I'm sorry, Jack, but the man sounds like a nut." She paused very briefly, then hurried on. "I'm sorry. That was stupid, too."

Erthmun shrugged. "My father was a nutty man. He was crazy. He did crazy things and said crazy things. He beat my mother. She forgave him. So he beat her again. And she forgave him again. He said that she was a devil. He said that the devils around the house had made *her* into a devil. So he beat her to beat the devils out of her."

"And you saw all of this, Jack?"

"Sometimes. Yes. I saw it happen sometimes." He frowned. "And I wanted to do something about it. I wanted to help her." His hands gripped the steering wheel hard. "But, shit, how could I help her, Patricia? I was as small as a pebble." He had begun to breathe heavily; his tone had become clipped, harsh. "I yelled at him, once. When he was beating her. I yelled, 'Stop it, you!' Those words exactly. 'Stop it, you!' So stupid! So weak! He ignored me. He beat her and ignored me!" He had begun to speed again.

Patricia said, "Jack, watch your speed."

He looked quickly left and right, as if she had told him to watch something at the side of the road. "He was no monster, my father," he said as his speed crept up, his words barely intelligible through his clenched teeth. "He was no monster. He was human. My father was *human*! And that is monster enough!"

"Jack, you're going too fast. We're going to get another ticket. Please slow down!"

He looked at her. His eyes were wide, his jaw set; she thought he was going to hit her. He looked at the road again. He sighed, let off on the accelerator.

Patricia glanced behind them. No Barney. "Jesus!" she breathed. "I had no idea how much you hated your father."

He was near the speed limit now. "No. That's wrong," he said. "I didn't hate him. I wanted to kill him. I should have. But how could I hate him?" His voice was less strident. "How could I hate the man who might have given me life?"

"Sorry?" Patricia said. "The man who *might* have given you life?"

"Yes," Erthmun said.

*   *   *

Villain was as fast as the tongue of an auctioneer, and Vetris realized he had no hope of catching him. And even if he *did* catch him, he wouldn't dare hold him for even a second. He—Vetris—would be a bloody mess afterward.

"Good Lord," Vetris whispered, "I've got to get rid of this animal!"

Vetris' hands and ankles were alive with scratches and bites. Even his nose had a scratch on it, which had resulted when Vetris had peered under the couch while looking for Villain. He'd found him, but Villain's claws had found Vetris.

Vetris was in the small narrow kitchen. Villain's food bowl sat on the floor at the opposite end of the kitchen. It was empty. An opened can of Friskie's tuna fish sat on the counter above it. Every time Vetris had attempted to pick up Villain's bowl to put food in it, Villain had appeared—as if out of nowhere—and lashed out at Vetris. This, Vetris thought, was completely irrational. If Villain was angry because he hadn't been fed at the proper time, then why in the hell was he preventing him—Vetris—from feeding him? But what was he thinking? There had never been anything rational in Villain's behavior or, for that matter, in the behavior of any cat, beyond the rationality of eating, sleeping, fucking, and hunting. Vetris had called out to Villain often, this night, though calling to the animal had never had much effect before. Vetris felt certain that Villain knew his name; Villain wasn't stupid. Villain was a cat—he answered to his name when it was in his best interests, usually when food was being made available.

But not tonight.

Vetris wondered then if Villain might be sick. If Villain

might have distemper. He'd seen distemper in cats, when he was growing up. It was an awful disease. It made a cat completely unpredictable. Then it killed the cat. Jesus, that would be an awful (if poetic) way for Villain to die. But what if Villain didn't have distemper? What if it were something far worse? Like rabies. Though, on second thought, how would Villain have contracted rabies? He never went outside. He was oddly afraid of going outside. And all his shots were up to date.

"Villain," Vetris said in a small voice.

Erthmun said, without looking at Patricia as he drove, "I can quote my mother's suicide note. I would like to quote it for you."

Patricia said nothing. Erthmun looked at her, said, "May I quote it for you?"

She nodded solemnly. Erthmun look at the road again and said, " 'The element of truth in all this is the rape, of course. The rape is not a kernel of truth. The rape is a hard and grim truth, with which I have tried to live peacefully within myself for a very long time. But the hard truth of the rape has jumped on me like an animal, and I cannot rid myself of it." He glanced at Patricia again. She was looking straight ahead. They were on a stretch of rural road. Erthmun went on. " 'Because I wonder, of course, what the rape has produced.' " He stopped.

After a few moments, Patricia said, "Jesus, you think you were the product of that rape, don't you, Jack?"

He said, "I know that I am."

"How do you know?" she asked.

"The same way I know that when I dream," he answered, "it's my dream. The same way I know that when I feel pain, it's my pain."

She said nothing.

"Sometimes," he said, "I'm as poetic as my mother was. I'm her son. I know that. But I'm not my father's son." He glanced quickly at her again, then at the road. "I'm one of those," he said.

She looked at him. "One of those, Jack? I don't understand. What are you saying?"

"Patricia," he told her, his gaze on the road ahead, "I'm one of those who stuffs chocolate in the mouths of people they murder. I'm one of those."

"Oh, Christ!" Patricia whispered.

"Except," Jack said, and there was the ghost of a smile on his lips, "I don't murder anyone. And I do like chocolate, yes, but I don't believe that I've stuffed it in anyone else's mouth but my own."

Williamson the Loon was very confused. He thought he had never been more confused—even when he had applied for a job as a shoe salesman several years earlier, and, Lord, *that* had been confusing! Being asked all kinds of stupid questions about his attitudes toward people— "Do you enjoy dealing with the public?" "Do you enjoy being of service to people?" "Do you work well with others?" Because what in the *hell* did all those questions mean, for God's sake? *Being of service to people? Dealing with the public?* It was like asking him if he enjoyed cleaning windows or smiling or waiting for an elevator. Who enjoyed such things? And why would they?

But this was even more confusing. After all, what had he done but responded to his inner self? What had he done but been true to his inner self? And wasn't that something that *people* harped on all the time—being a true and good and loyal representative of one's own self and of doing what nature, mother, and father intended and *required*! Responding to impulses as if they were desires, and responding to desires as if they were necessary to survival? If anyone was human, it was *he*! As human as the insidious predator, as human as any hunter of the weak and deformed, as human as the faithless deranged involved in the debauchery of Mother herself! And didn't *they*—the people who needed shoes—applaud all of that? Didn't they *require* it?

But here they were, in pursuit of him yet again, as if *his* inner self were somehow less important than their own inner selves, as if *his* needs and desires were somehow *different* from their own?

Didn't they know that the woman had been unnecessary to the earth, their mother, a burden to the air itself, and beneath it all, untidy and dying, as well? So it had been his clear duty to rip her throat out, just as it had been his duty to eat the pawnbroker.

"Jack," Patricia said, "I need you to stop the car. Now!"

He glanced at her. He thought that she looked incredibly earnest, even a little frightened. But why would she be frightened? He was merely telling her the truth, and wasn't that part of his job (and hers)—to ferret out the truth, to *learn* the truth and deal with it in the way it demanded? He said, "I'm sorry, Patricia, if I've upset you. . . ."

"*Upset* me! Oh, for the love of Christ, it goes beyond that! It goes way, way beyond that!"

"I don't understand." He looked at the road again. They were in a very rural area, now; high, tree-covered hills lay ahead.

"No, I imagine that you don't understand," she said. "It's suddenly too damned easy to realize that you don't understand. Please stop the car, Jack!"

He looked at her. She had her .38 pointed at him.

He reached out, as fast as a cobra, or a mongoose, and snatched the gun from her.

She screamed.

He brought the car to a screeching halt.

She threw her door open and ran into a field choked with tall summer grasses and dogwoods.

What in the hell is going on? Erthmun wondered.

Vetris knew that he could not go to bed until he found Villain. He wasn't at all sure what he'd do with him if and when he did find him, but if he simply went to bed, he knew with near certainty he'd wake up to find the cat tearing at his jugular. He was convinced that Villain was possessed by the spirits of its feline ancestry—the lynx, the ocelot. And these were beasts that no thinking person toyed with (and, he realized, which no thinking person took as a *pet* either).

He called the cat's name. It sounded foolish. He'd named the cat *Villain* because it was a playfully evil name—the same reason people named their large dogs Killer. But he was not a dog person (as the state police investigator had pointed out), he was a cat person; he was interested in covert displays of evil, which described this cat, any cat.

"Villain?" he called again. It was a futile gesture, Vetris knew, because the animal had never responded to his name, although Vetris was certain he knew it. "I know you're hungry," Vetris called. "And I know you're upset with me, but I was delayed by unusual circumstances." He felt very foolish, now—trying to explain himself to the cat.

He saw a flash of black fur at the far end of the kitchen.

"Villain?"

The phone rang.

* * *

As she ran through the fields of tall summer grass, Patricia thought (though not in so many words) that certainly it mattered how Jack Erthmun saw himself, and it mattered very much that he saw himself as someone aligned in an odd way with murderers, and it mattered just as much that he allowed for distance between himself and these same murderers, but it mattered most of all that she had never really known him.

She could hear him far behind her. Although he had told her more than once about his almost preternatural running abilities as a child, those abilities had apparently not stayed with him into adulthood and early middle age. She thought she could even hear him breathing heavily, though this had to be her imagination because he wasn't nearly close enough for that, and she knew that it would be difficult to hear anything above the sound of her own body crashing through the summer grass, and her own heavy breathing.

And she thought it was good that she was not in a complete panic. She may or may not have been fleeing for her life from a man she thought she had known, but who, she realized, she had not known at all. But she was *thinking*. She was analyzing this situation as well as she could under the circumstances. She wasn't simply tearing her hair out and making a complete ass of herself. That, of course, was because of her training—*Always keep your wits about you. Always assess the situation and react to it, not simply to your fear.*

She realized that something was running alongside her in the summer grass. She turned her head quickly. She saw a tall shadow not far off. Far behind her, she heard Erthmun call, "Patricia, stop running!" She thought for a moment that what she was seeing was her own shadow, dogging her footsteps. But this couldn't be true, she realized, because the sun was in front of her.

And she knew at once that it was the tall shadow's heavy breathing, as well as her own, that she had heard, and was hearing now.

She lurched sharply to her left, stumbled on a clod of earth, nearly fell, straightened, felt a hand on her back as she ran, felt it lower to her waist, screamed quickly, glanced around, saw a man's naked body, a face at her shoulder. The man was smiling—not in the way that a naked man might smile, but in a way that a man anticipating something tasty might smile, as if he were incredibly hungry and would soon be satiated.

"Get away!" she screamed at him. "Get away!"

"Patricia?" she heard. "Where are you?"

She pitched forward head-first into the grass and earth, tasted the soil, rolled once, twice, came up quickly to her feet, looked right, left, behind, saw Erthmun running toward her.

The naked man was gone.

Chapter Twelve

Erthmun said, "You're afraid of me, aren't you? I can see it in your eyes. Please, don't be. I am no more to be feared than an old basset hound."

She gave him a questioning look. They were standing together at the spot where she had pitched and rolled and she had yet to tell him about the naked man. "I'll reserve judgment, okay, Jack?" she said stiffly, voice quaking. "Could I please have my weapon?" She extended her hand for it, saw that her hand was shaking. "Jesus," she whispered.

He gave her the weapon; she put it in her shoulder holster and said, "The things you told me were very upsetting. More than upsetting . . ." She sighed. "There's someone else here, in this field. There's a naked man in this field. He . . . goddamnit, Jack, he attacked me!"

267

"Yes," Jack said, "I saw the naked man. I saw him running with you. Running after you."

She looked wide-eyed at him. "You *saw* him? You *saw* him, Jack? My God, you saw him and you didn't go after him?"

He shook his head, as if in confusion. "I lost sight of him, Patricia. He was there one moment, he had his hands on you one moment, I think, and then he wasn't there. I thought I should tend to you first." He nodded once, twice. "But you're all right. I think you're all right. Are you all right?"

"Yes. I think so. A little dirt in my mouth, but I'm okay." She spit.

"Good," Erthmun said. "Good. So I'll go looking for him, now. I'll go looking for this naked man."

"Yes," Patricia said. "We both will." She unholstered her weapon. "Jack?"

"Yes?"

"Stay where I can see you, okay?"

He nodded.

Williamson the Loon thought that he was a powerful son of a bitch, like his father, who had been a very powerful son of a bitch, whose father had been an even more powerful son of a bitch, who had been the product of a never-ending line of awesomely powerful sons of bitches.

And it was altogether possible, and quite possibly even true that he, Williamson, was the most powerful son of a bitch who had ever sprung from the earth, penetrated its women, and eaten of its fruits.

Oh, that was a chuckle deep inside, where chuckles had properly to reside and originate, within his gut somewhere, his lower intestine, no doubt, which was long and thick, red and blue and gray. Sunset and midday and twilight. Shit, shit—he was a poet, too. An awesomely powerful son-of-a-bitching poet!

He was in the grimy men's room of a grimy gas station southwest of Albany. He'd gotten here with the help of friendly people who had, they'd told him, hitchhiked, too, when they were young; "You don't see many people like you, anymore," one said. "Hitchhikers, I mean."

"That as well," said Williamson.

There was a knock at the rest room door. It was a soft knock, not urgent, and Williamson ignored it.

He was looking at himself in the rest room mirror. He worshipped what he saw in that mirror. It was perfection, the perfection of mathematics and poetry and biology and fucking madly, madly fucking, fucking in anger and retribution and . . .

There was another knock, not as soft.

Williamson looked away from the mirror and quickly around at the door. "Be patient," he called. "You'll live longer!"

"I'm sorry," a female voice called back. "I'll wait."

"Damn fucking straight you'll wait!" he called, and felt that chuckle again in his lower intestine; *Damn fucking straight you'll wait!* Poet, poet! Poet, poet! He was a fucking, all-powerful, son-of-a-bitching—

His hearing was so acute that the crash of the door being kicked open made him wince and cover his ears with his hands, which was enough time for the two state troopers who'd been outside the restroom door to wrestle him to the floor and throw handcuffs on him.

"You have the goddamned right to stay good and goddamned silent," one of the troopers said as they hauled him to his feet, "and if you give up this goddamned right . . ."

* * *

T. M. Wright

Erthmun called across the dozen yards that separated him from Patricia, "He's not here. I know he's not here. I can feel it."

She called back, "You're wrong. He is here. *I* can feel it!"

"But why would he stick around, Patricia?" Erthmun called. "He's got both of us looking for him now."

"That wouldn't scare him, Jack."

He hadn't heard her, so he shouted to her to repeat herself.

"I said, the fact that we're both looking for him wouldn't scare him."

"How do you know that?"

"It was in his eyes. I don't think he was scared of *any*-thing. I could see it in his eyes!"

Erthmun sighed. Naked men with fearless looks in their eyes running around in a field of summer grass and attacking police detectives. It was ludicrous.

He called back, "I know of such men."

She looked silently at him.

He repeated, "I know of such men. My father warned us about them, so long ago."

She walked toward him, asked him to repeat himself.

"I said, the person who called himself my father warned us often about naked men in the fields." She was only a dozen yards from him, now, and was keeping her eyes locked on his, as if she were wary of him. "He said there were naked men running about in the fields around the house."

Patricia said, "And were there?"

"And were there? I think there were." She was within arm's reach, now. Her eyes were trained on his. He said, "I think that I was one of them. One of those naked men in the fields." He grinned. "But I was a boy, then. I wasn't a man. I was a boy."

Vetris Gambol thought he was dysfunctional. Why else would he be living with an honest-to-goodness killer? A very small killer, certainly; a killer who purred and kneaded and acted, at times (all the *wrong* times, he thought), like . . . a *pussycat,* but a killer nonetheless. A creature that was born to be a killer and lived its life as a killer (though Vetris had to admit to the dearth of dead mice or moles in and around the house: but perhaps those creatures *knew* about the killer who dwelt within the house and gave it a wide berth). And now he—Vetris—was, damnit, afraid to go to bed and leave the killer loose in the house. Jesus, he had to get rid of the animal. But he knew he wouldn't. In a loopy way, Villain taught him something about human killers, about their predilections and habits and obsessions. Because the predatory nature was as much a part of Villain as it was a part of any human killer. Jeez, it was an interesting theory, wasn't it? But it was bullshit. He knew that he kept Villain around because he *respected* him. Because he *loved* him—predatory nature and all. Because Villain represented *purity.* Vetris sighed. God, he really *was* dysfunctional!

Erthmun saw a naked man on a low hill a quarter of a mile from where he and Patricia were standing. The man was looking at them, Erthmun guessed. The man's hands were flat against his ears and his legs were spread wide. Erthmun started to tell Patricia about the man, but then she saw the man, too, and said, "Good Lord, there he is!"

"There he is!" Erthmun echoed.

"What in the hell's he doing, do you think?"

"He's holding his hands on his ears."

"Yes, I see that. But why?"

"I don't know."

She glanced at him, said dryly, "Rhetorical question, Jack," and hollered to the naked man, "Stay where you are! We're police detectives and we're armed." Then she started sprinting toward him.

Erthmun called after her, "Patricia, you won't catch him, you can't catch him!"

"Watch me," she hollered back.

He went after her.

Williamson the Loon did not like handcuffs. It wasn't simply that they were confining; he was used to confinement, had been born of the warm, liquid, and confining belly of the earth itself, so he had grown to accept confinement—the confinement of his skin, the confinement of his years (which equaled a slow but implacable disintegration), the confinement of his strength (which was considerable but not invincible), the confinement imposed by his probing but necessarily inefficient intellect, and by his unquenchable desires. But handcuffs did not simply represent confinement, they represented the cold, hard imprint of human authority, too, which Williamson could not accept or bear, because, by their very nature, humans exercised authority unfairly and without *authority*—from the earth, or from him.

And now that the imminent end of his existence was pulling the magic from within his gut, he knew that he no longer needed to accept confinement of any kind.

The two state troopers—one male, one female—who had thrown him into handcuffs, and then into the back of their patrol car, were talking outside the car while they waited for backup. They needed backup, Williamson had decided, because the stories about him were clearly approaching the stuff of legend—stories that said he was a man of daunting power and even more daunting ferocity, especially when it came to handing out necessary pain and death to those whose continued existence would be an affront to the earth.

He could hear the troopers talking; they were very animated, and every few moments, one of them glanced warily at him, as if at a caged tiger. He loved catching their eye. Loved grinning at them as if he hadn't a care in the world. He knew that such grins were very upsetting because they spoke either of madness, an overarching self-confidence, or both, which were things that sparked fear in many humans.

Just then, the male trooper bent over, so his angular, handsome face was almost pressed against the car window, and he growled, "You wanna just look somewhere else, buddy!"

Williamson shrugged. It was the kind of shrug that was neither submissive nor acquiescing; it was the kind of shrug that said clearly that he didn't give two shits about anything the person speaking—in this case, the trooper—was saying and that the speaker could go piss in a hurricane, for all he cared.

It was a shrug that was simply too much for the trooper, who had seen one too many such shrugs in his ten years as a law enforcement professional, so he threw the door open, reached madly into the car, grabbed Williamson by the collar, pulled him close enough that Williamson was repelled by the man's breath, and growled through clenched teeth, "You know what I want, asshole! You know what I want?"

Williamson grinned.

The trooper brought him an inch closer. "I want *you* to be as quiet as a dead man! You got that!"

Williamson grinned again.

"You *got* that!"

Williamson leaned forward and bit the man's nose clean off below the nostrils. This caused the man to lurch backward, screaming, which made the back of the man's head hit the door frame very hard, which knocked the man out and sent him sprawling and bleeding into Williamson's lap. Williamson looked questioningly down at him (Williamson had already spit the man's nose out, and it lay white and red and ragged between the man's shoulder blades), then at the female trooper, who was leaning over, into the car with her .45 pointed directly at Williamson's temple. "What the fuck did you do?" she demanded. "What the fuck did you do? Get outta there, now!"

Williamson shook his head. "How can I?" he asked with a little catch of innocence and incredulity in his voice; he inclined his head toward the trooper sprawled out on his lap, and gave her a charming, boyish grin. "I'm not a miracle worker."

"Goddamn you!" the female trooper shouted, spittle flying, reached in, hauled her partner by the back of his shirt collar off Williamson's lap, and tried to set him down gently on his back outside the car, but the effort of keeping her eye on Williamson and dealing with her partner's limp body at the same time was too much for her, and she dropped her partner face-first into the asphalt. He hit with a soft *whump*, a groan, and a fart.

Williamson said, "Listen to that. He has no class. Your partner has no class, ma'am."

"Shut the fuck up!" she shouted. "Just shut the fuck up!" Her gaze fixed on something on the seat between Williamson and the door. "Oh, my God!" she breathed, and leaned over to get a better view. "Oh my heavenly

God," she said, "you bit his goddamned nose off!" She straightened abruptly, deftly avoiding the door frame, and pointed her .45 stiffly at Williamson's temple again. "Don't even *think* of moving!" she commanded, and slammed the door.

"Clichés, clichés," Williamson muttered.

The naked man watched as Erthmun and Patricia closed on him. His hands were still clasped to his ears, his legs were spread, and he sported an incredible erection.

Patricia said to Erthmun, who was only an arm's length away, walking quickly—as she was—though not running, so they were less likely to spook the naked man, "Jesus, look at that! That's damned unnatural!"

"Is it?" Erthmun said.

She glanced at him, saw a little grin play on his mouth, sighed at the chutzpah of the male animal, and shouted to the naked man, who was no more than a hundred feet away, "I want you to get down on your stomach, and I want you to do it now! If you don't do it, then I will be forced to fire on you." She had her weapon drawn, but she was holding it so it pointed upward.

The naked man made no response.

"Maybe he can't hear us," Erthmun suggested.

"He can hear us!" Patricia said.

"But he's got his hands on his ears."

"He can hear us, Jack. Look at him."

Erthmun looked closely at the naked man. He saw a face that was as unremarkable as chewing gum, a face no more remarkable—Erthmun thought—than his own. Except for the eyes, which were strangely distant and as opaque as stone, despite the man's libidinous grin. Yes, Erthmun realized all at once, the man could indeed hear everything that was being said, *had* heard everything ever since he and Patricia had come after him. Because this man, Erthmun knew, was one of those his father had warned him about decades ago. One of those who had moved with such exquisite and supernatural grace through the fields that surrounded the house Erthmun had lived in as a child. One of those who'd found Erthmun's mother and had had his way with her.

In a flash, Erthmun took his .45 from his shoulder holster, aimed it at the naked man, and fired.

"My God!" Patricia shouted.

The naked man clutched his chest, looked alarmed, fearful, fell backward down the little hill, and was gone.

Chapter Thirteen

Vetris Gambol could not believe that Villain was dead. But there he was, in the closet in the upstairs bedroom, on his side, not breathing, mouth open, tongue lolling out. Very dead. Vetris realized that he had always believed that Villain—as odd as he was—was simply not capable of being dead. Even now he could not believe it. He believed he'd bury Villain and that sometime in the night he'd feel Villain kneading his chest, and hear Villain's furious purring, and when he opened his eyes, he'd see Villain's golden eyes staring with great hunger at him. This was not altogether an impossibility for a cat who had been possessed by all the feline predators that had lived throughout history.

Vetris bent over and gingerly touched the dead cat's rib cage, found it cold and stiff. *What in the hell killed him?* Vetris wondered. *Old age?* Not possible. Villain was barely five. Cats lived a good long time—much longer than dogs. Poison, then? But from where? Villain never went outside, and there was no poison in the house. Heart attack? A chronic illness that had masked itself all this time in Villain's fearsome and bizarre behavior? Distemper? Feline leukemia?

Shit, what did it matter? Villain was dead, and he—Vetris—certainly wasn't planning on getting another cat to take his place because, simply, no other cat *could* take Villain's place. No other cat would be as *interesting* as Villain.

Vetris realized something, then, that unnerved him. He realized that he had seen Villain—or a creature he had thought was Villain—dash between the refrigerator and cupboards not even a half hour earlier. And here was Villain lying cold and stiff, now, in the closet in the bedroom. Clearly, Villain had been dead for more than a half hour. So what had he seen below, in the kitchen? Another cat? Obviously.

He decided to bury Villain in a custom-made box. He had constructed many such boxes, of various sizes, for his dead pets through the years—starting when he was a child of seven. The last pet he'd buried had been his aged cockatiel, Omo, a year earlier, shortly before he had acquired Villain at a garage sale ("You want to *pay* me for him?" said Villain's owner. "Hell no. Take him. He's too damned much for us to handle.").

"Why in the *hell* did you do that?" Patricia shouted, and broke into a run toward the spot where the naked man had fallen.

"Because he's guilty!" Erthmun shouted, and ran after her. Patricia glanced around at Erthmun and gave him a quick, disbelieving glance.

"Because he's guilty, Patricia!" Erthmun shouted, louder; she was outdistancing him. "Because he's *guilty*," Erthmun shouted.

Then Patricia was at the spot where the naked man had fallen. "Jesus!" Erthmun heard her say; he was within twenty feet of her. "Jesus!" she repeated. She gestured with her left hand as if to tell him not to come any closer; but this, he thought, was foolish. He'd seen far worse in his career than she had seen in hers. She gestured again, more urgently, glanced at him. "No," she said. She looked angry. "You can't!"

"Can't what?" he said.

She looked away again, at the spot where the naked man had fallen. Erthmun came up to her, stood beside her, looked at what she was looking at: "Patricia," he said. "He's just a boy."

"Yes," Patricia said, at a low, confused whisper. "A boy."

Some things are not a problem for a magician. Pulling a rabbit out of a hat, a dove from a sleeve, an ace of hearts from behind someone's ear. But these are sleight of hand; they have no more to do with reality than do bubble boys or fairy dust.

Williamson was no magician.

His reality was not a trick of perception. His reality was malleable because he was malleable. His reality seemed like magic, but it wasn't. It was deadly, but it wasn't magic.

"You're amazed, aren't you?" he said to the female state trooper, because her eyes were wide, she was quivering, and as she backed away from Williamson, she stumbled a bit over the limp body of her partner, who was still groaning, and kept herself from falling by

279

T. M. Wright

straight-arming the asphalt. "How in the fuck did you get out of your handcuffs?" she managed, and straightened.

"Or even," Williamson said, "out of the damned car. Aren't you wondering how the fuck I got out of the damned car? I mean, getting out of the handcuffs was one thing. Houdini could do that. Easily! But how in the name of all you call holy could I have gotten out of that backseat with the doors locked and the cage intact between the front seat and the back. And if you look"—he turned a little and pointed stiffly at the car; his voice rose in pitch and intensity, as if he were angry and was trying to make a point to someone who was impossibly stupid—"you'll see that the damned car door is still locked, and the cage is intact!"

The trooper glanced at the door.

Williamson backed up a step, reached for the door handle, grasped it, and pretended to try to pull the door open. "See now, see now!" he shrieked. "It won't open! It's locked! It's locked!" The trooper had her .45 leveled at him, though her body was trembling, her hand, too, and she didn't know why this man scared her so much—certainly not simply because he had gotten out of his handcuffs, then had gotten out of the locked car, or because he had bitten her partner's nose clean off. . . .

She thought that she should pull the trigger, be done with it. The man was obviously psychotic! But she had never fired her weapon at a suspect before, and had drawn it only once, though even then she had held it pointed straight up.

"I want you to do exactly as I tell you to do!" she barked.

Williamson took his hand from the car door. "Sorry?" he said, as if he hadn't heard her.

"I want you to get down on the ground with your legs

spread and your hands clasped behind your head, and I want you to do it *now*!"

"You mean this instant?"

"Now!"

"Do you mean before or after I make a meal of you? And oh, oh, what a tasty meal that's going to be, Officer, because I see that you are very certainly well worth eating—"

She lowered her gun a little.

"Don't do what I know you want to do!" he told her.

"Shit!" she whispered.

"Because I can assure you that the consequences will not be what you intend. When one stops caring about existence, because it will soon stop being something to care about, one is . . . freed up to ignore its foolish rules. One can be a magician without the top hat and rabbit. One can breathe and not breathe. One can murder and dissolve."

"I don't know what you're saying. I have no idea at all what you're saying," the trooper said through clenched teeth.

Williamson shook his head slowly, as if, strangely, with malice, and grinned.

"Fuck you!" said the trooper, and pulled the trigger.

Williamson looked down at his leg. He saw the huge, jagged hole her bullet had made in his pants, just above the knee, and the blood seeping from the hole (it stained his jeans the color of sunset), a few small shards of bone sticking out left and right from the hole. He looked blankly at the state trooper.

"You were saying, asshole?" she said, and tried to forget, for the moment, that the bullet which had apparently shattered his leg had not sent him reeling to the ground.

"I *was* saying, wasn't I?" he said.

T. M. Wright

* * *

Vetris had brought the dead cat into the garage and set it on a towel on top of a two-drawer file cabinet near his work bench. It was while he was cutting a piece of half-inch pine that he realized there was something not quite right about the dead cat who seemed to be staring at him with its eyes half closed, though he couldn't imagine what that not-quite-right thing could be. He stepped over to the body of the cat, which was still stiff, so the cat looked, in profile, as if it might be running, and gave the cat a once-over. He shrugged. No, other than the fact that the animal was dead, there was nothing that was not-quite-right about it.

He turned back to his workbench, began sawing again. "Shit," he muttered, and looked over at the cat once more. What in the hell was bugging him? It was almost as if this cat wasn't really Villain. But there was no mistake—long black fur, golden eyes, sixteen pounds of deadly predator. Dead itself, now, which was a consummate pity.

Vetris began sawing again. An hour and a half later, he'd fashioned what looked pretty much like a miniature casket, had installed the dead cat in it—the towel wrapped around its body—and had buried the miniature casket in a sunny spot in the backyard. He had even said a few words: "Villain, you were unique. You made life hell, sometimes, but it was always interesting. I'll miss you, killer." Then he glanced about to make sure none of his neighbors, who weren't close by anyway, had seen him, and went back into the house.

The phone rang moments later. It was Myrna Guffy. "Vetris," she said, "you've got to come down here ASAP. These guys from the State Police Investigator's office need to talk with you some more."

282

"Shit," Vetris said.

And Myrna Guffy said, "No, it's not what you think."

She knew that she had seen what she had seen, but because it was not possible to have seen it, she believed that she had seen something else, something she had forgotten. Or, which was more likely, she decided, she had been the victim of a mental trick or lapse, or a waking dream, or an hallucination. She believed that all of these possibilities were . . . possible, but believed that none of them were probable. She believed, on balance—if there really was a *balance* to be found in all of this—that she had actually seen what she had actually seen. But she believed, too, that what she had actually seen could not actually have happened.

Although there was the bullet hole in the car door to deal with and think about. And the blood on the ground in front of the car door. And the suspect, Williamson, doubled over in the backseat of the car and moaning in pain from the bullet wound in his lower thigh. And the blood pooling around him on the seat.

And her partner lying prone on the ground. He was silent, now. She reached down, felt his jugular, got a weak pulse, threw the driver's door of the patrol car open, and grabbed the mike, gave her location, glanced quickly back at Williamson—*No human being can do what he did. Only smoke or water or air could do what he did!*—and found herself thinking that reality was not all that she had been brought up to believe it was. That, in reality, apparently solid objects were not really solid. That people were capable of strange and awful things other than murder, or rape, or incest. They were capable, some of them—this man, for instance—of magic that *wasn't* magic because it was *real*. They were capable—this man, for instance—of disobeying laws that were not his or anyone's province to disobey, because they were laws that God and God's universe had lain down, so they were not laws at all; they were reality, they were fact, they were immutable. But they weren't. This man—Williamson—had proved it, and *that* fact started a hard knot of fear deep in her belly. Because, she asked herself, what else was this man capable of? What other kinds of magic that weren't magic at all was he capable of? And what would he do with it? What would he do with *her*?

Grigoli said, "Her name was Tabitha Reed. She was a suspect in some bizarre murders in New York."

Christmas said, "The Chocolate Murders. They were called the Chocolate Murders."

"Why?" Vetris said.

"Because the killer stuffed chocolate in the mouths of his victims."

"And," Christmas began, "your girlfriend, Tabitha Reed—"

"My girlfriend?" Vetris interrupted.

"Yeah, the one you hit."

"I didn't hit her. She hit me. I told you that. She ran into the car."

"Whatever. It's not important. We don't think you had anything to do with it. We don't think it was premeditated."

"We don't?" Grigoli said. "Jerry, we have to have a little discussion."

"Shit. Forget it," Jerry said. "She was involved in these killings, the Chocolate Murders, now she's missing. *Dead* is more likely. And everybody thinks it's damned strange."

"And you're telling me this because?" Vetris said.

"Because we share information with the local constabulary, Detective. That would be you and your captain."

Grigoli said, "And we really want to know if you were involved with her somehow. You'd tell us, right?"

Vetris sighed.

"Listen," Christmas said, "there's two NYPD detectives on their way here and they want to talk to you. Can you stick around? Just tell us if you can't. We'll put them up in a motel and you can talk with them tomorrow."

Grigoli said, "You never heard about the Chocolate Murders, Detective? It was in all the papers."

"I don't read the papers. They're not delivered where I live and it's too far to drive every morning to pick one up."

"Shit, read the paper at work. You don't have a TV either?"

Vetris shook his head. "As a matter of fact, I don't."

Christmas said, "Well, correct me if I'm wrong, but as a homicide detective, I'd think you'd be interested in what's going on."

"I am. Here. In South Oleander. And I'm not strictly a homicide detective. . . ."

"You have a cat, right?" Christmas said.

Grigoli said, "Jesus, what's that got to do with the price of tomatoes?"

"Just making conversation while we're waiting for those people from NYPD."

"We both saw him," Erthmun said. "We both saw him. He was a man. He wasn't a boy. He wasn't *this* boy! For God's sake, he was a naked *man*!"

"I'm going back and call this in," Patricia said. "You stay with the body." She leaned over, checked the boy's pulse, straightened. "He's dead, yes," she said, in answer to a question Erthmun hadn't asked.

"You checked already," Erthmun said.

"I had to recheck. You've got to be sure." She sighed. "I'll be back. You stay here." She turned and started across the field of summer grass, toward the car.

Erthmun called after her, "He was a *man*, Patricia. We both saw him."

She called, "Stay with the body, Jack. Just stay with the body."

And he did.

The female state trooper was having trouble. She found herself glancing—too often, she thought—at the suspect in the backseat of the patrol car. She knew why she was doing it, of course. Because she couldn't trust her senses. She couldn't trust the earth, the universe, even God Himself, after witnessing what she'd witnessed in the past fifteen minutes. She might as well have watched the sun rise in the west, she thought. That would have had the same impact on her. It would have meant that the universe had changed, or that she had simply never understood it as completely as she thought she did, or that she had never understood it at all. Which made this place, this small piece of the universe, a very, very dangerous place to be. By all that was holy, it made *any* place a very, very dangerous place to be.

She glanced at Williamson and told him, "You don't make even a move back there, okay? You make a move, you do *any* goddamned thing, and I'll kill you. I swear I will."

Williamson grinned at her.

"And don't *smile* at me like that. You *smile* at me like that and I'll kill you! You breathe too hard and I'll kill you! You *think* about doing anything to me, and I'll kill you."

"Is that a promise, Officer?" Williamson said, still grinning.

She was having trouble. Reality could not be a thing she did not recognize. Reality could not be something she couldn't cope with, or control. Reality could not be *this man*! She felt herself reach for her .45, felt herself grip it, hesitate, pull it from its holster, felt herself lean back from the cage that separated her from Williamson, felt herself hold the .45 out straight, heard herself whisper, "Yes, that's a promise," felt herself pull the trigger, heard the report as the gun fired, saw Williamson's head all but shatter, saw his blood splatter in a wide *V* on the back window, and on the passenger window, on Williamson's shoulders, on the back of the seat, heard herself whisper, "Oh, Good Lord, oh, Good Lord, what have I done?"

Chapter Fourteen

Something deep inside Patricia had whispered to her that she couldn't trust Erthmun, that she wouldn't find him waiting with the boy's body when she returned. But it was a whisper she had decided to ignore, because she badly needed to trust Erthmun, though there was little evidence that she could. But she had never expected to find what she found—Erthmun standing at the spot where she had left him, and the boy who had been lying dead nowhere in sight.

Jack glanced confusedly at her and said, "He got up and ran away, Patricia."

She looked open-mouthed at the spot where the boy's body had lain. She could see a very rough outline of the body in the tall grass, and a narrow area leading from it where the grass seemed to have been shoved aside. As she looked, several blades of grass snapped up straight again.

Erthmun repeated, "He got up and ran away."

Patricia nodded. "Yes, I see that."

"I watched him," Erthmun said. "Patricia, he wasn't dead. I watched him run away."

"I believe you, Jack. Come on." She started for the area where the boy had apparently run off. "We'll find him."

"Yes," Erthmun said, "perhaps we will."

Myrna Guffy stuck her head into the interrogation room and said, "Those detectives from NYPD are going to be a while. They ran into some trouble."

"You mean we can have dinner?" Grigoli said.

"Sure," Myrna Guffy said.

"How about we send out for pizza?" Christmas suggested.

"I'm lactose-intolerant," Vetris said.

"Really?" said Christmas. "So's my wife. Can't even have milk in her coffee. Makes her throw up. Are you like that?"

Vetris shook his head. "No, I'm not." He paused, then went on. "Listen, you guys get whatever you want. I'm going to go home, okay?"

Christmas shrugged. "Sure. We'll call you when we need you." He grinned. "Just don't leave town."

"Well, I have to leave town in order to get home," Vetris said, and grinned back.

It was past nightfall and several dozen searchers had failed to locate any sign of the boy that Erthmun had shot. Erthmun had been asked by the head of the search team— a state police homicide investigator named Stevens—to wait by his car while the search was conducted because, Stevens had said, Erthmun was a principal in the case.

T. M. Wright

Patricia was asked to wait by the car, too, in order to keep an eye on Erthmun.

So Erthmun and Patricia had waited in silence as night had fallen. No one talked among the people searching either, and the view that Erthmun and Patricia got was of a dark blue sky and dark grass punctuated by the intermittent glow of flashlights, as if huge fireflies were loose in the field.

For some time, as he stood silently, Erthmun had been wondering about his name. *Erthmun.* He had made endless apologies to himself for dwelling on something so mundane while something so momentous—the search for a boy whom he, Erthmun, had apparently shot—was going on before his eyes. But he couldn't help thinking about his name. It was such an unusual name. As far as he knew, no one else on all of God's green earth had it, except his mother and the man whom he had called his father, and his sisters. He had once asked his father about it: "Where did our name come from?"

"It's German," his father had answered. "We're all German. Even your mother. She's German. So we're completely German. And that name is German."

"Oh," the young Jack had replied. "I didn't know we were German."

"German as the Kaiser," his father said. "German as Volkswagens."

"Oh," said the young Jack. "I don't know about those things."

"No need to," his father said. "A boy like you."

Young Jack had wondered what his father meant by that, but had said nothing because he hadn't wanted to appear stupid. Certainly *he* should know what kind of boy he was; he shouldn't have to ask someone else.

His father said, "You're German, too, I think. Half

German, probably." The young Jack thought that the man looked suddenly annoyed, or bothered, hurt, or angry. It was difficult for the young Jack to sort out such emotions; it was not nearly as difficult for the middle-aged Jack to sort them out, and he realized—looking back thirty-five years at the face of the man whom he had called father—that the man had been hurt and angry at the same time, as if some great wrong had been done to him and all he could do about that wrong was simply bear it.

And so many people had asked him how he spelled his name. People to whom he had to give his name—store clerks and people carrying out official business—and though he spelled it carefully, they almost always misspelled it as "Earthman," or "Earthmun," and he had given up trying to correct these misspellings. Even the name on his driver's license was misspelled—"Jack Erthman," which was, at any rate, a unique misspelling.

He said now, breaking the long silence between himself and Patricia, "What do you think of my name?"

She glanced at him, and he at her, though he could see little of her face in the darkness. "I think it suits you," she said. "It's a strong name. A male name."

"Erthmun?" he said.

"Oh." She shook her head. "No. Jack. That's a strong name. I don't know about *Erthmun*. I've often wondered where the hell it came from."

"It's German," he said. "My family was German."

She shrugged. "Sure. It sounds German."

The search went on for another three hours. No body was found, and no further signs of the missing boy.

When he woke at 3:00 A.M. and did not find Villain on his chest, Vetris was disappointed. And relieved. He enjoyed the idea of leading a basically uneventful home life, which was one reason he had never married. But he also enjoyed the possibility of the strange and the unpredictable finding its way through the door and into his house. And what could have been more strange and unpredictable than the ghost of his psychotic cat waking him early in the morning? He wondered how he'd react. Would he scream and attempt to throw the creature off? Would he jump from his bed and run from the room? Would he and Villain stare at one another for a minute while the wide-eyed Villain let him know that nothing as insignificant as death was going to get in the way of their bizarre relationship, and while Vetris tried to understand where his ideas of reality had all gone astray?

And yet, Vetris thought, he had indeed awakened only a few hours after going to bed, and he had awakened because it was about the time that Villain had always awakened him. Old habits are hard to break, especially when they're lodged in the subconscious as tenaciously as a virus.

He heard movement in the room, and he thought at once that mice were taking over the house again, now that Villain was gone. The mice, he supposed, could sense the departure of an enemy as lethal and as omnipresent as Villain, so they thought that it was time to party.

The movement continued. Pitter-patter sounds, similar, Vetris thought, to the sounds that a large cat on the prowl might make, or several mice on the retreat might make.

He didn't like the idea of mice overrunning the house. It presented him with agonizing decisions about how to get rid of them. Another cat? Where would he find one with the lethality and lordly demeanor of Villain, whose very presence kept the mice at a distance? Traps? What kinds? He didn't at all like the idea of getting up to find mice nearly cut in half by the classic mouse trap, and the "Have-a-Heart" traps were too much work; he'd tried them. Plus you couldn't catch all the mice. And the ones you did catch had to be taken at least five miles from the house, otherwise they always found their way back. God knows how.

The sounds in the room became louder, Vetris thought, as if the creature making them had suddenly gained fifty pounds. But the sounds were still pitter-patter sounds, the sounds of something moving stealthily. He wished he could see better without light. His night vision had been deteriorating ever since he had hit forty and he sometimes believed it was a precursor to blindness. His father and two of his uncles had succumbed to early blindness caused by an esoteric illness, and the idea that he might go blind scared the hell out of him.

Perhaps he should turn on a light, he thought. Perhaps he should know what was in the room with him. Perhaps he should know if it was a fifty-pound mouse, or Villain being what he always knew that Villain could be.

A small face, nearly lost in darkness, appeared just above him. "Oh, my God!" it whispered.

Chapter Fifteen

Williamson the Loon knew about the Chocolate Murders. Everyone knew about the Chocolate Murders. Everyone whose mother had great oaks growing out of her forehead and hollyhocks growing from her feet and rivers flowing through her belly. And everyone who knew intimately about the Chocolate Murders—and, of course, everyone else with the same mother knew about them intimately—thought that they were strange, perverse, and unacceptable. That they were a waste of food and resources and too similar, far too similar, to the foolishly complex actions of those whose mothers had red lips and breasts brimming with milk.

Williamson the Loon thought that way, in those words, and he thought in other ways, too, when the occasion required. He thought in less lyrical ways, in direct ways, like an apple hitting the ground, or a honeybee, heavy with pollen, lumbering from one flower to another, or a man in pursuit of his survival pursuing women to impress and penetrate. There was nothing calculated about anything Williamson did. He did what was necessary to him, without embellishment, introspection, afterthought, or regret. He was not a man driven. He was simply not a man.

He wanted to pity the female state trooper whose body he had left behind in the front seat of her car. He wanted to pity her because he knew that *pity* was an emotion worth cultivating, because many in that other culture—the one born of women with red lips—seemed to value it in others, and seemed to know when it was offered without sincerity. But he wasn't absolutely certain what pity was. Could it be a feeling of sadness or regret in the face of another's misfortune? If so, what really were sadness and regret all about, except—as far as he could see—becoming emotionally entangled in the fate of someone else. And to what end?

But still, cultivating the emotion of pity, after he found out what pity was exactly, could be an asset. It might enhance the few days and nights that were left to him in ways he could not imagine now. It might give him greater access—at necessary times—to the bodies and vaginas and wombs of women of that other culture whom he required to bear his children, which promoted his own survival, as well as the survival of his species. Oh, it was such a heady time, this time of transition, from being to nonbeing to existence all over again.

But for now he was hungry for a cheeseburger, fries, and a Coke, and the idea of cross-species, cross-cultural philosophy simply stopped appealing to him.

He had grown to love cheeseburgers, but found that their appeal was enhanced tenfold by the addition of French fries and ketchup, and enhanced ten-fold again by the addition of a tall, cold Coke, half-filled with ice, and served in a genuine Coca-Cola glass that had been chilled. The whole meal was as heavenly as any that a vegetarian such as he could dream of, though he had often considered substituting Coke with Starbucks Mocha Frappucino, though Mocha Frappucino, he decided, was best drunk all by itself, unencumbered by other flavors and textures.

He had, however, drunk a bottle of Mocha Frappucino while devouring a housewife named Betty, who had very willingly let him into her house because he had told her that he was a representative of the TV show *Who Wants to Be a Millionaire,* and that she had been suggested as someone with an unquenchable appetite for knowledge and, thus, the possible winner of a million dollars. Perhaps more, depending on how well her appetite for knowledge had been satisfied.

When Williamson's appetite for her had been satisfied, and his bottle of Mocha Frappucino drunk, he had made his way back to the place where he stayed so that he could wash his hands, mouth, and face, and to change his clothes, which were unsightly with much of Betty herself, and then back to his job as a shoe salesman. He had always loved his job as a shoe salesman. It kept him close to the earth. God but he missed that job.

The face was the face of a boy who spoke in Vetris's voice, "Oh my God!" it said, then vanished into the darkness of the room, leaving Vetris breathless and shaking from the surge of adrenaline that had pushed through him.

He did not leap up, though he knew that he should, because he had seen something strange and threatening in the boy, who might, he knew, still be in the room, as he—Vetris—lay in the bed, quivering, trying hard to peer into the darkness above him, trying to make out, at least, the overhanging lamp on the ceiling, or the color of the ceiling itself—bright white—as he tried to push the darkness away by sheer force of will.

But his hearing had shut down, too. Or his brain's ability to process what he heard in the room had shut down. A big windup alarm clock ticked loudly on the nightstand next to his bed, but he couldn't hear it. And he thought that if the boy were still in the room, he wouldn't be able to hear him either, because he could hear only his pulse in his ears, and it was deafening, maddening, too fast.

Damnit! he was a fucking cop! And the image of a spectral child in his room, mouthing only three words at him, had made him almost comatose. Where were his balls, for Christ's sake!

His stomach muscles tightened—his body was readying itself for action, he knew. Fight or flight.

"Shit!" he whispered.

"Shit!" he heard from somewhere else in the room. In his voice.

An echo! he thought, and knew that the idea was foolish. There could be no echo in a small, furnished room.

Oh God, he was being what he had once been, long ago. A small boy frightened into inaction by what most small boys are frightened of—an unseen and unknowable, fantastic and deadly something that had invaded and corrupted the sanctity of his bedroom.

He threw himself from the bed, stood by it for a moment, glanced about frantically. "Where are you?" he whispered. "Where are you?"

And he heard, from somewhere in the room, from *everywhere* in the room, in his voice, as if it were an echo that could not exist here, "Where are you? Where are you?"

God, he was out of the bed at least. He was standing naked in a room without light and addressing a boy he could not see who spoke in his voice. But he was out of the fucking bed! He was no longer comatose. He had taken action. He had stopped being the small, frightened boy he had been so long ago.

"Turn the light on," he whispered to himself.

"Turn the light on," he heard.

He cast about for the source of the voice. He saw large, softly dark lumps that were his dresser, his bed, his bedside table.

"Turn the light on," he heard.

"Goddamnit! Shut up!" he screamed.

"Goddamnit! Shut up!" he heard.

He felt something touch the small of his naked back and he whirled about, groaned "Uh!" grabbed for whatever had touched him, grabbed only air.

Something touched his naked stomach, his naked legs and buttocks, and he whirled about and whirled about, groaning, "Uh!" again and again, told himself frantically that whatever was touching him could not be a threat, that it was only a boy who had gotten into his house and was playing tricks, playing with the naked man, making him grunt and groan and grab the night air.

"Uh! Uh!" he heard.

Only a boy had gotten into his house, and that boy was having fun, that boy certainly was having fun, laughing, certainly laughing . . .

But he wasn't. The boy wasn't laughing. He *wasn't* laughing.

"Show yourself, goddamnit!" Vertris shouted, and got the words back, in his voice, from the corners and walls and the ceiling and the floor of the dark room.

Something touched his face quickly, lightly. And his chest, too, at the same time. And his genitals. His legs. His buttocks. His back again, his neck, his arms. All at once. This was not just one boy, he realized. It was several boys. Several pairs of hands.

"Jesus Christ!" he screamed.

"Jesus Christ!"

"Jesus Christ!"

"Jesus Christ!"

"Jesus Christ!"

"Jesus Christ!"

Patricia and Erthmun were staying that night in Room 13 of the Wee-Welcome Motel, a couple of miles from South Oleander. They had gotten to the motel at 1:00 A.M., and though both of them were beyond exhaustion, they couldn't sleep, because the incredible events of the day just passed wouldn't allow it, so they had sat up—Erthmun on the bed, with his back resting against two pillows propped up against the headboard, and Patricia in a blue club chair across the room—and they had talked. Their talk was not about the incredible events of the day; that could wait. Their talk was about inconsequentials, about the motel, which Erthmun called the "Wee-Welcome Roaches Motel," and about Patricia's family—three brothers and two sisters; father dead, mother ailing—and Erthmun's predilections for Western literature (Louis L'Amour was his favorite) and ghost stories, particularly those of M.R. James and Peter Straub, which, he said, "have entertained me into fright on many a night"; the comment made Patricia smile: "I didn't know you were a poet," she said. And he said, "I'm not. My mother was."

Which, Patricia thought, seemed to invite her into a topic that she was not up to at that moment.

After a long silence, after it was clear to Patricia that she was at last ready for sleep, but that Erthmun didn't seem ready yet, and, she supposed, that he'd require her company until he *was* ready, Erthmun said, "Something is happening around here."

After a moment, Patricia said, "That's very cryptic."

"I mean," Erthmun said, "around these woods and fields, in these hills that the people here foolishly call mountains, in some of these houses. I feel that something is happening."

"Do you know what it is?"

"Yes," he said. "Somehow I do. In some way I do. But I know so little. It's clear to me, now, that I have never known anything very much at all. If you were to let me loose in the deep forest, I would die." He adjusted the pillows, then looked at Patricia again. "I think they got these pillows from a highway project."

She smiled.

He said, "But the thing that's happening here is a very small thing. It's not a meteorite blasting into the atmosphere, or a global conflagration, or a virus that makes us all into morons."

Patricia smiled again.

He smiled. "I've discovered my sense of humor only in the past few years. Before that I was as taciturn and unfunny as a roofing tile. Now I know what humor means. Even in the worst of times."

"Like these?"

He cocked his head. "Are you asking, Patricia, if these times we're in are the worst of times? No, I don't think they are. Do you?"

She shrugged. "I don't know."

He shrugged, as if in imitation of her. "Every generation's times are the worst of times. Don't you believe that? Every generation looks around and crows about its problems and troubles and grievances."

"Yes, I understand. I agree."

"Someone's going to knock at the door," Erthmun said.

"Huh?"

"Not now. Not right now. But in a while. Someone's going to knock at the door and they'll be agitated."

"Jesus, did you suddenly become a psychic?"

He smiled. "Yes. Just now. A few minutes ago."

"I like your smile," she said, surprising herself.

"I've practiced it," he said. "It used to be a smile that was no more entertaining than ketchup. Now it's the smile of a man who likes to smile."

"I'm sorry, Jack." She looked away a moment, looked back, caught his eye. "I seem to be flirting with you."

He shrugged once more. "And I with you. It's the setting, the hour. The people." He smiled once more.

She smiled, thought it was inviting, thought that was okay. "Yes. People flirt. It's one of the things they do, isn't it? If someone is even mildly interesting or attractive . . ."

"Meaning?" Erthmun interrupted.

She looked embarrassed. "Oh, no, I didn't mean that the way it sounded. No. You're more than mildly attractive, Jack. I'm sure you realize that."

There was a hard double knock at the door.

Erthmun said, "Continue."

She looked questioningly at him. "Jack, someone's knocking at the door."

"They'll wait. They'll have to."

She got up, started for the door, said, as if as an aside,

"Later, Jack. Much later." The hard double knock came again. She opened the door.

A tall, stout man dressed as if for hunting, in a red and black checkered jacket and orange pants, who had a rifle slung over his shoulder, and whose eyes were wide and dark, as if he had just heard something that was beyond startling, said breathlessly, "You got to get outta here right away!"

"Sorry?" Patricia said.

"I mean now!" the man said, turned quickly to his right, and, in a moment, was knocking loudly at the door to Room 14.

Patricia leaned out her door and called to the man, "What are you talking about? Why do we have to leave?"

Erthmun came up beside her. "Get back inside, Patricia. I think he's right. I think we have to leave."

"Jesus H. Christ, Jack! What in the hell is going on?"

"I'm sure that even that man doesn't know," Erthmun said.

Vetris Gambol watched through his living room window as the children scattered as quickly and as soundlessly as cats into the early morning light. It did not seem unnatural to him. What seemed unnatural was looking through glass at them, caught in his house the way he was, in his comforts, in his skin. He did not question this way of thinking. He realized it, accepted it, watched the children scattering into the morning light. And when they had scattered and were gone, he knew well that they weren't gone, no more than the pines on the hill behind his house were gone, or the blue sky that had arched over his civilized landscape a day earlier was gone, or Villain, his beautiful and psychotic black cat with golden eyes, was gone.

Nothing, he realized, was ever gone in this place, on

the earth, a dreaming ground for life and magic. He smiled. Had he actually thought those words? He'd never thought that way before. Why now?

He'd have to think about it.

Or maybe not.

He looked down at himself, looked out his big window again as the naked morning twilight became morning in full dress.

In time, he thought, he'd hang some clothes on himself.

Williamson the Loon was certain that there was no *never* and no *ever* and no *not* and no *possibility* or *probability* or *perhaps* anywhere in the universe he breathed in and fucked in and ate in and died in; and he was certain that there was no *died* either. Ever. Never.

For the first time in his existence he smiled a true smile.

So many non-possibilities among the possibilities and improbabilities, and impossibilities brimming with *nots* and serial magic and the lasts of nothing. He might as well have been a flower blooming underwater or a planetoid caught in an hourglass or a blade of summer grass contemplating Nietzsche. Because he was the nothing that was all. He was the poet. He was the mother and father of poets and magic. He was the child of sandstone and night music. He devoured the soul-less and became another evening or another afternoon.

He was Williamson the Loon. Great evaporator. And resurrector. A small part of the bacterial whole. The bacterial whole turned to crude language and cruder gestures and a need for exposition.

He was Williamson the Loon holding spleens in his teeth. He was Williamson the Loon following the blood around his body like a lover. He was Williamson the Loon needing to recreate. Himself. And all the whole. The subterranean bacterial self of himself that slipped naked through fissures and openings in granite to bustle about on streets built by that other species, the one transplanted on the earth from stardust and Mars meteorites.

He was Williamson the Loon who, like that other species, had gotten it all wrong, and so needed to return and resurrect on another day. On the long day that was night and day. In the long year that was decade and century and millennium.

What could end what?

He slipped away, smiling his first-ever true smile.

Knowing he slipped away to nothing from nothing and so became everything. In the long day, in the long year.

This is what Jack Erthmun said to Patricia as they drove away from the Wee-Welcome Motel in the naked early morning twilight: "It is the magic of being."

Patricia was driving. She liked to drive. Erthmun didn't. He found artifice in it that he couldn't understand or explain. If he had thought about it, he would invent this metaphor to describe it: That it was like a snail riding a bicycle.

Patricia glanced confusedly at him and said, "Again, cryptic?"

"Yes," he said. "Of course. People enjoy it. People enjoy cryptic. They need to know and not know all at the same time. They want answers but are always unsatisfied."

"Not always," Patricia told him.

"At the end, I think."

"The end?"

"When the earth comes alive again and swallows them up."

"Oh."

He said, "It is the magic of being. It is all the magic of being."

She glanced at him, said nothing, watched the twilight change to something grander and less interesting.

Erthmun said, "A rock might see us flexing our toes and declare that it was magic. But it would be magic only for the rock."

"Jack, it would be magic simply for the rock to speak."

"Oh, yes, wouldn't it," he said.

She said nothing. She had no idea what he was talking about. But she thought that *he* knew what he was talking about.

He went on, "Chocolate murders are an aberration, Patricia."

"I think I know that."

"They are such a thing as *we* do. Do you understand?"

"On the face of it, yes." She turned the headlights off. Morning was upon them.

"As if a rock were to come along and flex its toes," Erthmun said. "It would be magic for the rock to do that. But it would be a magic that needed to pass away. Do you understand?"

"No."

"Because only creatures such as ourselves flex our toes. Rocks don't. And shouldn't."

Patricia came to a stop at a red light that seemed to have been placed, she thought, in the middle of nowhere. A semi loaded with car parts whizzed around her and through the light. "Jesus," she breathed. "He'll kill someone."

Erthmun said, "He already has."

She glanced at him. "Huh?"

"Or someone else has. Someone also with a brain between two ears and genitals waiting to be put to their

305

proper use and hands to caress and also to do murder."

She glanced at him again. "Good Lord, Jack, you're being almost . . . Shakespearean this morning."

"I wouldn't know that," he said.

"Read him, you'll understand."

Jack shrugged. "I will."

Patricia leaned forward, noted that the light was green, looked right, left, went through.

Jack said, "We never stay. Patricia, we never stay. We always come and go. We always try to get it right."

"What do we try to get right, Jack?"

He looked out his window. "Living on the earth," he said.

T. M. WRIGHT
Sleepeasy

Harry Briggs led a fairly normal life. He had a good job, a nice house, and a beautiful wife named Barbara, with whom he was very much in love. Then he died. That's when Harry's story really begins. That's when he finds himself in a strange little town called Silver Lake. In Silver Lake nothing is normal. In Silver Lake Harry has become a detective, tough and silent, hot on the trail of a missing woman and a violent madman. But the town itself is an enigma. It's a shadowy twilight town, filled with ghostly figures that seem to be playing according to someone else's rules. Harry has unwittingly brought other things with him to this eerie realm. Things like uncertainty, fear . . . and death.

___4864-7　　　　　　　　　　　　　$5.99 US/$6.99 CAN

Dorchester Publishing Co., Inc.
P.O. Box 6640
Wayne, PA 19087-8640

SPIRIT
GRAHAM
MASTERTON

Peggy Buchanan is such an adorable little girl, all blond curls and sweetness. Then comes the tragic day when her family finds Peggy floating in the icy water of their swimming pool, dead, her white dress billowing around her. Her sisters, Laura and Elizabeth, can't imagine life without Peggy. They know from that day forward their lives will be changed forever. But they can't know the nightmare that waits for them. Peggy may be dead—but she hasn't left them. As the sisters grow up, a string of inexplicable deaths threatens to shatter their lives. No matter how warm the weather, each corpse shows signs of severe frostbite . . . and each victim's dying moments are tortured by a merciless little girl in a white dress, whose icy kiss is colder than death.

___4935-X $5.99 US/$6.99 CAN

JOHN SHIRLEY
Black Butterflies

Some nightmares are strangely sweet, unnaturally appealing. Some dark places gleam like onyx, like the sixteen stories in John Shirley's *Black Butterflies*, stories never before collected, including the award-nominated "What Would You Do for Love?" These stories are like the jet-black butterflies Shirley saw in a dream. They flocked around him, and if he tried to ignore them they would cut him to shreds with their razor-sharp wings. Shirley had to write these stories or the black butterflies would cut him up from the inside and flutter out from the wound . . . into the world.

__4844-2 $5.99 US/$6.99 CAN

This Symbiotic Fascination
CHARLEE JACOB

Tawne Delaney has never been what men consider beautiful. Still a virgin at thirty-seven, she's lonely and fantasizes about someday meeting her dream lover. But the man she meets is no dream—he's a nightmare. Desperate to change her situation, Tawne lets an ugly little man change her into something powerful and immortal. Yet the loneliness persists until Arcan Tyler enters her life.

Arcan Tyler is no ordinary rapist and murderer. He is possessed by three animal spirits that he must constantly fight to control. If they are fully unleashed, he will cease to be human. For the time being he is still all too human, and he finds something new in Tawne—someone who loves him. But love among creatures like these is not romantic, it is parasitic. Together they find a life not of happiness, but of terror.

____4966-X $5.99 US/$7.99 CAN

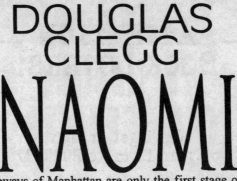

DOUGLAS CLEGG

NAOMI

The subways of Manhattan are only the first stage of Jake Richmond's descent into the vast subterranean passageways beneath the city—and the discovery of a mystery and a terror greater than any human being could imagine. Naomi went into the tunnels to destroy herself . . . but found an even more terrible fate awaiting her in the twisting corridors. And now the man who loves Naomi must find her . . . and bring her back to the world of the living, a world where a New York brownstone holds a burial ground of those accused of witchcraft, where the secrets of the living may be found within the ancient diary of a witch, and where a creature known only as the Serpent has escaped its bounds at last.

___4857-4 $5.99 US/$6.99 CAN